Praise for Award-Winning Debut, *Swimming Through Clouds*

"In *Swimming Through Clouds*, Rajdeep weaves a poignant but realistic tale of an abused teenage girl trying to live between 'what if and what is,'...trying to leave the reality of the mess of her life behind and fly to a place in her mind where things are peaceful, where fear is gone, and where dreams are possible."
~ Sheila Wray Gregoire, Syndicated Columnist,
Canadian National Award-Winning Speaker,
Blogger, and Author

"Paulus is an exceptional writer! The essence of the human spirit are illuminated through the characters who come to life in each page. Paulus captures the heart of the reader in *Swimming Through Clouds*."
~ Diana Mao, President of Nomi Network

"*Swimming Through Clouds* is a heartfelt story that, at times, is difficult to read but even more difficult to put down. This is a beautiful, not-so-average love story and [has] an ending that stays with you for days after you've finished reading the book."
~ Brown Girl Magazine Book Review by Atiya Hasan

"*Swimming Through Clouds* is what I would like to call a very brave book. In my opinion the purpose of this incredible story is to raise awareness about violence against women. The author, in a very creative way outlines this reality. This book should be read by everyone ... men and women, the young and the old."
~ Masala Mommas Book Review by Angie Seth

"*Swimming Through Clouds* is a heart-wrenching story of both suffering and courage. This book will haunt you long after you finish it."
~ Darby Karchut, Award-Winning Author of
Griffin Rising and *Finn Finnegan*

Seeing Through
Stones

RAJDEEP PAULUS

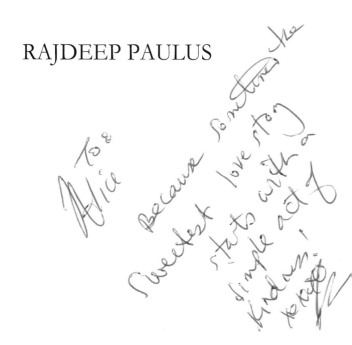

To Alice

Because sometimes the sweetest love story starts with a simple act of kindness!

xoxo

SEEING THROUGH STONES
Copyright © 2014 by Rajdeep Paulus

Published in association with
Playlist Fiction
158 Laneda Avenue
Manzanita, Oregon 97130

Scripture notations in this publication are taken from THE
MESSAGE. Copyright 1993, 1994, 1995, 1996, 2000, 2001, 2002.

ISBN-13: 978-1495413797
ISBN-10: 1495413799
Cover design: Angela Llamas
Back Cover Photo & Design: Deepa Elizabeth Paulus
"Lightning Eyes" Lyrics notation used with the expressed
permission of Evan Chambers
"Lightning Eyes": Copyright © 2013 by Evan Chambers

First printing 2014
Printed in the United States of America
Author represented by MacGregor Literary, Inc.

DEDICATION

For my parents, Sohan and Charanjit. Mom and Dad, thank you for all you poured into me to become the woman I am today. You continue to inspire me, make me laugh, and drive me to become my best.

And to Santhosh's parents, Samuel and Suseela. Amma and Appa, thank you for loving me like I'm your own daughter. Your fondness of stories connects us, and your marriage reminds me daily that love is a verb.

I love you.

1
~ Jesse ~

I dream in color. Orange and red glue my eyes shut, and I see no way out. A wall of fire before me. A sea of blood behind me. Asleep or awake, escaping means I burn or bleed.

"Jesse!" Talia's voice breaks into my dreams, but I roll to my side and squeeze my eyes shut, facing the wall instead of my big sister.

"Jesse. Get up." I memorize the warmth of Talia's hand on my shoulder over my shirt, etching each fingertip into a picture frame in my mind. I can't take her with me. I can take this moment.

"You're right." The first words I say when I push the covers off and open my eyes are not, 'Good Morning,' because nothing good can come of this day. Nothing.

"What did you say?" Talia stands over me, fingers running through her long brown hair, twirling a lock, then pulling it across her mouth. I know she hates her lips, but I often wonder if she's also trying to hide the part of her that looks the most like Dad—her face.

Talia tugs her green long sleeve past her wrists as she sits on the edge of my bed. I know what she's hiding underneath her sleeve. I also know she won't have to hide much longer. Today marks the last day either of us will ever get burned. Ever.

"You've always been right." I repeat as I sit up in bed, sliding hands down my face, drawing imaginary curtains over my brown eyes.

"Right about what?"

"About leaving without Dad knowing a thing." Two years have passed since the accident. I'm done hiding in a wheelchair, pretending I still can't walk, silently watching Dad destroy us. I thought telling him the truth, that I taught myself to talk and walk again, could lead to opportunity. College. Freedom. Talia reminded me last night that a positive response from Dad was as likely as Mom coming back from the grave. Impossible.

I lay out the alternative plan I mapped out in my dreams. "We'll set the house on fire. Make it look like we died in the fire. Dad thinks we're dead. We'll run away. Free. End of story."

Talia's face contorts with worry as I wait quietly. I need her to believe she's a part of the master plan. To get rid of Dad—the master. The king will burn down with his throne today. That's the plan.

"End of story." Talia repeats my words. "And the beginning of a new life." Talia rises from the bed, her gaze fixed on the door. "Where would we run to? How will we survive on the streets?"

"Anywhere but here is all that matters. We'll make it. We'll find jobs. Google our options. Figure it out. Together." I watch Talia's shoulders rise. And fall again. "The main thing is to get as far away as possible from Dad, right?"

"Right." Talia nods her head slowly, but her darkened hazel eyes and stiffened body say, wrong. "I need a day. One day."

Talia wants to say goodbye to Lagan, her slam-dunk, Bollywood prince who would risk it all for her. He is her out. I get that. And that's why I know I have to carry out the plan myself. No one will miss me if they think I'm dead. But

2

Talia…after all this time, my sister found something I'm still not sure exists. Friendship. A friend. And when I think about the way they look at each other—probably more.

"One more day." I lie. Because I know like I know my first name is Justice that this is it. No more nights wondering if I'll live to see another day. No more dreams where I fall asleep and wake up lying next to Mom in her coffin. Enough.

"I have to get to class." Talia hugs my neck as I grip the sheets with my hands. Then I throw my arms around her back and hold tightly. It's the closest to goodbye I can say.

"You okay?" Talia asks.

I don't answer. And I don't want to let my sister go. I still stutter when I get nervous, and I can't chance giving myself away.

"We'll be okay." Talia answers her own question. "We just have to remember what Mom said. To stick together."

And therein lies my dilemma. Being on my own scares me more than the idea of this house on fire. I can't remember a time my sister and I didn't navigate our mad lives together. With the exception of my short stay in the hospital, Talia has always held my hand, metaphorically and literally speaking.

"We'll make it happen." She keeps talking when I don't. Not too different from all the months when my voice fell asleep. The accident. She did all the talking back then, and her voice was medicinal, reaching places no one else could.

"And we'll leave this place forever. Together. See you after work tonight," she says, as she loosens her hold first. "Jesse, you have to act normal around Dad today. So he won't suspect anything. Okay?"

As I watch my sister leave my room, I run my hands over the top of my legs. Today we walk our separate ways. The sound of the front door closing alerts me—I'm alone, and I can take the mask off. I stumble into the bathroom, retrieve the broken shard from under the bathroom sink, and lay it on the vanity counter before peeling my scrubs off. My shoulders stiffen as I lift the jagged remnant from an old hand mirror, turn, and stare at my tan back in the reflection of the bathroom mirror.

Sandwiching the broken mirror between my hands, I curse the scars for still being there. Do-over. Put that on my Christmas wish-list of the last seventeen years. After filing the mirror back under the sink, I return to bed, lay on my back, and stare at the ceiling as I list the things I'd place under coulda, shoulda, woulda.

If I could do it all over again, I'd start by telling my sister I'm sorry sooner. Telling my mother that I loved her more often. And telling Dad to go to hell.

Knowing I have to wait until after Dad makes his lunchtime run, I close my eyes and draw out my plan, because sleeping is out of the question. As I lay in bed, lists cover every inch of my imaginary whiteboard, one for every one hundred lists Dad penned to trap Mom, Talia and me. Except that by the time I retrace the words several times, everything blurs together in my head.

Having spent close to a year laying in bed for most of my hours, I remind myself—one step at a time, like how I learned how to move my legs again. The waves on top of the covers help to still my pounding heart as I wiggle my toes and bend my legs. They still work.

Taking a deep breath, I clear my mind and start over, forcing myself to slow down, until I organize every item into three columns: what I'll take with me, what I'll leave behind, and what must burn. The first is the shortest list. The last—the most complicated. Because there are places Dad touched that I cannot reach. Not even with fire.

The clock reads 2:07 PM when I get out of bed and part my bedroom curtains. Driveway's empty. Grey clouds sweep across the sun, the sky changing from dark to light, back to dark again. If Dad hasn't showed up for lunch by now, he's probably stuck in a meeting at the office. Maybe he crashed his Acura on Lakeshore Drive, and he's burning up in a car fire, his briefcase of precious lawyer documents feeding the flames.

Embers cloud my vision as I throw on a pair of jeans and a black t-shirt with a grey silhouette of the Chicago skyline painted across the chest. My chest of drawers holds six identical shirts and seven pairs of generic blue hospital scrubs—Dad's choice in my wardrobe is about as predictable as the buzz cut he insists on giving me once every three weeks. So I can look like him in form if not in shade, Dad's Dutch South-African heritage giving him his blond hair and pale skin. Mom gifted me with her South-Asian black hair and brown skin, two things Dad could not steal from me.

Pulling my sneakers out from under the hospital bed, how many times did Talia return home after school to pick up the TV remote or a dropped blanket, my legs virtually useless those early months after the fall? If she only knew how often she lifted me out of a dark place, the way she took care of me, never punishing me for the stupid choices I made. Facing Dad alone is one way I can thank her.

Thankful for one of yesterday's storms, I make my way downstairs to the garage to find gas cans. This past winter's snowstorm marked one of Chicago's worst, and gasoline hoarding accompanied the Midwest panic during the weeks it took for the windy city to recover. Lucky for me, Dad would never again be unprepared for a citywide gas shortage.

After setting two five-gallon canisters down on the kitchen counter, I clasp my hands and swing my arms like a bat at the teakettle, sending it to a floor-clanging crash as I blink away the picture of Talia's arm stretched across the sink, Dad pouring out his anger with boiling water over my sister's skin. The throbbing sting in my hands will subside eventually. The memory of my sister counting one to ten while her arm sizzled will never leave me. Giving the teakettle a swift kick, I curse my legs for the times they failed to move and stand up for my sister. Payback was never a question. The only unknowns were when, how, and how to walk away.

The red container feels cool as my thumb and forefinger fiddle with the white, twist-top cap. When I break the seal and the top spins off the canister, the scent of gasoline fills my pores in that first whiff. A little splash here and there, and everywhere. The kitchen instantly smells like a Shell station.

Making my way from the kitchen to the dining room to the living room, I swing my magic lamp full of sleeping flames over Dad's perfectly organized house, kicking over chairs and vases, knocking lamps off end tables, and lifting paintings off wall hooks. The canister lightens as gasoline glistens around me. Curtains. Check. Carpet. Check, check. Wooden chairs. Triple check. I toss the empty jug in the mudroom, knocking several boots out of line before making my way back to the kitchen to open a second one.

Entering Talia's room upstairs, I feel a little guilty when the gasoline splashes over her beloved books. Whatever. Stupid stories. Not like fairy tales exist.

Standing in the doorway of my parents' room, gasoline soaks every corner of Dad's pillow before I turn and step toward the closet. Two of the longest days of my life, the memory of Mom's soiled body falling out of the closet lands on me like dumbbells across my chest that I cannot lift. The jug slips from my fingers clumsily to the carpeted floor, landing upright, gasoline splashing out of the open spout. Instinctively I punch the wooden slats, the door collapsing inward, pain shooting through my knuckles up my forearm.

"Stupid business suits and shirts and ties. Cutting all ties with you, today," I say to Dad's perfectly-organized wardrobe. My eyes play tricks on me as I douse the clothes, a line of Dad clones jeering at my inability to burn up my past. I place the canister to my right to clasp the closet doors closed.

Jug almost empty, I pile clothes, books, and papers on my bed and pour gas on top, leaving a trail as I backtrack, bumping into my wheelchair with my heels at the top of the stairwell. Turning, I douse a generous helping on the seat that held me captive. The charade is over, Dad. I'm done playing the mute paraplegic you know me as. You don't know me at all.

Kicking the chair, I watch it roll off the top step and bounce and bang its way down to the bottom, landing upside down, the wheels still spinning. I run down the steps and halt the spinning with my free hand before pushing it out of the way and heading toward Dad's office, my final stop.

"Jesse! Where are you?" I hear the familiar voice yelling before I see his face. Lagan. What the freak is he doing here?

"How'd you get in here?" Stepping on my toes, I arch my back to look over Lagan's shoulder, toward the doorway. "Where's my sister?"

Lagan follows me to the front as I scan the empty driveway before closing the door. "I'm alone. Talia's...she's the reason I came. She asked me to talk to you."

"About what? We already made a plan. One that didn't include you." I push past Lagan to retrieve a chair from the kitchen.

"What the heck are you doing? This place reeks." Lagan follows me, still talking. "Talia told me to get you out of here."

"Hold up. I just need..." I stop myself in mid-sentence. I can see the mahogany of Dad's desk through the office window. The desk with the drawer. The drawer with the gun. "I'd back up if I were you," is all the warning I give before lifting the chair and hurling it right into Dad's office window, the sound of shattered glass forcing us both two steps back.

"What the—?" Lagan's forearm lowers below his goatee-bearing chin, still raised in defense of a second hit. "Are you out of your freakin' mind?"

After two more blows to the office windows with the now splintered chair, the jagged frame opens wide enough for me to climb in. *Who's gonna clean up the mess for you this time, Dad?*

"You're nuts!" Lagan says, shaking his head as he steps over broken glass.

"Give me a hand." I ignore Lagan and boost myself into Dad's office with one grip on the chair and the other on Lagan's shoulder.

"We have to get outta here," Lagan says. "Before your dad gets home. If he finds out..."

I put on my best everything's gonna be okay voice and tell him, "This will only take a minute, and then we can jet, okay?"

"All I'm sayin' is..."

But, I can't hear another word. Focused on the task at

hand, I find the gun exactly where I saw it last. I shove the 9mm pistol in my pocket and unlock the office door, now face to face with Lagan. "Ready," I say, and march past him toward the back door.

"I came to tell you something." Lagan's talking behind me, but there's no time for conversation.

"Wanna do the honors?" I use one foot to keep the back door propped and open my palm inches from Lagan's face. A single book of matches lies on top for his taking.

"Talia wants you to know she's safe." It's Lagan's turn to ignore me. "She wants you to know you can be—uh—that you can get out too. And you don't have to do it like this." Lagan's hand motions to the house, and knocks my hand to the side, but I close my fist around the matches before they fall.

"It's too late." As far as I'm concerned, the house is already on fire.

"It's never too late."

"Sure. Whatever you say." I speak calmly before striking a match.

Lagan snuffs it out, his enveloped fist swallowing up the tiny match. Hands gripped to my shirt collar, Lagan shoves me up against the wall, his dark eyes piercing into mine, and the book of matches slips from my hands to the floor. "I said, Talia wants you to get outta here and not leave a trail." Lagan's not asking for my opinion. "A fire will leave a trail. Screw this place. I promised her I'd get you out, so let's go already."

Lagan's grasp tightens as he shoves me toward the back door. I feign falling to reach for the matches, but Lagan kicks them out of my grasp, his black Nikes just missing my hand. The ping of the gun in my pocket startles me, and I swallow relief that it didn't go off.

"Who asked you? I was doing just fine on my own." The feel of my cheek against the cool floor is all too familiar. How many times did I fall when I was first learning to walk again? Too many to count.

"So you think setting the house on fire is the answer to all your problems?" Lagan picks up the matches and pitches them over his shoulder. "You'll go to jail. And that's just stupid. You can't hurt your Dad without hurting yourself. For the last time, let's get outta here."

I rise to my feet, aware that my strength is no match for the six-foot tall athlete, and mechanically nod. If Lagan thinks he can just walk into my life and tell me how it's going down, he has no idea who he's talking to. Dad's thrown enough curve balls at my life. It's my turn to take the pitcher's mound.

"So Captain Lagan wants to just swoop in and save the day." I dust off my pants with my hands. "How 'bout I handle my business, and you stick to keeping my sister safe? After you." Opening the back door, I wait for Lagan to walk through.

"I'm not leaving without you." Lagan hasn't budged. "I made a promise to Talia, and I plan to keep my word."

"Fine. Have it your way." I take a final look at the place I call home. "Where's my sister?" The cool metal in my pocket gives me options. Plan B it is.

"I'll tell you one thing. She's never coming back here." Lagan eagle eyes me till I step outside, then slams the door behind us. "Race you to the train."

As I jog next to Lagan several blocks toward the Main Street Metra train in silence, I brace the gun in my pocket against my gut to keep it from bouncing while a mantra beats between my ears. *You can blow the match out of my hand, but you can't bully the goal out of my head.* If there's a way to hurt Dad without getting burned, I plan to find it. And next time, no one's gonna stop me.

2
~ Jesse ~

April 25ᵗʰ Afternoon

"You pump gas for a living?" The middle-aged woman with an oversized handbag on the train platform asks the question as she moves past me in the other direction, not waiting for an answer.

Lagan looks up from his phone, shakes his head, then faces me. "Gimme a minute while I figure something out," he says and turns his back to me as he returns his attention to the small screen in his palm.

A young couple facing each other leans against the pillar and makes out, blind to the world around them. Several men and women wearing business attire stroll onto the platform, each person enraptured by their phones, oblivious to the couple that continues kissing, the girl's backpack slipping off her shoulder to her feet.

More and more people file onto the platform—the train coming soon, I'm guessing. Distancing myself, I edge closer to the platform ledge. The railroad lies on top of a bed of grey stones, a shade lighter than the sky above. I look down the length of the train tracks. Then turn my head and follow the path down the other side, the Chicago skyline barely visible in the haze. *Does the direction really matter?* Distance from Dad while I rethink my plan is all I need. And to know for sure Talia is safe.

"Where is she?" I ask Lagan when he moves next to me at the edge of the concrete.

Lagan waits a beat till a man wearing a Bears jersey passes behind us. "Your sister's checking into a DVS shelter for women. I didn't think it could happen so fast. But…it's happening."

Talia used to tell me Lagan had a thing for acronyms. "And DVS stands for…?"

"That's one I didn't make up, actually." Lagan looks left and right before saying, "Domestic violence survivors." Lagan wipes his mouth like he just cursed. "And the thing is, technically, no one can know the location. It's for the safety of the women—they keep the site confidential."

Like a punch in the gut, the news that Talia left me first stings even though I planned to leave her today. The only nights I slept under a different roof than Talia were those few weeks in the hospital. Today it'll be by choice.

"Can I talk to her?" I ask, turning to the sound of the whistle in the distance. The silver train approaches from the north, the first car blue with red diagonal stripes on its face.

"I think so. I mean, I dunno. This is all new to me." Then he adds, "I hope so."

The tracks intoxicate as the train barrels closer, and the front of my feet teeter on the edge, remembering a time when it seemed so easy. To. Just. Fall. Lagan tugs on my sleeve as he tries to show me something on his phone. "I think I found at least three places for you."

I step back as the train screeches to a stop, and the doors spread open. "So where exactly are we going?"

Lagan steps on the train and says, "You gotta trust me. Come on," his hand holding back the door.

A clap of thunder in the distance nudges me forward onto the train. Lagan climbs a few steps to the top level and takes a seat on the semi-crowded car. The motion of the train cements

11

my feet to the train floor, the chill of the steel pole in my grip as real as the feeling of falling. Because I fell once. Leaned into the offer of "The End" and sailed off the roof. Only thing is, I woke up in a hospital instead of the morgue.

***

The first time I tried to open my eyes, the whitewashed ceiling above floated by like a sea of clouds. Snowflakes began to fall, and before the first one landed on my face, I exhaled, and my breath helped her take flight again. But then the next fell. And the next. And I couldn't keep up. I blew upward, trying to push back my cold reality. But the memories avalanched me back as I lay here, unable to escape, buried in my fall. It was a cold winter that night. The night I fell off the roof.

"Talia!" The scream never left my lips. I felt my throat constricting, tasted the salt of my breath as I exhaled, and discovered something stuck in my mouth. A tube ran past my teeth and down my throat. The scent of iodine filled my senses as I tried to yell again. Nothing.

Not even a whisper. *What the?* Why couldn't I speak? As my fingers slowly pulled into fists, my arms felt like lead. And my legs? Did I still have—? Lowering my eyes down my torso, my toes peeked out of the thin, white sheets, but my legs didn't move, like someone built a wall between my thoughts and my actions.

"Somebody!" I tried again. Nothing. Curses slashed across my mind. *What happened?* The whir of monitors, tubes, and lines mocks me with the answer: You, Justice, are still alive.

***

"Ticket?" The conductor's voice startles me, his hand stretched toward me, palm open.

"Uh…?" I search for an answer like the days I searched for my voice. I turn to see Lagan walking over, steadying himself on the moving train.

"One's for my friend here." Lagan hands the man sporting a striped cap two ticket stubs, and the conductor continues down the aisle to other passengers.

"Thanks."

Lagan nods, his fist wiping his goatee as the other takes hold of the same pole I'm holding. Stepping toward the window, my moving legs remind me the winter of my fall is in the past. Spring's speeding toward summer, and like a child lost in a toy store, I turn my attention to the blur of graffiti-covered walls whizzing by on Chicago streets, dizzy with the duality that I don't know where anything is, and I don't know what I'm looking for. The clouds break up above and red fingerprints streak across the evening sky. Maybe the storm will pass before it rains after all.

The train jolts to a stop and a recorded voice overhead announces, "This is Riverside Station. Next stop: Harlem. Harlem Station is your next stop."

"So, the plan?" I mutter under my breath, my eyes glued to the speaker overhead where the muffled voice sounded the station names.

"We stay on till the end of the line," Lagan says.

"Downtown?" The skyline, more intricate than the one painted on my t-shirt, grows taller and clearer as the train approaches the city.

"Yep. Union Station."

"And then?" I ask.

"We find you a safe place too." Lagan makes eye contact, perhaps searching for a sign of agreement in my face. The city lights brighten as we approach downtown, and I'm torn between trusting him and finding my own way. The sheer magnitude of the buildings shrinks my courage to face the future alone, but the weight of the revolver in my pocket decides for me. I can't risk going somewhere someone might find it and take it away from me.

I go back to staring out the window, fewer trees lining the streets crowded with people and high-rises. I shift my attention to inside the train to slow the rising panic inside me. A billboard advertising, "Accidents happen, but we'll help you get back on your feet," displays a woman in a wheelchair, the man next to her wearing a suit, his hand on her shoulder, smiles plastered across both their faces. I picture Dad walking in the front door to find my empty wheelchair, cursing the gasoline-soaked furniture, and setting the house on fire since there's no way to salvage anything. Then slipping on the broken glass of his office window, breaking his leg, and cutting up his beautiful face. Unable to stand, he burns down with the house.

"This is us." Lagan's voice extinguishes the fire as he moves toward the doors. The train enters a dark tunnel, lights flooding the indoor station seconds later, then we slow down as the platform nears.

Watching people exit the train as they pick up purses, shopping bags or backpacks and move through the parting doors, each person knows exactly where they're going. All I know is I'm not going back. For the first time in my life, the decision to go anywhere, do anything, and be anyone, is really mine.

"Union Station. Last stop. Please check your seats for your belongings." The only things I have with me are the clothes on my back and Dad's gun. "Everyone must exit the train. Union Station. Last stop."

Stepping off the train, Lagan and I follow the crowds past the tracks into the waiting area, a huge room bordered by cathedral-sized columns, lined with wooden benches covered by a dome glass ceiling. Lagan stops, scans the room for signs, and says, "This way."

I trail him outdoors, unsure when I should go my own way. A couple blocks of walking, and we pass the entrance to a familiar name—Quincy Station—the Brown Line that Talia used to say she took to work. I slow my stride then stop in my tracks, pedestrians passing me from in front and behind, the bump of shoulders making me second-guess my decision to go solo.

It takes a moment for Lagan to look over his shoulder and notice I'm not behind him. "Coming?" he asks.

"Going, actually," I say, my heart pounding as the words leave before I agree with them.

Lagan retraces his steps and stops in front of me. "I looked up this place. I think it could work for you. Get you away from your dad and give you time to get on your feet, ya know."

I taught myself to walk again. I'm thinking I know a thing or two about how to get back on my feet. "And then what?" I'm not looking at a one-week fix to my life. I'm thinking next month, next year, heck, the next decade. Even bears know that winter still comes when they hibernate. Dad isn't gone. Out of sight, for now, but who knows for how long?

"And then…" Lagan's palm rests on his forehead, his fingers disappearing in that thick head of black hair. "And then, you'll figure it out. Main thing is you have a place to start." His hand drops down, and he crosses his arms over his chest.

"Here's as good as anywhere." Anywhere not walled in by Dad is good. I shake my head, no, thank you.

"Whaddya sayin'?" Lagan wants me to spell it out.

"Thanks." Because that's all I really need him to know. "Thanks for taking care of Talia. I know you won't let anything happen to her."

"I can't promise…" Lagan catches himself in mid-thought. "What am I gonna tell her? When she asks me where you are? If you're okay?"

"Tell her." I need a moment to think. "Tell her…I'm good. Tell her she doesn't have to take care of me anymore. Tell her…it's my turn to stand up for her."

"You're kidding me? After all she went through for you? All you went through together. You're just gonna up and leave her? No details? No way for her to find you?" Lagan shakes his head, his arms still crossed over his chest, like he means to block my way along with my plan.

I straighten my stand, my hands shoved in my pockets, and look Lagan in the eye. "What do you know about what we went through? Besides, you're the one who told me I can't know where she is. Just tell her she doesn't have to worry about me anymore." I look away when I add, "Tell her she's…free." Even as the last word leaves my lips, I feel a yank like a dog collar, the smooth metal of the gun in my palm, pulling me in the direction of Dad. I won't be free till he's six feet under.

"I'm sorry." Lagan's voice lowers again. "I don't claim to know what you went through." Lagan uncrosses his arm, one fist under his chin again. "What if you just come and stay with me instead? You can do your thinking there."

His house. His parents' rules. Rules that probably include: no guns. I shake my head, no. "Thanks. But I can't. Your parents will ask questions."

"I meant my dorm. You can crash on the couch for a few days. I'm sure my roommate won't mind."

Sounds inviting. Maybe that life—the one with friends, roommates, and college—can be mine, someday. For now, I force myself to shake my head no again, and avoid eye contact with Lagan.

Lagan swings one of his long legs, sending a rock sailing off the curb. "Fine. If there's no convincing you, at least take my phone. So you can call Talia and let her know you're okay." Lagan slaps his iPhone in my palm then pulls out his wallet. "I have, like, a little over a hundred and fifty. Take it. And, and you're gonna need some kind of I.D. Here, take my license. And subway card, my library card, and—"

"Get outta here." I return the phone, arch back slightly, and wave both hands in the air. "I never asked for a handout. I look nothing like the picture on your license, and like I said, knowing my sister has you is enough."

Lagan puts the cash, subway, and library cards in my right hand, holding them in place till I take hold of it (them?). "Just take it. You can always pay me back."

Staring down at my closed fist, I say, "I will pay you back." *How can I ever repay you for taking care of my sister?*

"If you need anything? Anything at all?" Lagan's eyes narrow as he kicks the sidewalk again, missing the small pebble sitting still.

"I'll find you." If I can convince Lagan, maybe I can convince myself. "One last thing, if you could, wouldja tell my sister that I..." I watch for a few passersby to move on ahead of us.

Lagan pulls me into a quick chest to chest. "I'll tell Talia that you love her, okay?"

I let go and step back, picturing Talia's face as we stand eye to eye. "Thanks."

Lagan nods, and I turn and ascend the steps up to the L, searching for a wall map to find my bearings and figure out my next step. I watch several train-goers insert their transit cards into the slit above the turnstile and push through. After reading and rereading the signs to make sure the line is headed north, I insert the card Lagan gave me, retrieve it, and push through.

I could be wrong, but I have a pretty good hunch where to find Dad once the fit hits the shan. He's gonna fly outta the house with one goal in mind—to find Talia. And we both know where she's supposed to be.

3
~ Talia ~

April 25th Evening

I live in the in between. Between yesterday and forever. The way forward haunts me. The gap I must cover daunts me. And hope beckons, "Run to me," but I just learned to walk. I walked away from my life hours ago, and I still doubt the decision to walk alone.

As I unpack my backpack in my new bedroom at the Hope Now safe house, I tuck my thoughts inside my books on the wooden desk, *Hamlet* below *Gatsby* below *A Beautiful Fight*. Tracing the image of the green sword on the top book, the blank Post-its remain intact, marking Lagan's favorite parts. *Lagan*. The boy who opened my heart with his Sticky Note-sized love letters and loves stories about gardening and war. *Gardening. War.*

Dropping everything, I retrace my steps through the hallway to find the room with the community telephone and call the Garden office. It rings on repeat till the voicemail kicks in. The boom of thunder outside the window rattles me, the receiver nearly slipping from my fingers. Maybe they closed the garden early because of bad weather.

I listen for a dial tone and press Jason's cell phone number from memory. The same Jason who taught me the difference between a rake and a hoe when I started volunteering at the garden. *Please pick up.*

"What?" Jason yells into the receiver.

"Jason? It's Talia, I was just—"

"The willow! It's on fire, Talia. On. Fire!"

My eyes blur with flames I cannot see. Under the branches of the willow tree, where I first met the gardener, the silent voice spoke into my dreams and listened to my fears, especially the ones I couldn't tell anyone.

"What are you talking about?" My hand shakes uncontrollably.

"I dunno what happened," Jason says, his words racing one into the other. "One minute, there's a stampede to the parking lot and people screaming, 'Fire!' And then your dad's here raving like a lunatic about his daughter missing and what if she's trapped in the fire. I told him, 'Look, the fire trucks are on their way and she's not around. She [meaning you] already came in today and left.'"

I'm sure Dad had something to do with the fire. He followed me to work and watched me like a hawk that first week when Jason gave me the assignment to restore the willow. Did he think I was hiding up in the willow, and he could just smoke me out?

"So he left?" I ask.

"Eventually. But not before pressing me, following me into the parking lot, threatening to sue the Garden if I didn't come up with some answers." Jason's panting as he spews out more details. "I finally said, 'Sir, with all due respect, I'm on staff here, and right now my number one priority is to ensure the safety of all the patrons. If you wanna know where your daughter is, go ask her boyfriend.'"

"Boy-friend?" I bite my lower lip. Is this what it feels like to be speeding down the highway—only to discover you're on the wrong side of traffic?

"...had to evacuate the garden." Jason's voice fades in and out. "...and I hate the smell of everything burning, and when the fire trucks finally arrived, they were able to sort of contain the fire, but it's not over. They're still out there, Talia, and I'm so sorry. All that time you spent bringing the willow back to... Hold on a minute. Boss is asking me something. Sorry."

Me too. Dad knows, and now there's no way I can see Lagan. Dad'll be on him like a hawk, trying to get to me. Where's Jesse? I need to call Lagan.

"Wait, Jason!" I hate the sound of my voice raised. "Did you tell him Lagan's name?"

"No. I mean, well, I might have said that Indian dude who biked here all the time. But I'm pretty sure I never said his name. Definitely not his last name. I don't even know his last name—hold up. I really have to go, now. The cops need me to go down to the station and make a statement. Bye Talia. Call back."

I place the phone on its stand, pick it up and dial Lagan's number once. Twice. A third time. Voicemail, every time. I hang up when I hear the prompting beep and walk back to my assigned room in the women's shelter.

Less than twelve hours ago, Lagan and I debated whether this was the best option. In the end, he convinced me to give it a try, a place where other women like me come to—a place Dad can't hurt me anymore. The willow on fire means one thing: Dad will find a way to hurt me, whether I live at home or not.

Diana, the woman who interviewed me at the downtown headquarters of Hope Now, is the second person I ever told about Dad. Second after Lagan. But I lied about Dad's name. I know she said she wouldn't contact him, but I don't know who I can trust when years ago, the mention of Dad's name brought an end to our one chance of escaping with Mom.

Diana is nothing like Mom. She speaks with confidence. She wears bright lipstick. And she doesn't seem afraid of anything or anyone. Diana drove me over here to give me a tour of the safe house, and while she outlined the house rules, I memorized the contours of her hair, long like mine, but wavy and black while my brown hair falls pin-straight. At the start of the drive, she wound her hair into a messy bun, revealing grey strands not visible when her hair is down. And Diana glanced over from behind her rectangular specs at each red light, maybe to make sure I hadn't changed my mind.

From the outside, this shelter looks like a regular house, just larger, with a yard bordered by a tall fence lined with rows of evergreens. The gated entrance must deter the neighbors from casually walking up to ask for a cup of sugar. There are nine women currently residing here—I make number ten. This particular site is now at max capacity.

Holding a paper cup of something steamy in one hand and no longer wearing the business jacket from earlier, Diana catches me in the hallway and hands me a packet, and I can't help but stare at her flawless skin, several silver bangles gracing her tiny ivory wrists.

"Everything okay, Talia? You look like you just saw a ghost."

"I'm...I have a lot to think about." I fan the stack of papers between my fingers. "How much time do I have to fill these out?" Time. Deadlines. The line that went dead when Jason hung up. And Lagan didn't pick up his phone.

"By the end of the week work for you?"

Will Dad try and set the city of Chicago on fire by the end of the week?

"Talia?" Diana's hand on my arm makes me shudder and pull away. My arm with the scars. The scars from the burns. "Did you hear me?"

"A week. Yyy-yes." I take a deep breath. Diana is not Dad, but this place has rules. "I can have these done by then."

The words on the pages in my hands blur together as I think about the initial waiver papers I signed back at the office, noting one part printed in bold: Residents will not disclose the location of the shelter under any circumstances. Failure to observe this rule will result in immediate evacuation of said resident in the interest of the safety of other residents.

Location. Safety. Failure.

I feel like a failure, because I can't keep Jesse and Lagan

safe from here. They can't even know where here is. At this very second, I don't know where my brother is, but from all that Jason said, it sounded like Dad came alone, so I have to believe Jesse and Dad are apart.

"If you need anything else, I end my work day by stopping by the safe house most days, okay? And take your time." Diana tucks a loose strand of hair behind her right ear and takes a sip, leaving a trace of pink lipstick on the rim of her coffee cup. When we reach the room, she repeats herself. "I mean it when I say take your time, all right? We've had residents stay up to even a year while their cases get processed, and they're able to get their papers in order and get back on their feet. We don't want to see our survivors return to abusive situations. Make sense?"

I nod, wondering deep down if anything makes sense right now. I've never had time on my side before, and now someone's telling me it's okay to take my time. Find my way. They want to help. Who's gonna help the garden? My dying willow? Jesse? And Lagan now that Dad knows about him?

Diana opens my bedroom door and lets me walk through first. "Wish we could just hug you into our place and never ask any questions," she says. "But the laws are in place to protect you and part of that process includes filing records. So, if you could return the paperwork and make sure to meet with healthcare and social work by the end of the week, I'll go over anything you're confused about, okay?" She takes a swig from her cup. "It's a lot to adjust to. A new place, a new schedule, new people. We expect everything to take time." Diana walks over, placing a hand on the dresser top. "There are clean linens in the closet and some clothes the girls put in the drawers to get you started. And Talia," Diana waits for me to look up. "You're going to doubt yourself a hundred times, today. For many days. Whether you did the right thing by leaving. I'm telling you that you did. And we're here for you, okay?"

The word, "Okay," gets stuck in my throat, so I just nod again. I want to believe everything she's saying. I need to believe this wasn't a mistake. Just can't pinpoint why I feel more alone than ever when I should be thrilled that I'm no longer near Dad. But even as Diana leaves, a familiar wave of emptiness washes over me, like the day Mom died. I lay the papers next to my books on the desk before I lie back on the twin mattress, nestling my head into the pillow. My fingers unravel the Post-it from my back pocket. The last one Lagan gave me. It reads:

you + me = us three

The words morph, and all I see are numbers:

$1 + 1 = 3$

He always did love math. But this equation stings a bitter reminder as I tuck it under my pillow and turn on my tummy to add up my options. For now, it's just me, myself and I. Three in one. Doesn't mean I have to like it, but I get it. No Jesse. No Lagan. No waterfall willow. I'm alone.

4
~ Jesse ~

April 25th Evening

It's too late. I'm too late. I smell the smoke before I see the billows of black swirling in the glow of the streetlights. The sound of thunder makes me look up and I half expect to see a fire where lightning rips across the sky followed by another ba-boom. The garden's gated off with caution tape at every turn, and police cars and fire trucks race past with sirens blaring. Dad's fingerprints are everywhere.

As I turn the corner toward the parking lot, more caution strips, and a City of Glenco cop redirects traffic on foot. I shrink back, stepping off the shoulder of the road behind the tree line, the gun feeling heavier in my pocket at the sight of a police uniform. A long line of cars crawl toward and away from the garden—I'm guessing a combination of visitors and gawkers since sirens tend to draw a crowd.

"Sorry, young lady." I can hear the officer talking to the young brunette in a black Mazda pulled to a stop close by. "The stargazer's show is cancelled, the garden has been evacuated, and I have no idea when the garden will reopen."

I can see her gasping at the sight of all the smoke, and for a second, I think she catches me staring at her. Something about the expression on her face reminds me of Talia, and I start to doubt myself. Maybe I should've insisted on seeing my sister first, taking Lagan's phone so I could call her, and making sure she's safe and not mad at me.

When the officer one-eighties back toward the parking lot, I retrace my steps to the road, unsure if I should stick around in case Dad comes out of the woodwork, blowtorch in hand. The cop did say, everyone was evacuated. For the second time today, my plans have been foiled. I have Lagan to thank for messing up Plan A. Plan B was simple. Following Dad as he roamed the garden in search of Talia, he'd find one thing—a bullet in the back of his head. I haven't given Plan C any thought, and it starts raining.

"He does not look like the guy in the movie we saw last week." The girls in the Mazda that pulls up next to me speak so loudly, I can hear their every word, the traffic still inching forward.

"Just cuz you see a guy walking in the rain does not make him a Hollywood star!" the girl in the passenger seat says. I keep walking, ignoring them while pulling at my shirt sleeves, unable to make them magically grow longer to cover my now wet arms.

"Need a ride to the train station?" Gal in the driver's seat leans across to speak to me. Up close her hair shows lighter streaks of brown through it as she turns to face the girl in the passenger seat, "Jump in the back, Winter." There's a girl already sitting back there.

"I'm okay. Thanks." I'm not ready to talk to anyone, and the scent of gasoline on my clothes reminds me I stink. "Plus I don't want to mess up—"

Thunder booms, interrupting me. Heavier rains come down, and the passenger door swings open, the girl in front cursing as she moves to the back of the car. "Jump in. You're gonna get soaked!" the girl in the driver's seat says. And I do.

"So where ya headed?" Girl behind the wheel asks, and I clear my throat once. Twice.

"The Metra's good. Thanks for the ride." I can feel the

water drip off my head onto my shoulders.

"You fall in a pool of gasoline?" The girl who sat in the back from the beginning asks the question.

Driver's seat gal shakes her head, glancing over at me. "Ignore my sister. She's nosy. Glad we could help. My name's Summer, by the way."

"I'd consider changing up the cologne, is all I'm sayin' since Summer won't." I turn and the girl originally in the passenger seat flashes a smirk.

"Yeah, like I said," Summer turns and locks eyes with me at the red light. "My sisters are a lot of things. Shy is not one of them. Meet Autumn [Summer cocks her head back] and Winter [Summer thumb-points to girl sitting behind me.] Go ahead. Ask me why our parents named us after seasons?" Light turns green, Summer hits the gas, the traffic finally clearing, and silence follows.

Your parents could name a fourth girl, Spring, but I don't know anyone named Spring. Like the winter of my fall, when my voice hid for a season, words fail me. And I don't say my name, either. Car sloshes through the downpour for the next few minutes, the sound of a Michael Jackson remix on the radio.

"I was born in July." Summer answers her own question. "Autumn in October and Winter in January. So yeah. There you have it."

"And no that doesn't mean I lose my leaves or hair on my birthday," Autumn says.

"Just your mind." Winter raises a palm for a high five, but Autumn ignores it.

"And that's why I say she's the coldest," Autumn quips back.

Making Summer the warmest. If the name fits…

Winter taps the back of my chair, and says, "And you thought you were safe getting in a car with three girls!" followed by giggles from all three siblings.

The rain still falls in sheets when Summer pulls into the Metra parking lot. The brick house waiting room with a cone-shaped roof looks dark inside.

"Want to wait in the car till the train comes?" Summer asks, fidgeting with her black skirt next to me. "You'll be soaked if you stand out there."

"I'll be fine." I open the car door and step one shoe right into a deep puddle and change my mind. "Then again, waiting is good. I could wait." Close the door as I sit back down, annoyed that my sock is soaked.

"You could take my poncho." Summer unbuckles her seat belt and pulls the navy blue rain gear off, holding it between us. A tattoo circles her upper arm, a vine of leaves above cursive letters spelling words I can't read in the dark.

I want to ask what it says. Instead I say, "How will I get it back to you?" I hate owing somebody.

"Are you kidding?" Winter darts in to respond. "Mom has been trying to get her to give that thing up for like a year. You're doing us all a favor."

"Haha. Whatever." Summer's blue eyes look into mine. "Ignore them. Just, umm, pass it on. I'm sure you'll run into someone who's having a rainy day."

The sound of the approaching train expedites my decision, and I open the door again. "Thanks." My hand brushes Summer's as she hands me her coat. "Gotta go."

Someone, maybe Autumn yells, "Bye, Amoco-Aladdin!" just before I slam the car door shut.

A whole new world, it is. Pull the poncho over my head, race over to the concrete platform and slide into the train car just before the doors kiss. Time to find myself a seat, because this is my bedroom tonight. At least I'll be dry and moving.

***

"Move." Dad's voice entered my thoughts before I pictured his face.

I was five years old, stepping off the bus and running up the driveway on my first day of Kindergarten, two steps ahead of Talia, because I could not wait to show Mom and Dad what I did in school. All the cool pictures of airplanes and trains I shaded in with blues and browns. Someday I want to fly a plane, Daddy. Someday, I'll drive out west, riding on top of a train, Mommy. I rehearsed the announcements in my head.

Beating my big sister to the front door, I was surprised Dad's car sat in the driveway. I pushed open the front door, panting, raced to Dad's den, and shoved my wrinkled drawings on top of his desk. On top of his papers. "Daddy, Daddy, you're done with work early! You'll never believe—"

"Not now." Dad cut me off in mid-sentence. "Move your papers off mine. Now." He hadn't bothered to look at them.

"But Daddy, I just want to show you the one with—"

"I'm only going to say it once, Justice. Move. Your papers. And move on outta here. I came home to fetch some files. I need to get back to the office once I find them."

"But this is important."

"No. You're not." Dad said without flinching.

And like a perfectly timed sprinkler system, I couldn't contain my disappointment.

"Fine." Dad picked me up and put me in his lap. "Show me your picture and then let me get back to my files."

My hope boomeranged back as I flipped the pile of loose pages till I found the one with my favorite airplane sketch, the name N.E.Where printed across its body. Because it could fly…anywhere. My teacher helped me choose the name.

"What is it?" Dad asked. He couldn't tell?

"A plane, Daddy. See here, the wings."

"No. But I'll tell you three things I do see. That I don't like. And I don't ever want to see again. Are you listening?" Dad moved me off his lap and placed the pile of papers back in my hands. "Number one: the papers are wrinkled, bent and messy. Not acceptable. No son of mine will ever again present me with such poor workmanship."

I nodded, confused by how my show and tell turned into a three-part lesson from Dad.

"Number two: I see a boy who has no respect for his father's time and how hard he works to put food on the table. I will not be interrupted again. Am I clear?"

I nodded again. I just thought…

"And number three. Listen very carefully to this one. Boys. Don't. Cry. No boy of mine is going to cry. Got it?"

"O. Kay, Dad." I sniffed up my runny nose, my zeal gone like a hot air balloon deflated and grounded.

"Now. Run along." And a firm nudge on my back directed me out of his office.

I stood on my tippy toes to look at Dad through his office window. Furious at the smile on his lips as he stared at his files and wrote his notes, I didn't bother showing Mom or Talia. Instead, I marched up to my bedroom, crumpled the drawings in my hands, and shoved them in the trash.

5
~ Talia ~

April 26th

Darkness envelops me and I can't see my hands in front of me. Crouched on the floor, I feel for the walls on the sides and in front of me, pushing hard. Harder. They don't budge. He's getting closer. *I have to protect her.*

Banging against the walls, my hands pulse with pain. *I have to escape before he finds us.* The sound of knocking halts my swinging arms. I feel the carpet floor below me, searching for Mom's hand. *If I could just hold her hand, it might hurt less.* But it's gone. She's. Gone.

I shrink into a fetal position, waiting for the first blow. Eyes shut tightly, a second knock makes me wince as I bite my lip to contain the whimper that threatens escaping. Footsteps. A stream of light.

"Talia? Are you awake?" Diana's voice seeps through the closet door like water from the barrel of a gun. The gun I thought was loaded with bullets.

"Talia?" The closet door unlatches behind me and I fall back onto Diana's feet, heat rushing to my cheeks. "Oh, honey."

As Diana braces my shoulders and helps me stand, I rub

the sleep from my eyes, unable to gauge how long I slept. The digital clock radio reads 9:03 AM, and the crick in my neck greets me like a gift. I'm not bleeding, and my arm doesn't burn.

"I don't usually stop by the safe house till after work, but I wanted to drop off a few things and check in on you. See how your first night went." Diana's eyes move past me to the closet. "Are you hungry? Want to get washed up for breakfast?" I can feel her stare studying me in my silence as I take a few steps and sit on the edge of the bed. "Wanna talk about it?"

I shake my head, no.

Diana waits a beat, then says, "Well someone was anxious to talk to you." I look up and meet her gaze, the crease lines at the edge of her eyes emerge when she smiles. "Someone by the name of Lagan called the main office and left a couple of messages for you last night."

Clearing my throat, I tiptoe past last night's cobwebs and find my voice. "Did you, umm, talk to him?"

"We only directly answer the hotline calls to avoid lengthy conversations with family members or possible perpetrators who might be seeking out information about our clients. And just so you know, the safe house lines block the caller I.D. of all outgoing calls to avoid verbal harassment our women don't need."

That could explain why Lagan didn't answer my calls. "What did the message say?"

"Here." Diana peels a yellow Post-it note off the desk and hands it to me. "Read it yourself."

"He left a sticky note for me?" I slip the square, yellow sheet into my back pocket. I fell asleep in my jeans last night.

"No, silly. I wrote the messages down." Diana smiles again and adds, "But he did leave this small box by the mail room at the downtown office sometime last night." She taps the checkbook-sized box sitting on top of the desk next to the paperwork I haven't touched.

Rising to retrieve it, the three letters across the top pop out: *SUS*. Underneath the acronym lies my name. Well, sort of:

Tall-E-A Grace. -L.

Lagan!

My fingers trace the letters SUS as I say the words in my head. See. You. Soon. Will I?

"You heard me, right?" Diana's question lassos me back to now. "Doctor's in this afternoon if you're up to her paying you a visit. All the residents are required to go through a routine physical. Should take less than an hour. Okay?"

"Do I have a choice?" I don't recall ever being examined by a doctor. As far as I know, Dad had his medical friends sign off all our school health papers, and Jesse's trip to the E.R. was the only time I ever stepped into a hospital.

"We want to make sure you don't have any immediate health concerns that you're, perhaps, a little wary to bring up. We just want to take the best care of you we know how." She's not asking. "She'll be by around noon, all right?"

I nod, picking up the small box. It weighs hardly anything and I place it back down as Diana walks back over to the closet.

"I'll put the sheets and towels on your dresser top, for now." Diana waits for my nod of approval before moving the items.

As she shuts the closet door, I picture my baby brother, only eleven at the time, wiping up Mom's vomit and urine and everything else she couldn't contain after two whole days being locked up by Dad. A task that probably crippled him long before he ever fell off the roof and lost the use of his legs. *What roof did you sleep under last night, Jess?*

Diana turns to me in the doorway before leaving and says, "Gotta get back to the office. If you need anything special, call me, but the ladies will walk you through meals and chores and answer any questions you might have, okay?"

After the door closes, I pull out and spread the Post-it over my left palm to read it. *Talia, I just want you to know everything's okay. Jesse's fine. I'll call back okay.*

Flip it over to read message two.

Talia, your dad called my parents' house, looking for you. Good thing is they told him they'd never heard of you. But I got an earful about keeping secrets from my mom late last night. Need to lay low for a bit. We'll talk when things die down. Stay safe.

How is he going to stay safe now that Dad knows who he is? If Dad tried to burn down the garden, how long before he burns down Lagan's house? Or his dorm room? This isn't something a little Post-it note can fix. Wishing I could go back in time, to our secret friendship fueled by Lagan's words on little square yellow sheets, I think about that day I found the first note under my desk.

All the games we played with Post-its, you'd think the guy read a manual on Fifty Ways to Win a Girl's Heart Through Sticky Notes. Maybe he'll author that book, sell a bazillion copies, and buy the moon. Then build our dream house out of stardust so Lagan can spaceship us there for our honeymoon. As long as there's one tree, I could be convinced to move to the moon.

Setting the Post-it aside, I open the box, imagining Lagan's strong, chocolate brown hands wrapping this tiny box in paper. For me. Pulling the lid off, a letter sits on top of a stack of multi-colored Post-its. No surprise there.

I sit down at the desk to read the letter.

Talia, my Dew Drop whom I miss more with each passing second,

I thought I'd send you something small. To tell you what I think about every moment as I wait.

Do you see the Post-its?

Pulling out the Post-it books, I separate them by color. The top sheets all have arrows on them, some in the same direction, some different.

Turning my attention to the letter again:

Find an empty wall and pull up a chair so you can reach up and stick the first Post-it up as high as you can reach. They're numbered, but the key is the direction of the arrows. Place the next Post-it below or next to or diagonal from the last Post-it based on where the arrows point. When a color runs out, leave a little space and start from the top again.

Love you, girl whom I dream about every night. And day.

Lagan

I reread the last line a few dozen times, like I did since the first Post-it Lagan ever gave me, before I realize that I don't have to throw this note away. Dad will never find it in here! *Oh God, please don't let him find Jesse.*

I take a deep breath and focus on the letter. I think I get it—Lagan's instructions. I take the yellow book of Sticky Notes labeled with the number one, pull a chair over to the wall, and start peeling and pressing the notes, one at a time. Down, down, down, across, across, across, up, up, up, and then I get confused because the next one says down. But the color hasn't changed yet, so I don't think I'm supposed to leave a space. I place it on top of the last one, and keep peeling and pressing. Down. Down. Down. Down. Down. Down.

There are no more yellow ones. I stand back and smile, the number four displayed across from me. I suspect I might know what the green Post-it arrows will spell out, but I play along. And sure enough, they spell out a question mark. Then back to yellow, and another Sticky Note-drawn number four appears on the wall. The lilac ones, I can almost do with my eyes closed. The letter U. And when they run out, the bottom note simply says in Lagan's handwriting,

Just let me know when we can start our 4-evah.

I flip the Post-it and the back reads,

Waiting 4 U. Didn't want u 2 4get.

Wish it was enough, I think over and over again as I stare at my Post-it love letter on the wall, but I want more than the memory of, "For what? For you? Forever." I want him. Lagan.

I slip my feet into my black flats and attempt to rise and start my day, but the weight of fresh uncertainty challenges my resolve, and I'm back on my bottom. Sitting with my face in my hands. I wonder if this is how Jesse felt when he knew he could walk again. Would walk again. But lay in bed for months.

Lying back down, my shoes slip off as I shift my legs under the covers. If this is what freedom feels like, I want to go back. To the place where I knew what to expect and what was expected of me, minus Dad's burns. The time I knew Jesse's whereabouts, and Lagan sat a cafeteria lunch table away. The time when every minute was decided for me, so I wouldn't have to choose which way to walk and turn and live. And find out what mistakes will cost me out here on my own.

I bury my arms under my stomach and concentrate on breathing. And as I exhale question mark after question mark, I sense his footsteps like the day we first met in the garden. I knew he was real even if I couldn't see him. The gardener is here, but the waves crashing inside me refuse to still.

6
~ Jesse ~

April 26ᵗʰ Morning

The growling of my stomach chases me out of my dreams, and with the sun arrive swarms of morning commuters. That was the worst night of sleep…okay, maybe not the worst. At least my shoe dried in the air-conditioned car, and no one swiped Summer's blue poncho while I snoozed.

I can't recall the specifics, but I know flames followed me all night as I searched for a way to burn Dad without getting caught with the matches in my hands. Lagan's warning that I can't hurt Dad without getting hurt rings true. Unless… I think of a way to strike where no one but Dad sees and feels pain. I think I know a spot.

The conductor sporting a squared hat walks right up to me, shaking his head. "Look son, I coulda kicked you off the train last night, but it was pouring. The storm has passed. It's time for you to go."

I stand up and as I start to make my way to the door, his hand lands on my shoulder. He's not finished. "Just so you know, this train is not a hotel. Go home or find a friend. I won't be so nice the next time."

When his grip lifts off my shoulder, I pick up my pace and wait by the doors for the train to stop. With one hand shoved in my pocket on top of the gun, I step onto the platform, and follow the crowd into the station, but stop short of pushing through the turnstile when I spot a map on the wall. The sea of street names and train lines brings little clarity even when I spot the "You Are Here" arrow. Like I'm back at the beach in Benton Harbor, the familiar feeling of drowning reminds me that swimming isn't the only thing my parents never taught me to do. Where do I start? And which way do I walk?

A tall, blond woman, wearing a camera around her neck, approaches from behind, stands next to me and examines the map too. Parched like I've been trekking through the Sahara, my throat tightens.

"Can I help you? You look kinda lost." A man sporting glasses and a business suit offers the woman help.

"Oh, that is so very kind of you," she replies with a European accent. "I'm looking for the famous Bean everyone talks about. I want to photograph it for my students back home."

"So, you're a teacher. Where's home?" the man asks, as he begins to trace the pathway to Millennium Park with his fingertip on the map.

"Germany." She smiles then turns her gaze to follow his moving hand. "Oh. I see. So if I head in the direction of Lake Michigan—"

"And walk north from Buckingham Fountain along Lakeshore Drive, you'll run right into it." The man pulls down on the bottom of his sport jacket, beaming a grin like he showed her a secret passage to China. "My office is in the same direction if you want company part of the way?"

"Thank you, so very much, sir. And my sister warned me about you Americans. You're the third person today who's been kind to me." The woman adjusts her bright orange handbag on her shoulder and the two strangers walk toward the exit sign, chatting coffee and deep-dish pizza.

The mention of food prompts a growl from my stomach.

Emptying my back pocket to examine the cash from Lagan, I decide a few dollars on breakfast might help me to think clearly. As I count the bills, a card slips from my hand to the cement floor. Shoving the cash back in my pocket, I reach down to retrieve Lagan's library card, and in that small act, an idea births to help execute my newest plan. Breakfast can wait.

Using my finger as the man had done moments ago, I count the number of blocks and memorize the street names and turns from the station to my first destination. Recount. Rehearse the street names with my eyes closed and then opened, making sure I remember every turn. Sucking in a breath, I remind myself that I can always come back here and look at the map some more before I step through the doors and out to a bright and sunny Chicago morning.

After walking six blocks down Adams, turning right on State Street, the Chicago Public Library stands in front of me. The tall, cathedral-type structure has heavy glass doors that don't budge when I pull on the handle. The opening hours etched to the side window let me know it's not nine yet. The 5:00PM closing hours cancel my plans to sleep among the stacks tonight. Peering through the glass, no books in sight, I wonder what kind of library this is? Judging by the sheer size of this building, books and hopefully some computers have to be in there somewhere.

A fresh pang of hunger nudges me to search for breakfast as I cross the street. The window on McDonald's displays a "Hiring Now" sign, reminding me that my resources are limited. Wondering if they'll hire someone without any experience, the fine print at the bottom of the sign reads, "Citizens and Permanent Residents need only apply." Without a real I.D., how will I prove where I was born? Panic surges inside me, and I'm tempted to run to Lagan for help. The gun in my pocket lobs back—*not yet.*

As I watch several people pay a street vendor money and walk away with drinks and food, I follow suit and stand in line. But my turn comes up before I'm able to determine which option is better, the breakfast special or coffee and a donut.

Plus, I've never even tasted coffee.

"Move to the side until you know what you want," short, balding man wearing a white apron over his clothes says, looking past me to the growing line behind me. And I do.

After three people order in front of me, all choosing the special, I follow suit, imitating their actions by sliding money across the counter and saying, "Breakfast special, please. Juice no coffee."

"Got anything smaller?" He wraps up the bagel in a paper towel and lays it next to a cup with an unwrapped straw on the counter already crowded with a napkin dispenser and bottles of ketchup and mustard.

I shake my head, no, and he huffs as he counts out change and slides the stack of singles over with the food.

"Thank you," I say, folding the bills up without counting them, and before I finish taking my food, the guy behind me slaps down a ten-dollar bill and says, "Special. Make that two. One coffee, one tea."

As I walk back to the library, sipping orange juice, instinctively, I check over my shoulder every few steps. Sitting on the bench across from the library entrance to eat, I stare up at the three towering arched windows on the red brick building and imagine the copper-washed, green owls mounted on every corner come to life, swoop down, and pluck me with their talons, flying me back to Dad. Sinking back into the bench, then startled by the brush of a paper bag against my leg, I drop the last of my bagel to the grassy floor. Two pigeons hop over and battle over their newfound breakfast, and I rise to toss my empty cup in the closest wastebasket.

Pedestrians of all ethnic backgrounds, shapes and ages race back and forth on the sidewalk, most either talking on or staring at their phones. Several young people, maybe college kids, line up at the library doors with backpacks in tow. Not wanting to go alone, I follow them when they file through the entrance. Dizzied by the ceiling-covered skylights flooding the lobby with sunlight, this place makes the Benton Harbor school library shrink to dollhouse size. Talia dreamed she'd own a dollhouse one day.

I'm gonna give you something better than a dollhouse when this is over, Big Sis. Turning slowly as I read signs in search of public computers, I'm itching to find some answers. Where are you, Dad? Because for once in my life, I'm looking for you.

7

~Talia ~

April 26th, Midmorning

A knock at the door stirs me from sleep for the second time today, but this time I'm sitting at the desk with my head on my arms, Lagan's letter under my elbow. "Talia, my name is Dr. Kane, and Diana called me to come and see you." The voice on the other side of the door reminds me of my Brit Lit Prof, who annunciates every syllable. "Do you need a few minutes, dear?"

Reading Lagan's Post-it letter on the wall and reasoning this Dr. Kane lady won't wait forever, I clear my throat and say, "Yes, please."

"Okay. Twenty minutes enough for you? I can do my rounds and return in twenty."

"Yes." This time I rise from the chair and spot the toiletry items on the dresser top next to the sheets Diana moved out of the closet. Not like I can wash away the past, but I'm ready to change out of yesterday's clothes. Without touching the Sticky Notes, I trace the Post-it letters on the wall with my index finger, noting the question mark seems larger than any of the other symbols.

Breaking the plastic link between black flip-flops I find on the dresser top, I place the pair on the floor and slip my socks off before sliding my feet into them. As I sort through the small stack of clothes in the top drawer of the cabinet, my heart sinks when I can't find a green top. Settling for a black long sleeve and black yoga pants, I fish out undergarments with tags still attached, and a white towel with tiny orange flowers weaved into the border. They remind me of the garden, and I need the familiar like I need oxygen right now. Tracing the little flowers with my thumb, I walk over and wait outside the restroom down the hall from my bedroom.

"It's all yours." As she exits the communal bathroom, the young, Latina lady smiles at me, her bathrobe as black as the long dark curls falling down her back.

I nod and as the door closes behind me, I push the lock in place, allowing my fingers to linger on the latch. Dad removed the locks in the new house. Besides the one he installed on his office door, of course, after that awful day when I knocked a pile of letters off his desk. The letter from Amit Shah, Mom's dad, that seems like a dream since I never found it to show Jesse. As I place the soap bar and clothes on the vanity counter and step into the shower, I try to think of what Dr. Kane will ask me. Without much knowledge of my parents' histories, making up answers is something I can manage.

After toweling off, I pull on strangers' clothes, then walk back to my room and sit on the edge of the bed, fiddling with the cuff of my left sleeve, leaving the door slightly ajar. A knock at the door announces Dr. Kane's arrival.

"Hi Talia." She stretches out the hand not holding her black bag, and I notice her French-manicured nails as we loosely shake. "Ready for me?"

I nod as Dr. Kane shuts the door, but my eyes are fixed on the camera hanging off her shoulder which she immediately unloops and sets on the table next to her clipboard. Diana's paperwork sits next to it, untouched.

"Can we start by just chatting?" she asks, and then turns the chair at the desk around so she can sit and face me.

Sure. Talk. Who brings a camera to talk?

"I need to document your responses, but let's start off the record, okay."

My throat feels dry as I focus on her navy blue, high-heeled sandals, peach-painted toenails peeking out. She's not wearing a white coat over her blue, short-sleeved dress and her wavy red curls momentarily tangle with the earpiece as she slides the stethoscope from around her neck and places it over her black bag on the floor.

"I'll share a bit and tell you why I'm here, and then I'll start with the routine physical, okay?"

I nod, okay, but somewhere inside me, I picture drawing a sword from its sheath, ready to lunge at the first hint of invasion.

"First let me tell you why I'm not here." Dr. Kane waits a beat for me to look up and make eye contact. Her emerald-green eyes squint as she smiles before continuing. "I'm not here to force you to share anything. I'm not here to hurt your feelings by making you talk about your pain. I'm not here to blame you for the pain that someone else has caused you. One last thing: I'm not here to fix you."

Another pause as my chin lowers to my chest and I place the invisible sword on the floor.

"So why am I here?" I glance up and manage a small smile. "I'm here today to tell you your options. And more than anything else, I'm here to tell you that I believe you, even if you don't say a word, I believe you came here, because you're hurt. But no one out there will believe you unless we show them proof." Her gaze shifts to the camera on the desk and then back to me.

As my heart reaches for the sword again, Dr. Kane asks her first question.

"What's your date of birth?" She crosses her legs and holds a pen and her clipboard now.

Eyes fixed on the camera, I swallow and answer. "May 6th, 1992."

"Father's name?"

I think of the name I told Diana. "Benjamin. Benjamin

Burns."

"Mother's name? Any siblings?" And on and on, Dr. Kane asks basic questions of my family history, but to most questions, I lie or shrug my shoulders. I don't know if Dad has any history of heart disease. Or if anyone on Mom's side of the family ever had diabetes. But I tell her Mom's name. I don't want that part of my story to be a lie. Gita was my mother. But she passed away when I was fourteen years old. This much I tell her.

"Before we continue talking, I'll do a quick physical exam." Dr. Kane unzips her black bag and pulls out a blood pressure cuff, looping the stethoscope back around her neck. "I can take your pulse and pressure at the same time, and then I'll listen to your heart, okay?"

The pounding of my heart quickens from a soft rap on a conga drum to a palm and fingertip-pulsing boom as my attention fixates on my left sleeve.

"Want to roll up your sleeve so I can slip the cuff to your upper arm?"

I shake my head no. Then shift on the bed so my right arm is closer to her and push up my sleeve, but it's too tight to slide past my elbow.

"It'll be easier if you take your shirt off," Dr. Kane says, rising to shut the door completely. "This'll only take a moment."

"I. can't." Lagan is the only person I ever showed my arm to.

"Is it your arm? Did he hurt your arm?" When Dr. Kane reaches for me, touching my arm on top of my sleeve, I flinch, tugging the sleeve past my wrist.

One glance at the camera lens, and Dad's voice growls inside my head: "I dare you to show her your scars."

Two swords duel away inside me now where only moments ago there was only one. The words "Anger" and "Shame" are etched in the sword handles, and what I know from all the battles growing up, especially the ones I fought silently in my head, is no one wins and everyone gets hurt.

Like she can read my mind, Dr. Kane says, "I'm not here to hurt you. Do you believe me?"

Why should I? I fiddle with the hem of my shirt, and I think I hear Dad saying, "Show her and I'll make sure the other arm looks worse than your left one."

"He can't hurt you in here." Dr. Kane lifts my chin so we're eye to eye, and says, "You are the only one who can make sure he never hurts you again."

"You don't know my dad." I say, my stare shifting to the bedroom closet. "What he's capable of."

"You obviously want it to stop. That's why you came here, correct?"

"Why do I have to show you what he did to me?" My words taste like salt on an ice cream sundae. I know she's trying to help, but I, I…"I hate looking at what he's done to me. I just want the reminders to go away."

"The bigger question is…" Dr. Kane returns to her seat and folds her arms over her chest. "Do you want the person who hurts you to go away? As in be put away, in jail, where he can't hurt you anymore?"

Silently I consider her questions. The possibility of justice. *Justice.* His name makes me want my brother, even just to hear his voice. A sound that disappeared for a season after he tried to end his life. Wondering how to get there from here, I close my eyes when I come out of hiding. Pulling my sleeve back, my nails scrape my forearm, slamming the brakes at the crux of my elbow. I'm holding my trembling, scarred arm out to Dr. Kane and shaking my head side to side, my eyes squeezed shut. I don't know what I'll hate more, her pity or her judgment. I brace myself for both.

"Can I examine your arm more closely?" I can hear her footsteps as she approaches the bed again. "Does it smart to the touch?"

"No." I say honestly. "It doesn't hurt to touch it. Today."

Dr. Kane picks up my hand first and when I open my eyes, she moves her fingers slowly over my arm, the scales and blotches and bumps disappearing and reappearing as she works her way from my wrist to my elbow, pushing and squeezing gently, the sound of us taking turns exhaling the only thing heard as seconds pass.

"Burns." The first word to leave Dr. Kane's mouth sums it up.

I nod, yes. Burns upon burns. So many, I lost count.

"Did he use a hot liquid?" Dr. Kane asks.

"Water." We both know it was hot. Too hot.

"How often?" she asks.

I suck in a breath before saying, "As often as I failed." I wait a beat. Then say, "Often."

"I see." Dr. Kane gently lowers my arm to my lap before she writes a few notes on her chart. Then looks up and asks, "Can I? Is it okay to photograph your arm?" Dr. Kane reaches for her camera.

"Why?" I yank down my sleeve. I don't need anyone else to see this. Why would I want these ugly marks to be recorded forever, anywhere? "No."

"Okay." And Dr. Kane places the camera back on the desk. "The thing is, if you ever decide to take any legal action against your dad, you'll need evidence. This is the hardest part. But I will not force you. I can't force you to do something you're not ready to do."

Legal action? Against Dad? "I don't want to ever see my Dad again. Why would I want to take my dad, a lawyer, to court? He'll win. I'll lose." I've lost enough to him.

"What if we just take the pictures, but never show them to anyone? They'll be a part of your file, but each person's medical records are confidential, and you're legally an adult. Not even your parents can request to see them without your permission." Dr. Kane tries a back door entrance, and my resistance wanes.

It couldn't hurt if no one ever sees them. They could remain in my records, a closed file.

"I'm not allowed to show anyone the photographs without your written consent," Dr. Kane answers my silent questions. "And I would never show them to anyone without asking you first."

I nod, yes. And silently, I slowly roll my sleeve up to my elbow and look away. The camera shutters click. Click. Click, and she's done.

"Anywhere else?" Dr. Kane asks. "Did he hurt you? Anywhere else?" And I want to rip open my chest and say, "Here. Right here is where it hurts the most," and crack open my skull and scream, "What about here? Where I'll never forget!" But I just shake my head, no.

"Can I photograph your face?" Dr. Kane wants a picture of my ugly, broken lips, but I did that to me each time I bit down on my lips in my futile attempt not to cry when Dad burned me. It never worked. I shrug my shoulders, sure. What difference does it make?

"Do you want to talk about your arm? What specifically sparked his anger?" Dr. Kane's green eyes invite me in, but I've done enough swimming for one day. I shake my head no.

"Want to talk about anything more, today?"

I shake my head no, then reconsider. "Actually, there is one thing? Can I ask you something?"

"Sure. Anything."

I'm staring down at my uncovered arm. Because I've lain awake many a night and just stared at my arm, running my fingers over my skin. Scales of bubbled, blotchy, sandpaper skin. Ugliness.

"Will they ever totally—? Will my arm ever be—?" And I can't think of the right word. Normal? Not ugly to look at? Soft to the touch? "Beautiful?"

"Probably not." Dr. Kane says, "You see, your skin is an organ. The largest organ you have, and although it is one of the human body's most resilient, the healing and regeneration of perfectly new skin depends on how deeply a person's been injured." Dr. Kane pauses, screwing the cap back on her camera lens. "Your burns are deep, Talia. Clearly past the superficial derma, at minimum you've experienced deep partial thickness, second degree burns, even if they've managed to partially heal on their own."

My blood boils at the realization that Dad scarred me for life. "So are you telling me that short of cutting my arm off, I'll always look like this?"

Dr. Kane surprises me when she shakes her head no. "There are options, nowadays. We can certainly look into the options as time goes on. Plastic surgeon is a pricey option, but insurance companies occasionally offer partial coverage in the cases of abuse. Every situation is different. When you're ready, I'll walk with you through the process. Okay?"

Like a pendulum swinging from one treetop to the next, I land on a branch that doesn't threaten to break when Dr. Kane offers me that word that still sounds so foreign: *Hope*.

8
~ Jesse ~

April 26th Morning

Sliding my palm across the skyline print on my shirt, I never imagined the real thing being so grand. Everything in downtown Chicago seems super-sized. The cathedral-sized foyer in the library makes my head spin as I try to blend in by copying the other visitors. After having followed the students carrying backpacks in, I note that no one pulls out his or her library card as they walk past the circulation desk, so I tuck Lagan's back in my pocket.

A heavy-set man wearing a security uniform approaches me before I can orient myself and runs his hand over his white head of hair. "How can I help direct you?" he asks.

"Umm. Is there a computer lab here? Somewhere I could do a little research." I gulp as he turns to the right to point me behind him, the gun on his hip suddenly visible.

"Computers for public use are available if you have a library card. Do you have one?" He looks at me, tapping a finger on his chin.

The way his eyes narrow at me, I worry he can see through my jacket, Dad's gun as visible to him as his is to me. I begin to pull out the items in my back pocket, silently thankful that

Lagan's library card doesn't bear his picture, but he stops me with an open palm in the air.

"Just show the staff at the Computer Lab Reservation desk. If there are any openings left today, you're allowed one hour. And son," he takes one step backward. "Find a new cologne if you want to find yourself a lady. Just my two cents." He chuckles to himself, his belly jiggling under his blue button-down, as he says, "Pun intended," and as he walks toward the entrance to help an elderly lady with the door, I can still hear him laughing and saying to himself, "Cents. Scents. I still got it."

The scent of the gasoline still trails me. Let me add finding a place that has a shower to my list right now, because that needs to be my next stop. I follow the signs like the guard told me to and push through the door to the computer lab. The lady at the desk doesn't glance away from her computer screen when I pull out Lagan's card, and just mumbles, "Sign in. Find an empty desk. You have one hour. The computer will log you out automatically, so you don't have to keep track of time."

I find an unoccupied cubicle, set my poncho behind my back, and turn my chair sideways. I know better than to ever have my back totally turned. Exhaling a deep breath, I want to pat myself on the back, a little intoxicated from how smoothly my first morning of freedom is going. After following the on-screen instructions to login, I scan my surroundings before punching in Dad's name under the Google search bar. And even as my fingers type the letters of Gerard Vanderbilt, I imagine each letter as a bullet with a beeline trajectory through his three-piece suit, aimed at his heart. Then, just as the metal pellet nears him, it swings to the right, to the left, over and under. Just close enough to freak Dad out.

The monitor lights up with a long list of links. Newspaper and magazine articles featuring his accolades in cases won as one of the country's most successful immigration lawyers. Vanderbilt, the voice of reason...Blah blah blah. Bunch of crap.

I click on an article labeled, 'Breaking News,' reading it silently for Dad's name. "Illinois State District Attorney

Matthew Bonds faces his biggest investigation to date in the coming months. Bonds' client, an eighteen-year-old woman from Nepal, is the prime suspect in the brutal stabbing of the former CFO of the Moon Over Deserts (MOD) Hotel Corporation in a downtown hotel room of MOD's newest luxury hotel. According to the Chief of Surgery, the CFO, in the ICU at an undisclosed hospital, hangs on to his life by a thread, one that weakens every day he fails to wake up from a coma. The accused faces deportation on top of attempted murder charges if arrested. Several Human Rights' Groups claim the hotel tycoon runs an underground human-trafficking ring from which the accused attempted to escape, accusations that, to date, have yet to be proven."

Interesting, but what does this have to do with Dad? Okay, here. I finally read his name: "When asked about the validity to the human trafficking angle during this morning's press conference, heading the legal team representing MOD Hotels, Attorney Gerard Vanderbilt said, 'The only human traffic I'm aware of is the gridlock traffic on Lakeshore Drive at 4:00PM, daily.' After the crowds' uproar to his initial response waned, Vanderbilt added, 'As far as my client's concerned, the bottom line is justice. And I will find justice. That's my job.' And with that, the attorney told the press he had no further statements."

As my eyes roam over four particular words, I hear Dad's voice in my head, his footsteps inching closer to me with each repeat of the words, "I will find justice. I will find Justice. I will find—" Sliding down in my chair, I half expect him to be standing behind me. Turning my head, and relieved to see no one, I quickly scroll down the list of sites, pushing myself to stay focused.

How hard can it be to find...? Two screens of links later, I find what I'm looking for, clicking on Dad's website. The Law offices of Gerard Vanderbilt, Central offices located in downtown Chicago with subsidiary offices in New York City, Las Vegas and Los Angeles. As I jot down the Chicago address on scrap paper I picked up next to the sign in sheet, my eyes catch a blurb on the side bar that mentions a new office opening shortly in South Africa. Huh? *Moving back in with your parents, Dad?* Or is this the Plan B for his life? TBD, I suppose. Doesn't alter what I have to do.

After minimizing all my searches, I try to open a new email account, but the name I want is taken. Darn all those people who already used the name ROOT. Whatever. Can't let a little setback distract me from the task. I alter the address until it mimics the lists one to ten that Dad left us: 1234567890ROOT@gmail.com. Looking over my shoulder, I carefully script my first email to gvanderbilt@perfectlaw.com.

Dear Sir,

How are you? I wanted to introduce myself and ask if you would consider representing my case. I've heard only wonderful things about your skills and expertise in the area of defending the cause of the hurt and harmed.

I hid my pain and injuries for so many years, but trust me, the scars never faded. What would I do without these beautiful marks all over my body, clearly signs that my husband loves me so much, he can't help but tattoo his affection over me with his force and his fists?

What would you suggest I do? Ignore my pain? Bury it? Bury myself? Well, as luck would have, I am.

Buried.

Sincerely,

Root – [Running Out of Time]

Finger hovers over the send button before I delete and retype the subject heading several times. I settle on short and bitter, going with my first instinct. "Dead or Alive." Send.

9
~ Talia ~

April 26th Almost Noon

The scent of fried onions lures me out of my room toward the kitchen. Running my hand along the hallway wall as I inch toward the kitchen, I turn and walk back to my room. Why does this feel harder than the first day of high school at Hinsdale South? Maybe because I know I can't hide when I meet these women. The simple fact that I'm here tells them something about my story. The story I've hidden my whole life.

Standing in my bedroom doorway, I steady my breathing and think about how Lagan first pulled me out of my shell, with the tiniest invitation to eat with him in the café during lunch. Eating, an activity that doesn't require talking. I can do this.

"Hey," a blond woman, college-aged looking, calls from down the hallway. "Want to join us for breakfast? We could use another set of hands in here." She's holding a knife in her hands, wielding it like a sword.

"Sure," I nod and look back in my room. At the Post-its on the wall. "I'll be right there." I peel one Post-it off the bottom of the question mark, crumple it in my hand and toss it in the trash before heading toward the kitchen. The sound of salsa music grows louder before I turn the corner into the breakfast buzz of pots and pans, chopping and slicing, dishes and chatter.

"First two breakfast burritos coming right up." The woman with shoulder length black hair has her back to me when she flips two tortillas with eggs spilling out of them from a long skillet to a glass platter on the counter next to the burner.

The blond who invited me stands over a cutting board of chopped tomatoes at the kitchen island where two other women slice onions and jalapenos.

"Can I have mine extra hot?" An Indian woman wearing glasses glances over and beams me a smile. "Anyone else want chopped green chilies in theirs?"

As I raise my hand, I stop, pulling a few strands of hair over my mouth, "Umm, what can I do to help?"

"Can you dance?" I recognize the Latino lady with black waves falling down her back from the bathroom this morning. She stops setting plates on the dining room table and pulls the blond to a stand, and the two salsa to the beat, the blond having trouble following her partner's lead, but giggling nevertheless.

"Talia, meet Ava." The Indian woman introduces the Latina. "She's our resident D.J. and dance therapy instructor so if you hang out long enough, you just might get a dance lesson or two during your stay."

Ava twirls the woman who invited me to breakfast, and when the blond faces me, she says, "I'm Nahida, by the way," her smile revealing a gap where her two front teeth should be.

"Nahida," I repeat. "That's. A pretty name."

The song ends and Nahida lets go of Ava to wash her hands at the sink before returning to her tomatoes. "Wanna beat some more eggs? It's kind of a favorite job around here, any time we get to beat something. But I'm sure we're willing to share to help the new girl feel welcome."

A few of the women laugh out loud as they chime in their "oh yeahs" and "uh-huhs." The Indian woman opens the fridge behind her, then hands me a bowl and a carton of eggs. "I'm Sunila. Nice to meet you, Talia."

I guess Diana told them my name.

"And I'm Addison." The Asian woman at the stovetop raises her hand holding the spatula in the air, but she's still turned toward the burners. "Sunny, your extra spicy is just about ready."

Sunila. Sunny. Only two ladies haven't spoken a word. The young, brunette with her hair braided down her back chops onions, her eyes visibly wet even as she steals glances my way, her stare anything but friendly. And an African-American woman placing silverware around the dining room table limps on one leg quietly from spot to spot.

"Where should I sit?" A soft voice from behind makes me stop short of cracking the next egg and turn to be greeted by the small smile of a short blond with highlights, tucking her shoulder length hair behind her ear with one hand and rubbing her very pregnant belly with the other.

"Next to me, Mija," Ava says, "So I can serve you two of everything."

Sunny giggles, and after the woman passes by me, she says, "That's Myrna. She's new like you, but she's been with us for about a week."

I count eight ladies including myself as I whisk the eggs. "How long have you been here?" I ask Sunila, then bite my lip. "I'm sorry. I shouldn't have pried."

"Not at all." Sunny takes a plate over to Addison who spoons a burrito onto it, the sharp scent of spice greeting my senses when she lays it down on the countertop near my bowl of eggs.

"Ready for the last batch," says Addison.

The woman with the onions walks over with her cutting board, and as I carry my bowl over to Addison, she turns, and we're standing face to face. I struggle not to stare at her patchwork cheeks, her blotchy, disfigured features, her nose missing its tip, her eyebrows penciled in under the bangs of her silky black wig. I can tell now. The wig. And her body, covered head to toe with clothes, like Mom used to dress.

The bowl of eggs in Addison's grip, I turn, nearly knocking the onions off the cutting board of the woman with the braid standing next to me. The one who hasn't spoken yet. She slides the board onto the counter top, narrows her eyes at me, then dashes out of the kitchen without eating. Did I do something to scare her off?

Like she can read my mind, Sunny says, "Don't mind Jaya." She cocks her head in the direction Jaya left, and adds, "The fact that she actually showed up today is progress. It's been four weeks, and today is the first day she left her bedroom long enough for anyone to see her."

One by one, the women take a seat around the table and Sunny nudges me to join the others, saying, "I feel like a permanent resident here." She chuckles, and a few of the woman smile and nod in agreement as they pass around dishes of salsa and sour cream.

Chitchat between neighbors carries on, but Ava lowers her gaze to her plate, perhaps thinking about her own history.

After swallowing her bite, Sunny says, "I don't know which is more fun? Choosing a new name for myself or picking a new birthday?"

"So your name's not Sunny? I don't follow." I lied about Dad's name. It didn't occur to me to change my own.

"Hey, when your husband destroys all your legal records and the U.S. Government never documented the day you showed up on this earth—I was born in Sri Lanka—then it's time to get creative."

Ava perks up and says, "Mija, last month she was twenty-five-year-old Susanna from Havana."

"And the month before that, she was twenty-nine-year-old Brielle from Montreal," says Nahida.

"Six months have passed while I wait for Immigration to sort out a valid I.D. for me so I can find a job. Move out. And move on with my life. Until then, I'm kinda liking Sunila. The nickname option makes it more fun. Sunny from the land of honey."

"So how old are you? This time?" I ask.

"Twenty-three." Sunny smiles widely and says, "Everyone in Chicago claims that is the ultimate, lucky number. Something about the River Jordan."

"Michael Jordan's number," Addison and Nahida say at the same time, and Nahida adds, "From the Bulls a few years back. Most famous player in basketball history."

Sunny shakes her head, doing a little dance with her shoulders. "Gets them every time."

The mention of the Bulls immediately brings my thoughts to Lagan, but he always wore the number one jersey. I keep the moment to myself and wonder how these women can joke around like this? How did they get to this place? Maybe they laugh so they won't cry. Maybe they're used to hiding.

Cutting a small piece off and stabbing it with my fork, I think about the woman who left the kitchen. I sink the tortilla bit into the sour cream and slide it around my plate. Jaya's not the only one. I'm in a room full of mirrors, each woman hiding behind her smile, but like Lagan once said about me, rain falls in their eyes.

I place a spoonful across my lips when Addison asks, "How are the eggs?"

Her face. The skin. It reminds me of how my arm looks. Bits of egg slide past my windpipe, setting me off into a coughing spell. I sip some water from a white mug before saying, "I. I'm. I mean, they're okay."

Sunny clears her throat and asks, "Seconds, anyone?" And small talk continues between neighbors. I eat silently, but in between bites, I sneak glances at each of their faces. Women who walked away. Ran. Fled. Escaped.

And I'm surrounded by daughters. Sisters. Mothers. My mother. Mom in every seat. Oh God!

I push back my chair, picking up my plate and my utensils, but as I fumble toward the kitchen sink, the white mug slips from my fingers. The sound of ceramic breaking on the tile floor pierces the air, and I buckle over to gather the shards scattered all around me. Blood red droplets paint the broken pieces, and I don't understand why the cup is bleeding. I just need to wash my dishes. Must. Wash—

"Oh girl, you're bleeding." With Nahida's hands on my shoulders, she tries to lift me, but a picture cements me to this spot. The image of my mother's broken back, cut by a hundred broken dishes, my trembling fingers unable to stop her bleeding. "It's gonna be okay. In time, Talia." Nahida spreads open my palms and begins to pick each broken piece from my hands. Setting them aside. Back on the floor.

"I'm. S. S. Sorry. I'll pay—"

"Shhhh." Nahida rubs my back with one hand, her blond hair falling around her face like a curtain. Picking the shards out with the other hand, she says, "There are no mistakes too big in this house, okay. Nothing we can't walk with you through. Okay? Nothing."

Through. Through. Through. I just want to get through this day and the day to be over. I just need...a mom. My mom. One by one, each woman rises from the table and each takes a broken piece to throw away and leaves the kitchen while Nahida nurses my cuts with moist paper towels—her arm over my shoulders like a waterfall willow. And I am weeping. And minutes melt away as Nahida rocks me to the lullaby of tears. Mine. Hers. Ours.

10
~ Jesse ~

April 26th, Midmorning

With only ten minutes left to my computer time, I quickly google, "Rooms for Rent in Chicago," and a long list of options appears when I hit the return key, except that my enthusiasm wanes when I read the prices. Page after page, my options dwindle, and I debate choosing a different train to sleep on tonight, gambling on a different conductor working the night shift. Then again, what if the next guy isn't as nice as the first one.

Just when I resolve to give up, a listing for a room on a site called, "Craig's List" displays a number I can swing with the money Lagan gave me. *Thank you, Craig, whoever you are.* Copying the train directions on the other side of the sheet with Dad's office info, I quickly jot down the address and exit the library, back out into the warm April morning.

"Get your t-shirts. One for five. Three for ten." A vendor wearing a muscle shirt and a burgundy beret on his head calls out. When he spots me a few feet from his table of shirts, he says, "For you, son, be my first buyer today, and I'll give you four for ten." He holds up a t-shirt, standing in my pathway. "Best deal in town. What size are you?"

"Uh…" I'm looking around, wondering if he'll pull the shirt over my head if I try to walk around. "How much did you say?" I suppose I could use a little bit of the money to pick up a few basics.

"Ten dollaz. I think Medium will fit you just fine." The vendor folds up the shirt he held up, picks out three more t-shirts from a stack, all similar to the Chicago skyline tee I'm wearing, and begins to pile them into a bag. "Thank you kindly." He practically shoves the bag in my arms and holds out an open palm. "If you need change, I gotchu."

I give him a twenty and he returns two fives, tips his beret, and turns his attention to another fellow walking down the street, shouting out the same spiel. As I walk past him toward the train station, tucking Summer's blue poncho in the bag, something tells me I wasn't his first customer today, but the bag feels like a trophy in my hand. I bought something. On my own. For me, for the first time ever. Second, technically, if I count the bagel and juice from breakfast.

En route to the El, I purchase two pairs of knock-off, brand name jeans, one sweatshirt, and a black Bull's hat from different stands on State Street. Passing a pharmacy, the display of toothbrushes and other toiletries in the window invites me in to search out a few more things. In addition to soap and shampoo, I find undergarments, two pairs of cheap shorts, chips, crackers, a six-pack of water bottles, and two candy bars. As I wait in line at the cash register, my eye catches a glass blue charm, in the shape of a heart, dangling on a thin steel bar with other chains, and I know it makes no sense to splurge right now. Not when I don't have a job and the rest of Lagan's cash will go toward a roof over my head tonight, but it reminds me of Talia.

"And this," I hand it over to the cashier, and he adds it to the grand total: "Thirty-two dollars and fifty-seven cents. Dude, you sure you don't want to change up your cologne. Just sayin'…." The scent of gasoline still clings to me like a tattoo. I pay and beeline to Union Station with bags in tow to map out the route I wrote down to the hostel I read about on Craig's list.

After taking the Red line five stops uptown, I never find the street I thought I read on the map, so I exit the train, and return downtown till I jump on the Green line and then back on the Brown line and I'm almost at the point of giving up and searching out a park bench when I try the Red line again.

The voice overhead announces, "Local Red Line. Making all stops. No more Express trains tonight. Local Red. Sheridan next. Next stop Sheridan." Realizing I probably jumped on the Express Red last time, explaining why I never heard the stop overhead, by the time I arrive at the address, it's dark outside.

I knock on the door with the words, Fred's Office, painted above and enter. "Name's Je-J-John." I catch myself. For all I know Dad's already circulated a missing person's bulletin with my name and picture all over the state of Illinois. The pale-skinned, skinny guy with disheveled hair and a five o'clock shadow hasn't looked up from his phone yet. "Um…do you still have a room for rent?"

"I don't care if your name's Toilet Grime. I'm the boss around here. Name's Fred. And yes. Just kicked the last guy out." Fred picks up a lit cigarette from the ashtray behind him. "So long as you keep your corner neat, pick up after yourself in the bathroom, and pay your rent on time." The cigarette dangles from his lips as he peers at me, blowing smoke from the side of his mouth. "Comprende?"

"Yes, sir," I say and hand Fred my last hundred as he pulls out a cash box and slips the bill inside. He lives above his office, attached to the three-story hostel where I'll sleep tonight.

Noting the grass outside needs mowing, I ask, "Uh, do you ever hire people to work for you? Jobs that pay cash? I could take care of your lawn. I'm willing to do just about anything."

"First time on your own, man?" Fred flicks the ashes off his cigarette with his fingers.

Before I make up some story about my parents moving to

England, he says, "Forget I asked. Sure. I have a guy who fixes up apartments on the West Side. Not the safest neighborhood, but if you work hard and mind your own business, Jimmy's always lookin' for an extra set of hands to paint and stuff."

"Wow. That would be…great." No place can be any more dangerous than living with Dad. And if it means I can save up faster and see Talia smiling sooner… "When can I start?"

"You're not looking for drug money, are you?" Fred inhales deeply from the waning cigarette. "Cuz, first sight of candy, and I'll call the cops faster than you can say, 'Shut up.' Got that?"

"Just looking for a way to pay next month's rent. That's all," I say, picking up my bags off the floor, Dad's gun in my pocket feeling especially heavy at the mention of the police.

"I'll shoot Jimmy a text, and if he has something for you today or this week, I'll call you. Your cell?"

"Umm. I don't have a phone."

Kicking myself for not taking Lagan's phone, I see my first job opportunity swirl down the drain when Fred says, "No problem. I'll leave the deets on your door. Fair enough?" Fred grinds the cigarette butt in a rusted metal ashtray on the window ledge behind him, turns back, and scrunches his nose. "If you're looking to get hired by anyone, for anything, anywhere, you need to shower up first."

I nod and say, "Thanks. Really appreciate it," and walk out of Fred's office, through the hostel entrance and up two flights till I find room 214.

The door unlocks with one turn of the single key, and I stand on the threshold for a moment, dropping my bags on the inside. It's a barebones room, just as the online ad described, with a twin-sized mattress, a simple, single-drawered metal desk, and a small wooden dresser near a square window bordered with chipped beige paint. A single, faded painting of a generic beach scene hangs crookedly above the bed. Two kids build a sand castle with shovels and buckets in the picture while two parents lounge nearby. Their sun hats cover their faces, but the painted toes of the woman and the swim shorts of the man spell mother and father to any observer.

I lock the door behind me before I reach into the plastic bags to retrieve an envelope, slip out of my shoes, and then climb over the bed to tuck the rectangular sheet into the top ridge of the frame so it covers part of the portrait.

"There" I say to no one in particular. "Much better." Now I can't see the dad in the picture.

Hop off the bed and walk over to look out the window. The brownstone a few feet away takes up most of the view, although I can see a few pedestrians on the sidewalk passing under the glow of streetlights if I crane my neck. Pull the gun out of my pocket, slide my thumb and finger into trigger position, and imagine Dad's walking below, and I'm a sniper hired by Talia. A knock at the door sends my heart racing as I shove the gun in the desk drawer and say, "Yes? Who is it?"

"Fred here." There's no peephole, but I recognize his voice, and unlock the door, waiting for Fred to talk as I block the entrance.

"Just wanted to make sure everything's cool." Fred rubs his stubble cheeks, his right sleeve rolled up over a square lump exposing his bulging bicep. Cigarettes, I'm guessing.

"Yep. Everything's fine," I say, looking over my shoulder to double-check I shut the desk drawer.

"Just holler if you need anything. Preferably during normal daylight hours, aw-right."

"Will do."

Fred leaves, giving my heartbeat a chance to return to normal as I organize my things in the dresser, using the top drawer for my snacks, the second for toiletries, and the third for the few clothes items I bought. I hang Summer's blue raincoat on the back of the desk chair, and as I pick out the bar of soap, shampoo and a change of clothes, I realize I didn't think to buy a towel. One of the new t-shirts will have to do. After washing down a bag of chips with a water bottle, I lock my door and walk down to the first floor, past a small room with a coin-operated washer and dryer, to the communal bathroom with the sign, "Dudes" on it. Pushing through the door, I place my things on a folding chair by the shower entrance, hiding the key under the small pile, and turn the water to warm before peeling off my clothes and entering the stall.

When I step out of the shower, a guy missing the urinal stares at me in the mirror. "Dude, what happened to your back?"

Ignoring the question, I skip drying off, pull a t-shirt and shorts on, grab my things, and charge out. Racing up the steps, ticked at myself for not seeing the guy before he saw me, I make a note to myself to dry off inside the shower stall and hang my clothes over the bar so I can change in there too.

"Hey, was just leaving you this." Fred's hand covers a note on my door, an unlit cigarette tucked above his right ear. "Jimmy says he could use your help tomorrow. Address is on the paper, John."

Who's John? Right. The stupid name I gave myself. Sheesh. Glad I didn't ask aloud. "Thanks."

Fred walks off and I unlock my door, pull the Sticky Note off the door, and lock it behind me before falling on my back in bed. The springs creak and the mattress gives way in the middle, but I stare up and exhale the word again. Thanks. Not sure who I'm thanking. Maybe Talia. For giving me the motivation to walk again. Maybe Lagan, for his gifts of money and two cards that have helped me get around. Maybe Mom, for leaving so I wouldn't have to see Dad hurt her anymore. Cursing when I think of the guy in the bathroom, I'm not sure if I'm relieved or resentful that Mom left before she saw what Dad did to me.

From this angle, the envelope flaps over the painting, and I can see the dad in the picture while lying in bed. A little tweak will fix that problem. I scoot off the bed, press the Post-it to the desk, then turn to adjust the edge of the envelope so it's tucked in at the bottom instead. The ridge is too wide, and the envelope slips to the left, falling diagonally over the mom's face, and instead of moving it back, I decide to leave it. As I smooth the envelope, my other fist punches the wall next to the frame, and I cradle my throbbing hand as I lay down to sleep. Mom's gone. Maybe things would have been different if we had escaped that night. The one night Mom tried to save us.

***

"Wake up. Get up, already." Talia's urgent whispers streamed out of my dreams into my ears. Her grip on my shoulders forced me awake.

"What? What? Did I miss my alarm? Am I late for school?" Fourth grade probably wasn't the most important academic year in one's life, but Dad wanted us to have perfect attendance every year.

"Keep your voice down. You have two minutes to get dressed. Meet me in the kitchen. We're leaving tonight. For good." Talia's hazel-green eyes looked wild. "Mom's waiting."

It was the middle of the night, and Talia turned just before she left my room. "Jesse, this might be our only chance. Don't mess it up."

And with that, I sat up in bed, wondering if I was dreaming. I'd never done anything against Dad's orders. No one ever disobeyed Dad, or else.

Talia's warning to not screw up motivated me to quickly slip on a pair of jeans and throw on my blue and black-checkered flannel over my Michigan t-shirt. Sports socks up, I grabbed my Tiger's cap and pulled it on. Eyes adjusted to the dark now, I kneeled down by my desk, opened the bottom drawer, and pulled out all my Harry Potter library books. Then I wiggled the drawer's particle board backing forward and reached back behind it to retrieve my only treasures, the action figures, Luke, Leia and Darth Vader. They were a gift from the lost and found box at school. Someone lost them, and they found their way into my backpack.

"Jess." Talia stood in the doorway, arms flailing.

"Coming." I pocketed Luke and Leia in my jeans and carried Vader in my hands. I'd tuck him away in my jacket once I got it from the mudroom.

Following Talia to the hallway, we passed my parents'

bedroom where I saw Dad sleeping, his snoring muffled with his head under the covers. Tiptoeing down the stairwell, I lost my footing and grabbed the railing to keep from falling down, but Darth Vader flew out of my fingers in the process. Past Talia, tumbling down, making a dull thud on every step until he landed face down on the white tile below the steps. The heat in Talia's glare rose just a notch.

"Sorry," I mouthed the word, reaching down to retrieve my black-suited figure. We waited at the bottom step, Talia's back and hands on the wall. Felt like I held my breath forever. Moments later, Talia beelined to the kitchen while I detoured to the mudroom to get my jacket and shoes.

"Jesse." Mom embraced me when I entered the kitchen, her eyes bloodshot and her hands trembling. "This is goodbye. Of this house." Mom whispered every word. "We're leaving tonight. Just the three of us. Okay?"

I cemented my feet to the kitchen floor. "Dad won't like this."

"Dad doesn't know," Mom said, pulling me into her arms. "Trust me, Jesse. We have to leave."

"But where are we going?" I wiggled out of Mom's hug. "And how will we get there?" Mom can't drive. And we have no friends.

Mom lowered her voice even more, tucking the last of sandwiches and apples into her tote bag. "It doesn't matter where we go or how long it takes. Just that we leave before he finds us. And that we're together."

Talia held the door open for me and said, "Come on." And I did.

We exited out the garage door that chilly November night, the three of us, at four something in the morning, and no one looked back as we walked briskly down the sidewalk on the empty Benton Harbor streets. Mom directed us toward the beach. I hoped she hid a boat, because we couldn't exactly live in a sand castle.

"This way! Hurry!" Mom said, grabbing my free hand and pulling me along.

My fingers, numb from the wind, felt like ice in my mother's grip, and after about thirty minutes of nonstop, silent trekking, we reached a border of prickly thickets.

Talia jogged ahead and turned to motion us to catch up. "Over here!" she said, pointing to the break in the brush wide enough for us to step through onto the beach.

Talia went first, reaching back to give me her hand. I made it over and just as Mom climbed up, her bag snagged on the bushes, and as she fell backwards, I grasped her arm. Talia grabbed onto my waist to keep us from domino-ing back into a tangled mess, and once we were all on the waterfront side, my sister and I ran clumsily toward the water. The full moon lit up the waves and shore, making me less scared than when we first left the house.

"Catch me if you can!" I screamed to Talia.

Talia ran toward me, swatted my back and took off past me, laughing. Mom trailed behind us, walking near the water's edge, skipping sideways any time a big wave rolled too far up the sand. When distance separated Talia and me from Mom, Talia dropped in the sand on her back, calling, "Time out! Let's wait for Mom."

Out of breath, I fell to my knees by my sister's side and joined her, lying down on my back in the sand. Hands behind my head, I loved that we were all sandy. Dad would never see us, and we could be as messy as we wanted to be. Talia's arms moved first, and like gears connected at the hip, I caught sight of her actions and began to move my legs in sideways scissor-kicks on the sand. Talia's head turned to face me, waiting for me to stop moving, then she spread her legs and I swooped my arms over the sand up to my head last.

Mom caught up to us, shaking her head and giggling. "Get up, you two. We have to keep moving."

Smiling, I rose first and offered my hand to Talia to hoist her up. We stepped back to look at our canvas. Two sand angels, side by side, holding hands.

"My angels!" Mom said. "Let's fly now." Mom hugged her tote to her and marched ahead of us. Talia followed, but I lingered. Running over the angels with my feet, back and forth, I broke their wings and erased their halos. Couldn't take a chance that Dad might find this.

Scurrying to catch up, Talia looked back, her smile disappearing when she saw the mess I made. "Why'd you go and do a dumb thing like that?" A shove from Talia and the edge of my right shoe stepped in the suds as they rolled over the pebbly shore.

"Enough you two," Mom said, "Just keep walking."

Onward we trekked, the wind off the water whipping as the moon set, until we reached an inlet disrupting the beach. High tide made it too deep to wade across. And the sand along the border piled high into dunes. Going up and around was our only choice if Mom's thought was to keep following the curve of the land.

"Mom!" Talia said. "I see headlights."

Off to the left of us, sure enough, the dim glow of two lights, probably from a car, moved over and across the sand. Instinctively, I dropped onto my chest, Darth Vader pinching my skin as I landed on the sand. Talia followed suit, but Mom stood there, a deer caught in..."Get down, Mom!" Talia beat me to the command.

Mom pulled her long winter coat off and threw it on top of us and ran forward, right toward the light.

"Mom!" I screamed, lifting her coat when I saw her stumbling away in the sand. "What are you doing?" Talia and I screamed the words together.

She stopped long enough to say, "Stay put," then continued to charge toward the dunes.

Talia snatched my hand to keep me from chasing mom and pushed my fist into the sand. "Listen to Mom," my sister said, teeth gritting but her hazel eyes floating in worry.

"What if...?" I was so ticked that Mom just up and left us. "What if that's Dad?"

"Hopefully not!" Talia said, covering our heads with Mom's coat but leaving an opening small enough for us to keep an eye on her.

Someone approached her now and light spanned across the beach from the person's flashlight, prompting me to pull the coat back over our heads completely. When we peeked out again, Mom was returning to us with the person carrying the flashlight. Made me think it couldn't be Dad. It just couldn't.

Close enough to make him out in the dark now, I saw the stranger next to Mom sported a uniform.

"Officer Daley here. You kids can get up from under there," the cop said.

"It's okay," Mom said. "He's a nice Police Officer. He's not going to arrest us for trespassing."

"No Ma'am, I promised I wouldn't, and I won't." Officer Daley tipped his cap to Mom, setting my fears at ease as I rose to my feet, brushing the sand off my chest while Talia stepped a few feet away to shake the sand off mom's coat. "But, you still haven't told me why you're roaming the beach at this strange hour. Is there somewhere I can drive you folks tonight?"

"No." Talia blurted out an answer. "We're fine. We'll be fine." She corrects herself.

"Actually sir," Mom chuckled nervously. "If you would be so kind as to drive us to the closest bus station, that would be a great help to us. Thought we were close, but I think we might have gotten turned around."

"Bus station?" the cop said. "That's clear the opposite direction of town. Next time bring a map with you. But sure, I'd be happy to drive you. It's much too cool a night for walking."

His smile widened before he turned, muffled something into his walkie, and led us back to his squad car.

"Mom," Talia pulled Mom's arm, and I heard her ask, "Are you sure?"

Mom shushed Talia and followed Officer Daley till he opened the car door for her.

"Ma'am can I just see some I.D." He said to Mom in the passenger seat. Talia and I sat in the back seat. "Just routine. Need to log my activity on the night shift."

"Umm. Sure." Mom began to fish through her bag.

She handed the officer a small blue book, and before he flipped it open, she said, "I can spell my name for you. G.I.T—"

"I got it." The policeman scribbled on his clipboard. "You do realize your passport is expired? Vanderbilt, huh? "

Something about the way he said our last name, I couldn't tell if he didn't believe Mom or if he'd heard it before?

"Yes, sir. It's a common name," Mom said, her speech shaky.

No one else ever had the same last name in school. Talia and I exchanged looks, and Talia shook her head no. Was that "Oh no!" or "No, Mom, don't lie," or "There's no way Mom will get away with fibbing."

"Funny thing is Dispatch just informed me of a call that came in from a Gerard Vanderbilt." My palms felt clammy when I grabbed the door handle to get out, but it was locked. Officer Daley eyed me in his rearview mirror, raising his eyebrows like he was doing the math.

"Anyway, must be a coincidence," the cop said. "Buckle in everyone. Seatbelts are the law."

Mom giggled nervously, not answering him, and turned her head to look out her passenger window. Talia bit her lower lip, her knuckles resting on her mouth, then her index finger straightened quickly and bent again. She was telling me to keep my mouth shut. I pulled the lever one last time, but the door didn't budge.

"So where you folks heading to? Catching an early bus ride to warmer parts, I hope." The officer smiled at me in his rearview mirror, but I didn't trust that smile, and I didn't trust him. "I hear Florida's nice this time of year."

Mom cleared her throat before answering. "Alabama."

"No way. Which part? I have family down in Birmingham." The squad car reversed out of the parking spot, cruising down a main road, past a cemetery and then our school, nothing lit except a neon sign of a twenty-four hour Dunkin Donuts.

"Umm." Mom's fished through her purse again. "Not too

far from Birmingham. Yes. We'll be stopping there first."

"And your final destination?" Officer Daley just shot the breeze as we pulled up to a stoplight. "Traveling kind of light for a road trip?"

Shoot. He noticed that we were not carrying any luggage. Talia's hand on the seat next to mine pulled back into a fist.

"Oh, we don't need much." Mom answered truthfully. "We'll be fine, sir. Thanks for your concern."

Handled nicely, I thought, but Talia shook her head, her hand on her window as I counted the seconds while the light stayed red. Our school bus stopped here every day.

"Ma'am, don't mean to intrude, but can I ask you something?" The light turned green. We're two blocks from my elementary school. Three blocks from home. The streets were desolate and his foot stayed on the brakes.

"Sure. Just please don't ask me about my husband. He died, and it's a very painful story to talk about." Mom lowered her head and from the sound of muffled whimpers, she sounded like she was crying too.

"Don't mean to pry." Stopped at a stop sign down the street from our house, Officer Daley leaned over and put his hand on Mom's shoulder. Then slid it down her arm, slowly. My stomach churned as I watched his hand linger on Mom's wrist, the way he stared at her, eyes glistening.

"Dispatch calling in, any sight of the three we're looking for?" The sharp crackle of the CB interrupted all conversation as Officer Daley picked up his piece to talk into it.

"Got them right here in my car, Dispatch. Driving them home now. Get some rest. Over." Like a noose pulled tightly around my throat, the word home choked out the last bit of hope I held onto. We weren't going to the bus station, were we Talia, I asked silently as my eyes began to tear up now too.

"Sir, please." Mom pleaded. "If you could just. Please. Help us."

"Ma'am. Sorry, but your husband is frantically calling the precinct every other second, threatening to sue the county for not finding his family. He's been worried sick that someone kidnapped you all. And, for the record," Officer Daley hesitated for a moment, then continued, "he informed headquarters that he will not press charges against you for abducting his children so long as you return home safely."

"Home? Safe?" Mom's voice broke, her fingers running through her long black hair.

Talia gaped at me, a tear escaping down her cheek.

He stepped on the gas, the car driving past familiar houses. Right toward our house. "He sounds real worried, Ma'am. And truth be told, Geri and I go way back. He's a good guy. One of Benton Harbor's finest."

I punched the back of mom's chair before I could stop myself. Why did you tell him your name, Mom?

Talia grabbed my hand and leaned into my shoulder. "Don't say anything, okay. Just remember one thing: It's all my fault."

I didn't get it.

The car turned the corner down our street and bile began to rise up my throat. I swatted the tears from my cheeks with the back of my hands. I refused to let Dad see me cry. Not now. Not in this moment of defeat.

The moment we pulled up into the driveway, Mom exited the squad car and stood outside facing down the street. The place where we fled not long ago, our yellow brick road vanished. Dad waited on the porch, dressed in a business suit, like he was ready to go to trial.

When I heard the click of the unlock button up front, I jumped out of the car to take hold of Mom's hand. Seeing Talia still in the car, I asked, "Should I get her, Mom? Of do you want me to stay with you?" I looked up, feeling Dad's glare from the porch. "Maybe if we say we're sorry to Dad and promise never to leave again?" I fished for a way to help Mom. I fished in the Dead Sea. Even at a young age, I knew punishment was inevitable, and Dad would strike Mom the hardest.

Mom's answer cemented our modus operandi for years to come. "Stick together you two. You only have each other.

Remember that."

I let go of Mom's hand reluctantly and returned to get my sister. From the cruiser, I watched Mom slowly walk past Dad with a downcast march into the house, no exchange of kisses or hugs.

"What are you waiting for?" I asked Talia through the open car door. "Come on. Mom needs us."

Officer Daley, on his walkie outside the squad car, clicked it shut and latched it to his belt before approaching Dad.

"Remember what I said, okay, Jesse?" Talia's eyes squinted and she pressed her lips together. "Go on. I'm waiting for Dad to come and get me."

"If you say so."

Officer Daley stood on the porch talking to Dad now. They shook hands, exchanged smiles, and chatted like they were talking sports' scores.

I walked up to the porch and waited. Dad rocked back and forth on his heels as he talked with Daley, then turned to me and said, "Justice. It's a little past your bedtime. I suggest you take a bath, get all that sand off you, and get to bed. I'll speak with you in the morning."

"Umm. Dad?" Does he not notice Talia's still in the car?

"Go on. Say thank you to Officer Daley and get to bed. No questions." Dad sounded like a stranger, the softness of his tone as unfamiliar as owning a brand new action figure. "And Justice," Dad's hand slips past my jacket into my shirt pocket. "You won't be needing this." He pulls Darth Vader, broken in two, out.

I moved toward the door, and his hand on my shoulder stopped me in stride. "Anything else you wanna hand over?" I silently said goodbye to Luke and Leia as I placed them in Dad's open palm. Wanting to obey Mom's wish to watch out for my sister, I crouched behind the front door so I saw the driveway but stayed out of sight. I could also see Dad's and Officer Daley's backs.

"Your daughter's still in the car," Officer Daley said.

"Don't get any ideas, Daley." Dad spoke sternly.

"No reward for bringing your family home safely? And I thought you'd show a little gratitude." Daley's hands were in his pockets. Now he rocked back and forth on his heels.

"I'll get you your due reward. But not Talia. Besides, she's damaged. Wouldn't want to give you damaged goods. Only the best for my team." Dad and Daley shook hands. I had no idea what he meant by damaged goods. And why was Dad calling Talia damaged?

"If it's alright with you, I'll just go ahead and take her for a little spin and bring her home before sunrise?" The cop asked for Talia again. I understood that much. But why would he choose a girl over cash? At least that's the reward I understood Dad was offering him.

"Did you not hear clearly? Or do you need me to call in to the precinct that I have an officer here who can't mind his manners. No means no. And for the last time, I said NO!" Dad's voice rose so, I wondered if the neighbors heard him.

"Loud and clear. Let me get her for you then." Daley darted to his patrol car, opened the door, and leaned in to talk to Talia. Not a minute later, he returned to the porch. Alone.

"How hard is it to get an eleven-year-old out of a police car? Do I need to do your job for you?" Dad crossed his arms over his chest.

"Sorry, Boss. She's a stubborn one. Keeps insisting I should arrest her and throw her in jail. That it's all her fault. That she forced her mother and brother to trespass on private beach property. That she should be arrested and her brother and mother left alone. Want me to carry her out into your house? I can do that, but she might start screaming."

After sighing loud enough for me to hear, Dad said, "I'll take care of it." Then Dad walked to Talia's side of the car, spoke to her for ten seconds, and the next thing I knew, Talia exited and ran up the driveway toward the front door. That was my cue. I raced upstairs, locked myself behind bathroom doors, my hand slipping off the knob when the water flowed into the bathtub. Initiating the shower switch, I sat down on the toilet lid to catch my breath.

Wondering what Dad said to Talia, I showered up, changed into my pajamas, and tiptoed to my room, startled to find Dad sitting on the edge of my bed in the dark.

"Dad!"

"Listen up, Justice." Dad stood, towering over me. "This will be the last time anyone in this house ever walks out on me."

Dad's hands covered my eyes as his pull guided me forward toward himself. I buckled over, wincing in pain, before my mind registered what happened. My feet. My bare feet. Stood on top of broken toys. Vader. Leia. Luke. Smashed to pieces. Dad's firm grip moved to my shoulders and held my ten-year-old frame in place.

"Clean up this mess and we'll review the rules tomorrow morning. And Justice," I heard Dad's voice but my blurred vision barely made out his shoes. My feet stung from the jab of jagged plastic shards as fresh wounds etched Dad's warnings into me. "I'm watching you, Justice. Every step you take."

11
~Talia ~
April 27th Middle of the night

"I trusted you." Dad's standing over my bed, shaking his head in disappointment.

He's here. I'm sure of it.

I shoot up in bed, hands gripping the sheets, sweat beading my forehead. Nothing. No one is in this room but me. As the pounding of my heart slows, I let my feet touch the wood floor and sit on the edge of the bed for a moment. Instinctively, my hand rubs down my arm. He's not here. The scars still are.

The digital clock on the desk reads 3:07AM. I'm wide awake. *Water.* I could use a drink. As I trace my way toward the kitchen in the dimly-lit hallway, I walk past the bathroom to the front foyer and turn the doorknob to the entrance, double-check the bolt, and tug a second and third time. Definitely locked. My forehead touches the metal frame, the coolness a sober reminder that I'm in here, while the world continues to turn—out there. Jesse. Lagan. They're my world, but for now, my world is silent.

I return for a second glass of water, taking it with me as I cozy up in the wicker chair lined with striped cushions nearest the front door. Legs folded under, I sip and watch. Watch and sip. If he finds me. Correction, when he finds me, I'll be the first to know.

***

"Good morning, Sunshine." Diana's voice greets me along with the empty glass in my lap. I fell asleep? Where's Jesse's room? And will I see Lagan today under our willow? Oh wait. This is not home. And yesterday burned down with my willow.

"You're not the first to play guardian for the house, but I assure you we have a sturdy alarm system that has a direct access line to the authorities, and in fifteen years, we've only had one instance where the police showed up. A nineteen-year old resident tripped the alarm when she tried to leave to return to her abusive boyfriend in the middle of the night."

"Hmm." I manage a nod. Why would she do that?

"Her mother made her leave him. Maybe if she had made the decision on her own, she wouldn't have run back so quickly."

It crossed my mind to return home. Thinking back to two days ago, I'm not sure if I made the choice or Lagan decided for me.

Diana offers me a hand to rise, her other hand holding a coffee cup. "How are your cuts? No stitches, correct?" She's examining my bandaged palm.

I shake my head no, and as she walks next to me, Diana says, "Most survivors choose not to leave the safe house for a good while. There's a lot of fear of running into their perpetrators or others seeing them and informing their abusers where they're living. That's why we don't allow even family in here, with the exception of fathers with visitation rights to their younger, biological children. Those visits are always supervised. In general the women meet friends, family and even lawyers in alternate locations." Diana touches my arm, the one without scars, and adds, "Talia. When you're ready, you can visit with whomever you want to, okay. By the way, you can contact your college and arrange for your assignments to be emailed to you. You remember the resource room I showed you, right?" Diana hands me an envelope. "This is your new email address and password which you can change once you log on. Because you need to keep busy. And of course, there are shared chores we all do in order to function as a household, so just take a look at the chart on the kitchen wall for your name and tasks."

Chores. A list. My name was next to dishes until I dropped that cup yesterday. We're at my room when Diana stops in the doorway and asks, "How'd it go yesterday? Did you eat okay? And your appointment with Dr. Kane?"

"Umm. Dr. Kane was nice." I fumble for words, still thinking about the list of chores I need to do. "Eat?" I think about my half-eaten burrito. "I ate enough."

"There's a group session later today." Diana looks down when she drinks from her cup, her blue mascara shimmering in the light.

"I think I'll pass." I say, looking away.

"Word of advice," Diana waits a beat till I turn and we're eye to eye. "Try things one time before you decide they're not for you. You might be surprised what helps. And what meets your needs."

Mom. Jesse. Lagan. I can think of a few needs. But no use voicing what I can't have. "Thank you," I say, because I am grateful. I decide to take Diana's advice and give the group session a try. Just not today. I tell Diana, "Maybe next time."

I need a few days to catch up on school, do my chores, get used to things around here. Plus Dad never allowed us to be a part of any group, club, or team.

"Just think about what I said, okay?" Diana says, tossing her empty coffee cup in the trashcan by my desk. "You can attend and observe the sessions without saying anything. The group needs you as much as you need the group. Trust me on this one."

Jesse needed me for the season he was bedridden. Mom needed me on days after Dad hurt her badly. Lagan told me he needed me like he needs peppermint gum. More, in fact. And he chews gum constantly. I'm still working on believing it.

What could these women possibly need from me, the newbie? Besides Jaya, who looks like she's fourteen, I'm probably the youngest resident too. After Diana leaves, I pull off a third Post-it note from the question mark, because today is day three apart from Lagan. And the third day I haven't heard my brother's voice. Hoping I see them before the question mark disappears. Because the questions won't vanish, even if the wall before me goes blank.

12
~ Talia ~

April 27th

Nahida stops by, dropping off a message from Diana that I'm scheduled to meet with Social Work after breakfast. I wash up before heading to the kitchen. Korean-style eggs are on the menu, and D.J. Ava is doing her thing with K-Pop beats pulsing from Pandora. I didn't know K-Pop or Pandora existed until I came here, my musical tastes expanding by the day.

"Ketchup is all you need to Asian-ize your eggs." Addison cracks a row of eggs on the skillet as she adds, "Over rice, of course."

And Nahida's two left feet, trying to keep up with Ava's stepping and swaying to the beat sets off laughter among several ladies, but I'm tired after my rough night of sleep. Jaya, the woman who stormed out yesterday, and Shandra, the woman with the limp, don't laugh either. In fact, if I thought Jaya didn't like me after yesterday, today, her evil eye stare nearly pushes me back to my room. Sunny's hand on my shoulder redirects my attention.

"Can you grab some forks for all of us?" Sunila points me

to the cabinets. "Second drawer down."

While Sunny scoops out steaming rice from a rice cooker on the kitchen island onto a line of plates, and Addison spoons fried eggs on top of each bed of white—I can feel Jaya's eyes on me like two heat-seeking missiles. When Nahida stops dancing to squirt ketchup on top of the eggs, Sunila covers her dish, but not before a swirl of red sauce lands on her wrist.

"I'm bleeding!" Sunny squeals, and nearly everyone laughs—Nahida, the loudest. I smile at Sunny's antics, and she turns to the woman with the limp. "Oh come on, Shandra. Why so serious?" Then she licks the ketchup off her wrist and says, "Unless you wanna be my next victim. Cuz I'm a vampire, now!" And Shandra shakes her head, side to side, as a small smile emerges right before a giggle escapes. And I laugh too. But Jaya storms out. Again.

As I clear the table, Ava puts the music back on as she does the dishes, her feet moving side to side the whole time. Sunny catches me staring and pulls me aside, lowering her voice. "Her hubby threatened to cut her legs off if she walked away. She didn't walk. She ran. She told us that for the rest of her life, she plans to dance every single day, even for a few minutes, to remind her that she still has her legs."

I pull my hair over my face. Slowly at first. Then ask, "Sunny, can I borrow your glasses for a second." She hands them to me as I remember something Jesse and I once made Mom do with her long hair when we were little and Dad worked late. I pull more and more hair forward until my hair covers my entire face and then I adjust Sunny's glasses over my face. Sunny giggles then takes her specs back as I brush my hair behind my ears and finish clearing the table.

Hair. That's one thing Dad never stole from me. Like he did from Mom. I need to remember that.

"Did I do something to offend Jaya?" I ask Sunny when we're the last two in the kitchen. I can't be the only one who notices her strange behavior around me.

"She doesn't say much." Sunny says.

Tell me something I don't know.

But before I dismiss my question, she adds, "The only thing she said the first day she met you was that you remind her of someone."

"Must be someone she hates…" I blurt out.

"More like someone she's not sure she can trust." Maybe Sunny feels bad, because she adds, "I wouldn't worry 'bout it. We all come in here with stuff. Some of us more than others."

Dad is the one person I know I can't trust. Do I remind her of her abuser? Thinking of Sunny's words "not sure she can trust," Mom comes to mind. Maybe I remind her of someone who could have stopped her pain but didn't. I accept that I probably won't know more unless I ask Jaya myself, and at the rate that we've exchanged words—yeah—that's not gonna happen, and right now, the wall clock reminds me that I have an appointment to get to. I excuse myself and head for the safe house office.

I barely walk in when the woman behind the desk says, "Sit down. Have you thought about what has been mentioned to you? Your next step? The options?" Before I get her name, visiting social worker, Margaret Williams, fires several questions at me. "You can't see this right now, but someday, you'll want to move on, and you'll be ready to move on with your life. My job is to make sure I help you lay the foundation for your long-term freedom and safety. Make sense?"

"Are you referring to putting a restraining order on Dad?" Tempted to ask her if she needs a bib, I notice her scooping neckline on her metallic grey blouse forms a perfect net to catch the crumbs from her coffee cake.

Ms. W. nods her head yes as she pulls a Kleenex from the box to wipe her hands. Then she begins to jot down notes on her chart spread out in front of her on her desk, a tiny, rhinestone stud visible on her upper earlobe when she turns her profile to type something on her computer to her left. Just like the clip in Ms. W's hair fails to hold her bun intact, dirty-blond curls falling out everywhere, I doubt a court will contain Dad and his explosive anger.

"With an emergency order in place, your father will be

restrained for thirty days pending a trial after which the courts can rule for his limitations for up to five years if the abuse threatens your life." Ms. W. lays out the details, taking turns flipping through the chart and typing away.

"So, I have to do this if I want to make sure he can't come within so many miles of me, my campus, my workplace, my everything?" Diana told me all this when I first arrived at Hope Now.

Ms. W. glances up, turning her right hand in the air. "And who wouldn't want that?" She glances at her phone, and looks up again. "So have you decided? Doesn't it sound like the best option for a person in your situation? I don't understand the hesitation."

Sure. Sounds divine if it weren't for the minor details that nail me to no. Because if I pursue an order against Dad, he has to be told. Which means he has to be contacted. Which means he'll know I told on him. And that's where I get stuck, every time I play out the worst case scenario, I'm vacuumed back into Dad's clutches, separated from Lagan and Jesse, or dead.

"How can you guarantee he won't ignore the order and come find me anyway?" I've asked myself this question a thousand times.

"Like so much of life, darling, there are no guarantees." She leans back in her chair, crumb cake in hand again. "But generally speaking, most abusers are afraid of the law, and the threat of prison convinces most men to stay away." She repeats her answer, but I know Dad. He'll find a way to skirt the law, and I'm not ready to give him any clues as to my whereabouts.

"He'll trace the paperwork back to here. He's really smart. And—"

"He's not allowed here. He can't come in." Ms. W. rises from her seat and places her palms flat on the chart. "The police are on your side. He would be immediately arrested, and if he is a smart man, he won't do anything to risk his career. Your chart says he's a lawyer. It would be career suicide, and your dad sounds too bright to do something like that."

"I never said he was a lawyer." Maybe I told Diana he was a

liar, but businessman is what I wrote on the Hope Now application. Benjamin Burns, Businessman. Flashbacks of a foiled escape attempt hurdle me back behind the caution tape. "You don't know him." I'm shaking my head, remembering the one time we tried to leave. The beach. The sand angels. The bust. "The Police have always sided with my Dad. I would rather he just think I ran away."

Ms. W. sits down, and I rise from my seat. This meeting is over. I have chores to do and a lot of homework to catch up on. Dr. Deans from Loyola's English Department emailed me a list of my backed-up assignments once they granted me permission to carry on as an online student pending a change in my present situation.

"You know Talia…" I stop mid-stride and hang onto the doorframe with one hand. "At some point, everyone gets tired of running."

I say goodbye and head over to the resource room lined with shelves of books. One wall lined with a row of desks, one of which holds a computer monitor, but Addison's currently using it, and I'm tempted to leave before she sees me. So I won't have to see her.

"Be done in a few minutes," she says.

Too late to go unnoticed, I spot the sign up clipboard, uncap the pen attached to a string and sign up for a two-hour window starting at 3:00PM. It's 2:00PM now.

Run my finger along the index of books to see if I can find a light read to pass the minutes, and I pull out the *The Fault in Our Stars* by John Green. As I skim the back cover, sounds like the author might have the inside scoop on who to blame for this mess called my life.

I flip to the last chapter and start reading, because if it doesn't have a happy ending, why bother? After a few lines, I file the book where I found it. Not because the ending disappoints, but for the simple fact that the paper grates my palms where scabs from the broken cup incident haven't completely healed.

"I'm done," Addison says. She's stashing her paperwork

into a backpack, and the zipper catches on her sleeve, exposing her wrist and forearm as she detangles the snare. A perfectly, smooth shade of tan covers her arm. Her skin is perfect.

Jealousy foolishly stunts my speech until I look up to see her face, no longer turned toward the monitor. Focus on her eyes, I tell myself, to keep from wincing at the sight of her flattened, disfigured features.

"Go ahead. Look," Addison says. "It helps you and me both out if we're not pretending my face isn't deformed. Once you take a few hard looks, you'll feel less awkward around me. And that's what I'd want. For us to get past the surface. Make sense?"

I clear my throat and stare at her forehead. And let my gaze wash over her, first her lashless eyes, blotchy cheeks and flattened nose, down past her shapeless lips and flaky white chin to her throat where my stare stops at the neckline of her black, long-sleeved top.

"But the skin on your arms—" I start to ask the wrong question. "I mean, what happened?"

"Where do I start?" Addison sighs and motions to a chair near hers, and I sit down. "Let's see. There are one hundred and sixty-four wall tiles, eighty-one floor tiles and one hundred and fourteen ceiling tiles. There are also two hundred smaller, white diamond-shaped bathtub tiles."

I wiggle in my seat, wishing I had left when I had had the chance.

"Why would anyone know that, you're wondering? Well, every day, for a total of ten years, two months, thirteen days, and twelve hours, my husband escorted me down to the basement bathroom, locked it from the outside and left for work."

Oh.

"But exactly three months ago, I decided I didn't want to count the tiles anymore. So I slipped a book of matches into my panties before the morning stroll down the steps and when I was sure he was long gone, I lit the tiles on fire." Addison chuckles to herself. "Unfortunately, they didn't burn so easily, but the rest of the bathroom did, and even from behind the locked door, I could hear the smoke detector going off somewhere in the house."

"How long before help came?"

Addison smoothes her wig down to her neck, her bright, toothy smile strangely beautiful, like a rainbow arching over a cyclone-hit city. "Too late for my face, as you can tell. When the fire spread from the bathroom door to the walls and to the floor, I hid in the bathtub and turned the shower on cold to cool my body, because the heat became unbearable. Then as the tub began to fill, I realized I could hide my body under the water, keeping the flames from making skin contact. If I were a fish, I'd have kept my head under water too, but I couldn't hold my breath long enough and even though I ducked my head under on and off, I couldn't stay immersed continuously. Moments after I resolved to drown rather than burn any longer, the firemen broke through the doors and found me. And here I am, alive but unable to cover the ugliest part of me." Addison rises from her chair. "But I guess none of us escapes without scars. Somewhere."

I tug at my sleeves, pulling them past my wrists and nod to the floor. I want to say sorry, something, anything, but I'm flooded with guilt for coveting her smooth healthy skin on the rest of her body. "What are you studying? Are you in school?"

"Started taking classes toward my Bachelor's a couple months ago. Hope to complete a degree in art history and eventually teach art therapy to child survivors." Addison walks toward the door. "The counselors who run the group sessions, they use art therapy a lot, and I know it's made a difference for me. Well, I'll let you get your work done. It was nice chatting, Talia."

"Yeah. I mean, I'm sorry. For all you went through." I pull a few strands over my lips. "You're so...brave. And smart to think of the water. Do you think you'll ever do, umm, plastic surgery or something like that?"

"Sure. When I win the lotto. Sunny's story isn't that different from mine although she's from India, and I was born in Cambodia. Most of us immigrant survivors are lucky the system doesn't deport us. I can't lie, though. There are days I wonder if I were better off letting him beat me. At least I'd still have my face." She breaks out into another smile. "But then I think about the day Diana said to me, 'You never have to go back,' and that first taste of real freedom. There's nothing like it, wouldn't you say?"

"I...I...I should get my homework done."

"Yes, yes. Of course." Addison slips out the door, and I sit down to open up my account Diana started for me, print out several pages of assignments, and return to my room to spend the rest of the day with Hamlet and Gatsby, preferring someone else's trials over my own.

13
~ Jesse ~

April 28, 29, 30

One week in and Jimmy hires me on for three more jobs after the initial test run to see if I could handle a little direction and work on my own. I painted five apartments one day, moved a truck load of furniture the next, and ripped off caked-on layers of wallpaper from the seventies on an old house he's fixing up to sell. The work's back-breaking at times, but gives me plenty of time to think.

"You gotta a good head on your shoulders, John," Jimmy tells me, his dark brown shoulders pronounced under his tight Bears t-shirt. "Natural instincts with tools and a sense of navigation as to what order to do things. Anyone ever show you the ropes? Your dad? An uncle? You have any big brothers you tinkered around the garage with?"

I shake my head no, focusing on the wood floor I'm currently tearing out to keep from making eye contact. Jimmy will show me how to put in a new one tomorrow.

"The hard part is getting rid of the old." Jimmy gets down on his knees next to me, wedges the curved side of his hammer under a slab of wood and pulls and pulls until the nails loosen, then pries it out like he's picking a piece of paper off the floor.

"Gotta clean it up real good if you want the new stuff to stick," Jimmy says. Then he rubs his clean-shaven head with a towel and asks, "Where are your folks? You doing anything for the weekend?"

Does formulating another disturbing letter to Dad count? "My parents are dead." That should end that line of questions.

But Jimmy says, "So sorry for bringing it up, man. I didn't know. Wanna join my mom and me for a barbeque?" Jimmy's chucking old wood into bins that we'll carry out to the dumpster in shifts. "She makes a mean burger. Swears it's better than a Rachael Ray creation any day. And her jerk chicken will set your mouth on fire. In the best way."

Who's Rachael Ray? "I'll think about it." Thought about it. Uh. No. "I'll probably pass," I add.

"Well, if you change your mind, I'll be heading over to Ma's to put up a new fence this weekend. You can always take a burger to go after we pretty up her yard." Jimmy waits a beat, but I don't say anything. "That fence she has there right now is like a century old. Rotting wooden slats that did nothing but fill my childhood with splinters. Like clockwork, Ma pulled one out of my hand every week till I stopped running around the yard with my buddies."

"Why'd you stop?" Were you through with splinters? Did one just hurt too much?

"To start chasing girls, of course." Jimmy grins as he crosses his arms over his football build of a chest, his pristine white teeth contrasting with his dark brown skin.

***

April 30ᵗʰ

I wake up Friday morning, and walk to the desk, pull out an envelope and count my cash. I've made two hundred dollars this week, and it's time to replenish my snacks, buy myself a towel, and maybe even splurge on three instead of two meals today. Two more weeks of working for Jimmy, and I should have enough money to buy the things I need to execute the last part of my plan. Letter number one has had five days to simmer. Time to find a new library in case Dad found a way to trace the first note.

I take my toiletries down to the men's room but leave last night's t-shirt on while I shower. I need nosy people in my life about as much as I need to forget how to walk again. Those days were rough back then. Falling. Lifting. Pumping out reps till my muscles burned and my arms shook like twigs threatening to break, but Talia never let up on me. And once I knew she needed out even more than me, I pushed my body past its limits. I was going to walk again if it killed me. And today's the day I make Dad wish I had died when I jumped off the roof.

Trekking back up to my room, hair dripping, I pull on the last of my clean Chicago skyline t-shirts with my last pair of clean jeans. I'll throw a load in the washing machine later. And someday soon, when I have a steady cash flow coming in, I'll change up my wardrobe.

Pulling out the Chicago transit and library cards from the desk drawer, my eye catches the glint of the gun. I try to push it back a little further, telling her, "Not time yet. But soon," but when I close the drawer, the Rite Aid bag snags on the metal top rim, tearing the plastic. I pull it out, dropping the necklace I bought for Talia out onto my palm but just as I pull out the dresser drawer to store it elsewhere, the sun streaming the room catches the blue of the glass heart and an ache I've buried for several days rises inside me. *God, how I miss you, sis.*

Slipping the silver chain around my neck, I tuck the blue heart into my shirt and silently vow to carry it with me until I see my sister again.

The sun shines, motivating me to walk a few blocks till I reach the entrance to the Brown line instead of transferring trains to get across town to Michigan Ave. Slowly getting less nervous about getting lost, but I routinely study the subway map before boarding the train, even if one or two trains arrive and leave without me.

The public library stands across the street from the Art Institute, and although not nearly as majestic and towering as the Harold Washington branch, the entrance boasts the dual functions of a military museum and a research institute. I'm not here to learn American history or check out books on artillery, although the display of war rifles behind glass cases stirs both thrill and fear inside me. With two computer labs to choose from, I make my way up the staircase to the third floor, but spot at least three people waiting their turn for an open spot. After writing the name John on a sign up sheet, I mosey around the library, surrounded by symbols of war.

The battles in my own life seem less fierce when I take in the posters and paintings that freeze moments in history. A soldier sheltering his buddy from oncoming gunfire, a pilot kissing his lover goodbye, uniformed men fighting with missing limbs, and a picture of a field of purple flowers covering a sea of graves, white crosses peeking out everywhere. I wonder if flowers grow over where we laid Mom to rest?

As I move from one stack of books to another, skimming titles, I think I recognize the brunette sitting behind the cubicle next to the windows. Summer, the girl who lent me her raincoat, slouches with her head leaned on one hand, but she's not reading or writing. Seems more like she's staring out the glass at the park or the lake beyond the grass. The poncho's back in my room, hanging off the back of the chair at the desk.

First things first. I retrace my steps to the computer lab and now only a guy wearing biking gear stands next in line. The ringtone of a cell phone goes off, and the redhead behind one computer rises from her seat and whispers loud enough for all to hear. "I'll call you right back. I'm in the library," and then she walks past me and the biker dude takes her spot.

I take a walk back toward the windows, arching my back from behind some stacks, I don't see Summer where I thought I saw her a moment ago. Maybe it wasn't her after all. Stay focused, Jesse.

I mosey on to the periodicals shelf nearby and open up this morning's Chicago Tribune to the business section, figuring I can find a few big words to throw into my next email to Dad. Seeing his face splashed across the business headlines, I drop the paper like it's on fire. Exhaling as I remind myself that it's just a picture, I pick up the news section and sit to peruse the article titled, "Game Changer in Biggest Investigation of the Year when MOD's CFO Dies."

I scan, searching for Dad's name. "MOD's CFO died...multiple surgeries could not stop internal bleeding... Undisclosed sources strongly suggest the deceased engaged in domestic abuse or human trafficking, forcing the suspect to act in self-defense... How can you ask a dead man anything? ... MOD's legal spokesperson, Attorney Gerard Vanderbilt, told reporters he and his client have no plans to drop the case. 'This is a time to lay down your human rights' sling shots and mourn the loss of one of Chicago's finest.' After a moment of silence to pay respect to the deceased, Vanderbilt added, 'Of course I plan to find justice, or else. Or else why did I choose this profession? No further questions.'"

Or else. Like an I.V. line, Dad said these two words daily to Talia and me, fear running through our veins. And even though it's just ink on paper, I can hear the intonation of his voice like he's standing over me, reminding me that he will find me.

The last thing I read before I notice a vacant seat behind a computer is: "Attorney Vanderbilt has his work cut out for him since witnesses who arrived early on the scene reported multiple bruises visible on the prime suspect's exposed skin. State D.A. Bonds said, 'It'll be interesting to see how Vanderbilt gets out of hot water this time.' To date, no arrests have been made."

Laying the newspaper back in place, I take my seat behind the empty computer cubical and login using Lagan's library barcode, momentarily relishing the image of a teacup, a shrunken Dad flailing his arms in hot water. Thank you for that picture, Mr. Bonds, whoever you are.

When I attempt to sign in to the email account I contacted Dad's office with, the screen reads, "This account has been blocked, reported for spamming." A smile creeps at the edge of my mouth knowing Dad read the email. I have Lagan to thank for my new plan. If he hadn't suggested I find another way, I would have never looked for a backdoor entrance to destroy Dad.

Scanning the walls for inspiration, a photograph of a blue jay flying over a boy soldier, the enemy cowering behind bushes, provides a light bulb moment. The setting sun casts shadows of the boy and bird on the mountainside, painting a Goliath-sized warrior and the blue jay with a hawk-sized wingspan. I need Dad to believe he's no longer facing his wheelchair-bound son, but rather the new, stronger and capable me—capable of shooting him in the heart without hesitation. Key word: capable.

I click on the option to open a new account as TIRO1toten@gmail.com before I type up my second letter to Gerard Vanderbilt, Esq.

Dear Sir,

How are you? I am writing to ask you if you'd take up my case. I'm a nineteen year-old female college student who's looking for representation against her father. I believe I have a case against him that could lock him up, but I need to ask your input on three things.

1. Is it legal to burn your daughter with scalding hot water each time she forgets to do her chores?

2. Is it legal to iron out your differences with your daughter. With a hot iron? Centimeters from her face?

3. Is it legal to imprison your daughter in your house, threatening her daily that her options are to stay or to stay...or to die?

Which brings us to a point of irony, really, since I left, and I'm still alive. But I do want to guarantee that I can live safely, free of any possible retribution from my father. How best should I proceed so I can nail his South African behind to the wall, figuratively-speaking?

My little bit of research suggests that he could go to prison for five to ten if the evidence is strong enough. And believe you me, the evidence is all over the place. All over my body. I have pictures of every cut, burn and scar from the last several years. Should I send them to you? Or do you just want to see them for yourself? I could come in today. Pull up my sleeves.

Let you take a peek.

Sincerely aware that I hate my father,

TIRO [Time Is Running Out]

For once, I want Dad to count one to ten and fret over every second he draws nearer to what he's due.

Before I hit send, I subject the message, "Hot or Cold" and google, copy and paste two gruesome pictures of severely burned, female arms under the words:

p.s. I hope this letter finds you in hell, I mean, well.

I log out of all the pages and restore the screen to the library homepage before I take a deep breath, cracking my knuckles as I imagine stepping from one room into the next, off-ing the lights where Dad consumes my thoughts and flipping the switch to on where a girl offered me a smile on a rainy day. A little part of me wishes I had run back to my place for her coat, but if it was her, she already took off.

I'm typing "affordable men's business suits" in the Google search bar when someone behind me says, "Hey. I thought that was you."

Summer.

I exit out of all my screens, relieved she only saw my last one, turn to face her, and say, "Summer, right?"

"You remembered my name?" Summer smiles, exposing an endearing small space between her bottom two teeth. "Glad to know you survived that crazy storm."

In more ways than one.

"Shhhh." An older lady leans to the side of her computer screen with her finger on her lips. "This is a library."

"Wanna talk outside?" Summer suggests.

"Umm. I don't want to bother you." I run my thumb along the neckline of my shirt, the feel of Talia's necklace a cool reminder that she's the only girl I've ever really talked to. I rise from my seat and make to leave. "Just wanted to say thanks. For the other day. And the poncho."

"I'm calling security." Miss I Cannot Concentrate threatens us again.

"No need. I was just leaving." I turn toward the exit.

"Wait." When Summer follows me, she smoothes down her beige skirt that falls above her knees. "I need a little air. I'll walk you out."

When we're outside the library, I face Summer, taken by her eyes. Don't recall them seeming this shade of cobalt blue that night we met. "I kinda have to go. But, how long will you be, uh, studying here? I can drop off your coat if you'll still be here in, say, an hour."

"Are you late to class?" Summer asks, tugging at her sweatshirt neckline, the afternoon sun blisteringly hot today. "My anatomy class doesn't start for another hour so I thought I'd read ahead, but truth be told, the human body is putting me to sleep."

Summer wears a black University of Chicago tank top, uncovering her leaf tattoo when she pulls off her purple long-sleeve. Inked on her upper arms are the words, "Leave the earth changed if you want to leave the world changed." When she catches me staring, I shift my gaze to her pivoting heels, revealing well-defined calves with each turn. A second tattoo of dainty leaves circles her right ankle. *I could study your body while you...*

"What'd you say your name was?" Summer asks.

"I didn't," I say. "Um, about your coat?"

"Oh right." Summer fishes out her phone from her sweatshirt pocket. "I'll be back after class to study for finals around three. Want to meet back here? There's a new churro vendor I've been eyeing for the past few days. He sets up shop at the corner in front of the Art Institute about that time."

She plans to change the world by supporting the small businessman? Oh wait. *Is she asking me to eat churros with her?* The request is as forward as anyone's ever been with me, and I'm tongue-tied for a moment. I do owe her, and a churro is one thing that won't break my bank account. I practice my response in my head a couple of times before I let the words out of my mouth: "My name's J-John. Three PM churro break on me, it is. I'll see you in a bit."

As I walk away, I imagine feeling her blue eyes on my back, but

I don't turn to look until I reach the corner, the light green for oncoming traffic. Summer's still standing there, and her fingers rainbow a slow wave goodbye at her waistline. I reach up and cover the tiny bump under my shirt, and with my fingers I find the blue heart and whisper a silent confession to my sister, wondering when I'll be able to tell her face to face. A smile crowds out the anger I woke up with. If only for a moment, I forgot why I came to the library today.

.

14
~ Jesse ~

April 30th Continued

When I arrive back at my new "home," I find a note on my door from Jimmy.

Ma wanted to have the fence up before the weekend barbeque. Hoping you can make it today at 4:00PM. The house is two doors down from our last project.

Before I unlock my door, I change my mind about twenty times. The only friends I've ever had sat across my computer screen, our time together spent gaming online. Hanging out like normal teens after school had always been out of the question with Dad's rules, so I never bothered talking to anyone in school. The invitation to spend time with Summer whets an appetite that went into hibernation with my fall but didn't wake up with my legs and voice. Not even when Talia told me about Lagan. I just assumed some things were out of reach. So I stopped reaching for them.

When I find her jacket, I realize I don't have any detergent. Improvising, I run down to the laundry room on the first floor, toss the poncho in the washing machine, and squirt in a bunch of shampoo. Fishing out some coins from my pocket, I push them in slots and exhale relief when the machine comes alive.

It worked!

As I watch the spin of the soapy water knocking the raincoat to and fro, I imagine how our conversation might go and make a mental list of ten things I can talk about with Summer to keep from talking about my family. Like a teacher with a red pen, I cross out the word list in my mind and replace it with "topics." Dad's lists made up more than enough lists for one lifetime, and the last thing I want to do is associate Summer with something that reminds me of Dad.

Guy who saw my back walks in while I wait for the cycle to finish with a canvas bag and empties the contents from the dryer into it. The room is not that big and he's squatting in a way that pretty much blocks the doorway. Not like he can see through my shirt, but I back up against the wall and study my hands like I'm a palm reader.

The spin cycle comes to a zooming finish while the guy cleans out the lint tray. "It's all yours, Dude," he says as he rises to his feet, slams the dryer shut and starts walking out. Right before he clears the door, without turning, he says, "I'd ask for my money back from the tattoo guy. Just sayin'." And he's gone, but I can hear his footsteps on the stairwell.

As I open the washing machine, the jacket smells great, but it's saturated with soapy water. Maybe shampoo wasn't the best idea. As I debate whether to run the cycle again or wring it out and let it hang in my room, the stinging words of the stranger play on repeat like a bad stand-up comedian stuck on the same joke. Me. The joke's *always* on me.

I decide I'll buy Summer a new poncho, hoping I can spot a vendor who sells them en route back to the library. I'll keep an eye out for a new place while I'm at it, because one more wisecrack out of that guy and I might be tempted to test out Dad's gun on him. Then we'll see whose mess is difficult to clean up. *Jerk.*

As I head back toward the library, I imagine Dad reading the second email, his smile dimming quicker than a match blown out, his face turning fire-red with rage. Thinking I'll let the two notes simmer for a week before I write a final email and pay my father a visit. Who knows? Maybe it won't take a third push to expedite Dad's departure to his South African Office for good. Because if Dad leaves, Talia and I won't have to. Maybe he'll lose the big trial and no one around here will want him as their lawyer, his perfect record shattered alongside his career.

An increase of people crowd the park as I approach the museum library, everyone excited to start their weekend, I'm guessing. Teens toss a Frisbee back and forth, little kids run under a huge mirror-coated, coffee bean-like structure, some take photos around it, and still others sit and chat, sharing drinks, reading on tablets, or tapping on phones.

The steps of the Art Institute come in view when I cross at the light and turn the corner, and there he is, just like Summer described. The Churro Guy concentrates on sprinkling a row of tubes of Spanish delight with powdered sugar while another batch rotates slowly behind the steamy glass. If I buy her a dozen, will it make up for the fact that I didn't bring her poncho back? Maybe the guys selling rain gear only set up shop when the weather forecast calls for showers.

"You're early," Summer says. She's a few feet behind, her brown hair bouncing on her shoulders as she picks up her pace to catch up to me.

"A pretty birdie told me they go fast." I put my hands in my pocket and look up to the Art Institute windows.

"You mean a little birdie?" Summer's blue eyes squint when she smiles.

"That's what I said." Didn't I? "Anyway, I'm really sorry about your jacket. I...I'll get you a new one."

"Don't bother. My mom told me I looked like a whale in it so she was thrilled when I came home without it." Summer fishes through her purple backpack and pulls out a compact, rainbow-striped, umbrella. "Besides, now I always carry one of these just in case."

I'm at a loss for words, forgetting everything I rehearsed in the laundry room. The topics. I draw a complete blank, so I simply nod, smile, and look away again.

"Buy me a churro and we'll call it even?" Summer takes several steps toward the churro stand, and I robotically follow. "I want the chocolate-cream filled please." She turns to me, I shrug my shoulders, and she says, "Make that two. Thanks."

Summer snags a few extra napkins, handing me a churro, and I follow her up the Museum steps, stopping two rows short of the door. "Wanna sit for a minute?" she asks. "We can't eat in the library."

"I have this thing." I thumb-point behind me like Jimmy's place is somewhere in that direction.

Summer leans in and brushes my cheek with a napkin. "Missed a spot. Some of the best things in life are messy."

Are we still talking churros? "It's a job. I could use the extra cash."

Summer moves past me, her hair grazing my arm, and she sits down, hugging her knees with the hand not holding a churro. "Are you late? Because it only takes me four or five bites to finish one off." Summer props the churro off her lips like a cigar. "Unless you decide to smoke it."

Grinning, I shake my head and join her on the steps, careful to leave space between us. "They say smoking is bad for your health."

Summer turns her body to face me, her knees bumping mine. "Unless you don't inhale." And we both start laughing as I scoot back on the concrete step to recreate the gap between us. Okay. I can breathe again.

"So...are you into stars?" she asks, and I swear I see one falling in her eyes. The sun is playing tricks on me.

I clear my throat. "Stars?"

"That night. At the garden. In the rain." She's nodding, twisting her head in a you-know-what-I'm-saying manner.

But I don't. Know what she's saying so I just shake my head back and forth, rising to leave. Jimmy will be waiting for me.

"There was a stargazer's show that night." Summer answers her own question, creating a shield from the sun in her eyes with her hand over her forehead. "Weatherman predicted a perfectly clear, moonless night, but then the clouds rolled in. And then the lightning which some are still saying was the cause of the fire. And now the news reports suggest the garden won't reopen till the fall with all the damage."

"It wasn't lightning." I mutter, turning to leave.

"What'd you say?" Summer rises too, popping the last of her churro in her mouth. I haven't taken a second bite of my churro yet.

"Nothing." I look at the sugar-coated pastry in my hand and consider telling her it's too sweet for me. Instead I say, "I really want to…umm…pay you back. How much was the poncho?" I pull out some bills from my back pocket.

"About the cost of ten churros." She says, her arms over her chest.

As I count out singles, before I get to six, Summer clears her throat and says, "But I only take payment in churros."

I start descending the steps back toward the churro stand when I hear her voice behind me, "Oh. I forgot to mention…" When I turn to hear the rest, she's smoothing the sides of her tiny waist with her hands. "No more than one a day. Have to watch my figure an' all."

I stand cemented to my spot, heat rising up my neck. If she wants me to buy her another nine churros, but not more than one a day, that means I'd have to see her again. As in nine more times. Which means she *wants* to see me again.

And like tangled up shoelaces, I fail to undo the knot I walked into by the time Summer catches up to me.

"So Monday? Same time-ish?" She's asking me and before I can respond, she says, "Unless you're busy. With school. Or another *thing* you have to get to."

I can't tell if my ears are hot because I want to say yes, or because I'm afraid Summer will bowl me over if I say no. The word, "Sure," leaves my lips a little louder than a whisper. I clear my throat, and add, "Three o'clock, right?"

"Oh wait. I forgot. The library's always closed on Mondays. And Tuesday, I have Bio after orgo and then chem lab always runs late, so five would be better." Summer pats her JanSport on her shoulder. "Always a workout."

I nod, tickled by her chattiness. "So you're a science..umm..major?" I ask, rubbing the back of my neck.

"Pre-med. What about you?" Summer looks at me, head turned ever so slightly as the sun dances in her sky blue eyes. "Are you working? Studying? Wait. What I really want to know is what do you want to be when you grow up?"

I don't know which is worse, the thought of telling Summer I haven't been in school since freshman year at Benton Harbor High, because I tried to end my life, or the only reason I didn't complete my GED was I was too busy setting the house on fire in hopes of killing my Dad.

I decide to answer without answering. "I'm working right now. I guess when I figure out what I want to do, I'll go back to school. Maybe." I look to the street, all the people going somewhere.

"Didn't you have a little boy dream? I mean every guy I know at one point wanted to be a fireman with a dog, ride on the back of a garbage truck, or play for the major leagues."

A smile creeps to my mouth as I remember the one time Lagan came over during a snowstorm, and we nailed Talia with snowballs until she agreed to bake us cookies. "A guy once told me I had a good pitching arm."

"But if you could be anything, the sky's the limit, money isn't an issue, and no one could stop you, what would you do? What would you be?" Summer has her hands up but her arms aren't raised enough. Her tattoo stares at me like an exclamation point to her enthusiasm.

"Free." *Who said that?* My eyes shift up, toward the cloud-dotted, blue sky. "You know...a free, umm...bird. Fly a plane, maybe. Like some of those Air Force pictures in the library. Yeah. A pilot. Want seconds?" A mostly untouched churro rests on my open palm.

Summer looks skyward, one hand guiding the leaf charm on her silver necklace side to side. "I'll pass. Only one a day. Gotta have a plan. Then stick to the plan."

"That's cool." I wrap the churro up in the paper, keenly

aware at how close we're standing to each other. "What about you? Did you always wanna be a doctor, hoping to find the cure for cancer. The secret ingredient hidden in leaves?"

Summer glances down at her chain, picking up the tiny silver leaf. "Oh this?"

I point to her arm, the side where her tattoo lies. "Well there's this." I motion to her ankle with a downward gaze. "And that too. I mean, you obviously—" and I catch myself, because I don't know the first thing about Summer. "Sorry," I say, shifting my focus to the Churro Guy who can't hand out his sweets fast enough for the growing line.

"I'll tell you my leaf story someday. Are you gonna come inside so you can google how to get your pilot's license? You could always call in sick." Summer combs her hair behind her ear with her fingers, her left hand fiddling with her earring.

"I would...except for the minor detail that I don't have a phone, so my boss is expecting me. And I have to save up a whole heck of a lot before I can afford classes and a phone." I shift my weight, feeling stupid for drawing attention to my lack of money. Remembering what we agreed to moments earlier, I say, "I'll do some research on Tuesday. After churros."

"I always forget to charge mine." Summer pulls out her phone. The screen is dark. "So I'm no help to you."

But you're helping me with…what? I'm not sure what the right word is. Because I don't know what to call this really nice feeling inside me.

"Right." I stuff a hand in my jean pocket, my gaze dropping to my shoes. My other hand still holds the crumbling churro.

Summer's arms suddenly wrap around my neck. "Thanks!" she says. "For the churro."

She lets go, steps back, and adjusts her bag on her shoulder, and I guess my gaping stare betrays me, because she fidgets on her feet, and says, "Sorry. I'm a hugger. I hug. Like everyone." Summer shrugs, spreading her arms open.

The only embrace I've ever known from a girl was my sister's, and I barely hugged her goodbye that last morning. For most of my life, she's been the one who hugged me.

Out of the corner of my eye, I see a jogger pass, his shirt soaked completely through. When he passes, I point to him over my shoulder with eyebrows raised, hoping to still my pounding heart with the little joke.

"Okay, maybe not everyone." Summer's doing that spinning on her heels thing again.

The grin on my face hurts my cheeks. Is that even possible? "You're welcome. So, 5:00PM, uh, next week, Tuesday?" I ask, a marching band having taken up residency in my gut.

"Rain or shine." Summer smiles and turns to walk, down the steps, across the street, and through the library doors.

15
~ Talia ~

May 1st

I pull the sixth Post-it note off the question mark on the wall, today marking my sixth day at Hope Now, and between the chores, the meals, and computer time, I find myself with a routine, and the ladies who speak to me make me feel more welcome with each day. The activities help pass the time and distract from the constant awareness that I haven't spoken to either Lagan or Jesse, and I'm just hoping that the two men I love are doing okay.

We had dosas for breakfast this morning, Sunny attempting to teach Ava a few Bollywood moves while Addison flipped the thin rice and lentil pancakes before stuffing them with potatoes. The familiar scents of masala ignite my yearning for Mom, the memory of her pointing to the round, silver cups and naming each spice till I knew them by heart. "Turmeric, coriander, chili powder. Garam masala, cumin, and paprika." How I wish Mom were still alive and I could fill her spice tins with joy, peace, love. Healing, hope, and freedom.

Three o'clock sounds the end of my computer time and I've reread the same page over and over again about

Shakespeare and historians' best guesses as to the premise behind *Hamlet*. Someone behind me clears her throat. *Nahida*. She's standing at the door, her gap-toothed smile in full effect.

"Do you need more time?" she asks. "I can come back."

"No. No." I log out and rise to leave, gathering my books. "I can't concentrate. I'll try again tomorrow."

"I was like that when I first got here. Always watching my back, wondering if my boyfriend would find me." Nahida pulls a lock of her blond hair across her mouth, and I'm wondering if she's making fun of me. Then I remember her missing teeth. "Want to do our nails together?"

"You mean you didn't come here to use the computer?" I ask as Nahida pulls out five vials of nail polish from her bag and lines them up on the table.

"In a little bit. I think it's more fun to type when your nails are pretty. Come on. Which color do you like?" Nahida's holding up two shades, hot pink and lilac purple.

I walk over and see the metallic blue and run my thumb over my finger nails. "I kinda like the blue." Nahida motions for me to sit, and I giggle, saying, "This'll be a first."

"Well, then, if you let me, I'll do your nails for you, cuz the first time's a mess." She turns my hand over in hers and without looking up, she asks, "Are the cuts better? Do they still hurt? I'll be gentle."

"Getting better," I say. And then I inch my chair closer and stretch my hand out, palm down. Makes me think of the time I played a game with Lagan, having to cover happy face and sad face Post-its with my hand. The invisible Post-it under my hand is currently happy. And as Nahida brushes blue over each nail, she tells me her story.

"Nails are something I can still pretty up, since my teeth. Well, I'm sure you've noticed by now." Nahida pauses and smiles, exposing the gap, and then keeps talking. "Crazy thing is, my boyfriend promised to erase my smile if I ever ran away." She pauses again, and says, "He found me hiding in the wooden castle at the park by his apartment the night I tried to leave. It was the place we first kissed. Then he dragged me home and punched my two front teeth out."

I accept that Dad isn't the only monster out there as Nahida stops and dabs the skin under my fingernail where a little excess polish spread.

"I hated my smile. And my life. Until my twentieth birthday came and my boyfriend completely forgot about it. When I casually mentioned, did you get me anything, he threw a Reader's Digest magazine at me, you know, the free ones that come in the mail sometimes, and walked away. I read while he was in the shower. And I read while he slept. I tried to sneak in a story whenever he wasn't watching. And then one day, I fell in love with a character in a book. A man who made me believe I deserved a second chance. So I left everything behind except the Reader's Digest novel that teased me a new life."

"What was his name?" I ask, placing my other hand flat, this time on a Post-it with both happy and sad faces.

"It was the character's job that swung my heart. He was a dentist who fell in love with a girl with crooked teeth." Nahida smiles, her eyes glistening. "He didn't try and fix her. In the story, he just loved her."

I turn to face her gapped smile. " Just before he punched out my front teeth, he told me, 'No one will ever fall in love with your new smile.' He was wrong."

"I don't follow." Nahida greets my question with a full open-mouthed, hearty laugh.

"I'm emailing this guy I met last month. We met at the library. We're working out the details of our next date."

"That's. That's so great."

"Like this," Nahida blows over her own nails and says, "Helps them to dry a little faster."

I imitate Nahida, blowing over my nails, one hand at a time. "Well I'll leave you to, umm, get to planning."

"You have a boyfriend?" Nahida asks as she opens up a neon orange and begins to paint her nails. "I bet there were some hot guys on your campus."

"There is one guy, but it's hard." I'm fishing for words. "I guess it was harder back then too, but somehow it feels harder to see him now. I hate that I don't know when I'll see him again." I gently stroke my nails over my bandaged palm. The cuts are still healing. My nails feel dry but a little sticky, so I blow over the blue polish some more.

"Go see him. This isn't a prison you know." Nahida shrugs her shoulders and resumes painting her other hand.

"It's complicated." I sigh, not ready to share details. "Maybe things will change tomorrow."

"Ya know, if Sunny offers to paint your nails, don't let her, cuz then she'll offer to read your palms." Nahida's laughing like she's experienced this. "She's a comedian, and likely to tell you that you'll win the lotto, buy a plane, move to Hawaii and live happily ever after."

I can read palms, I decide. Every story has both happy and sad face Post-its under its palm. That's one thing I'm learning. But note taken: avoid Sunny's predictions for my future.

"FTR, no one knows the future." Nahida closes up her polish and blows across her fingernails. "But, what would life be without surprises, right?"

The question hangs in the air as I gather my things and head out the door. I walk by the board to check which chores my name lies next to. With my hands not fully healed, dishes got slated to someone else, and I am in charge of towels and sheets, but it's an alternate day task, and I folded and stored the linens yesterday. As I walk back to my room, I think about Jesse and what he must be doing. Has he made friends? Is he eating well? Where is he sleeping tonight? And is he sleeping or still having nightmares?

A brown paper bag rests on my table—the size and shape of a hardcover book—with a simple envelope taped to the surface. My first name is written on it, but it's spelled Tall-E-a in Lagan's handwriting I know so well. I pull it off and rip open the envelope and pull out a folded piece of paper. Unfolding it, before reading, I silently say thank you for this surprise.

My Talia,

It's only been a week, but it feels like a lifetime since I heard your voice, saw your face, held you in my arms. Kissed those lips of mine. Okay, your lips are technically yours, but...where was I?

[A giggle escapes. *Lagan.*]

A lot has happened since we said goodbye. I offered to take Jesse to a men's shelter, and when he refused, I even gave him a chance to crash in the suite at my dorm, but he just seemed to need some space. So your brother took off on his own, but I don't want you to worry. I gave him some cash, my library and subway cards and told him he can call me if he needs anything. He taught himself to talk and walk again. Any guy who does that on his own will make it on his own, so don't go nuts worrying about him. He also asked me to tell you that he loves you. I know you already know, but I promised I'd tell you.

[A pang of guilt makes my insides contract. Why didn't I just go with Lagan to get my brother? What does he mean by he'll get in touch? When? And how do I know he's okay while I'm waiting? I feel like I've broken my promise to Mom. How can I watch out for Jesse while I'm in here and he's out there, only God knows where? I take a deep breath and reread the part where Lagan reminded me of Jesse's success with rehab. He really did do that on his own.]

I'm guessing you've heard about the fire by now, at the garden? Jason told me he spoke with you when I stopped by the other day. I missed you. Thought I would sit under our waterfall and just, I don't know, think about you. They're not sure they can save it, to be honest.

[I sit down on the edge of the bed, holding the paper to my chest and imagine Lagan sitting under an empty shell of a tree. From weeping to waterfall to once-was-a willow tree.]

Jason also apologized. He had no idea I was, well, we were trying to keep us a secret from your dad. I thanked him for telling me and left, and by the time I got back to campus, my parents were freaking out. Your dad called their house and threatened to sue me if I didn't tell him where you were. My uncle, the lawyer, told us that would never hold up in a court of law since you're already an adult, but my parents wanted answers, and I know I'm an adult too, but my Indian parents are acting like I kidnapped you and have you stashed away in some cave. It's taken a lot of repeating things and phone calls to calm them down.

But that's not even the hard part. I think your dad hired some guy to snoop around campus for him, asking my roommate and friends and even some of my profs if they've seen you with me. And now I wonder every day if I'll run into him every time I turn a corner, but so far, I haven't met him face to face.

[And I hope you never will!]

He warned my parents in a second phone call that if I pursue you, that I can just kiss my law career goodbye, because he will find something to pin on me since he's a world-renowned lawyer who has never lost a case.

But Talia, the news is blowing up these days with your dad's name. He's involved in some huge case that the media thinks has him cornered. It's crazy all the papers are reporting: Suspicions of human trafficking. Accusations of first-degree murder. And rumor has it, the CFO of the hotel your dad represents had enough money to pay for a royal wedding, but now he's attending his own royal funeral. My uncle, the lawyer, doesn't see how they will arrest the prime suspect with all these sticky side issues, because no one can win a case like this without something unexpected turning up to dismiss the case altogether. And that kind of stuff has apparently happened in your dad's cases before. I'm hoping I can make more sense of all this when I get to law school.

[That would be good. Then you can explain it all to me, too.]

Btw, my parents called the phone company to have your dad's calls blocked from our landline.

And for all I know, your dad's figured out a way to hack my computer and my phone, so I'm limiting my phone calls to the shelter office for now. I'm so sorry. I hate this. I feel like even though you're free, there are bars between us. I have to believe it won't always be like this. That he'll eventually leave you alone or maybe someday, you'll be ready to have him put behind bars for what he's done to you. Just think about it. Okay?

[Okay. I suppose I could *think* about it.]

This has to be a lot of information. I don't even know how you're doing in there? I hope you've made friends, and you're figuring things out.

Know that you're my first thought in the morning. My last thought before I lay down to sleep. And my every thought in between. Okay, maybe every other. If I don't keep up my grades, there's no telling what my parents will do.

Looking forward to hearing your voice. Seeing you. And another kiss.

Or two. Or three...thousand. :)
   Love you, my Talia, my dew drop from heaven. And don't ever 4get.
      4 what? 4 you?
      You know the rest.
      Waiting,
      Lagan.

Lie back on my bed, paper over my chest and stare at the ceiling. I close my eyes and wrap my arms around myself, and a moment from months ago becomes my now. Lagan's strong, dark brown arms holding me tight. My ear to his beating heart. The brush of his goatee tickling my forehead. His almond-shaped eyes looking into mine. The scent of peppermint gum in the air with his dimple in full effect. His fingers sliding off my lips.

"The present!" I say out loud, scoot off the bed and tear open the paper bag.

It isn't a book at all. The thin rectangular box has white lights in it, a Post-it stuck on top. It reads,

Hang these somewhere in a shape of a Z, please.

The words, *Your Lightning Eyes Won't Fade...Ever,* are printed on the back of the Post-it.

I unwind the string of lights only to realize I have no tape or clips to hang them on the wall with. I settle for forming a Z on my bed and then plugging the lights in. I shut the door, flip the lights off, and lay on my side.

As I trace the line of lights with my fingertip in the dark. Z. Zigzag. All lit up. Kinda like lightning.

My lightning eyes, huh? Lit up because of you, Lagan. Because of you.

16
~ Jesse ~
May 2ⁿᵈ (Middle of the night)

I'm standing in a pool. Underwater. At the bottom of the pool. And I'm breathing like a fish. A mermaid swims toward me, except her scales are purple. Purple like the color of Summer's backpack yesterday when I met her in the library. She backstrokes toward me, her long brown hair covering my eyes and tickling my chin as she passes by once, twice, then a third time.

I want to see her face. I want to see if it's her. But she's too fast for me. I have no choice, I have to chase her. Swim after her. I throw my arms behind me and swing them forward in Michael Phelps fashion. Nothing. I don't know how to swim. But I can swim in my dreams, I tell myself as I try to lift a second time. But not even an inch off the ground, I'm pulled back down. To the bottom. I can't move. Like my feet are chained to the pool floor. I can't look down, or I might lose sight of her. Where she's swimming. Which way she left.

Out of reach, my fingers grasp at bubbles. She swims further and further away, like she exits my dream through a trapdoor out into the ocean. Cursing my glued feet, I look down below me. Dad holds my feet in place. His hands are like cuffs made of stone. And no matter how hard I try to swipe and swing, I can't hurt him or get away from him. The chilling sound of his laughter reaches my ears underwater, and I hate him from keeping her from me. I fell asleep consumed by hate. I wake up hating more.

Hate drives me forward. Maybe there's no time for Summer. No space for her. Like I know she even wants me? If Dad ever knew about her, my spending time with a girl, he'd shoot us both. And ask questions later. Lucky for me, I have his gun. Somewhere between dreaming and waking up, I decide I want justice and a friend. Her backdoor request for more time with me fills me with hope like…a chocolate-filled churro. With my brown skin, I guess if the name fits.

The wall clock reads 9:45AM. I was supposed to be by Jimmy's at 9:30AM. Darn that brownstone next door that blocks the sunlight, my go-to alarm till I can afford a real one. Skipping a shower and breakfast, I race to catch the train to meet Jimmy. Headed to his Mom's house to finish the job we started yesterday, even though I'm flustered for not waking up on time, a purple mermaid swims through my mind, and a whistle leaves my lips.

"You're late." Jimmy says. He's leaning on a shovel, a row of white posts lying on the ground border the house. "It's a girl, isn't it?"

"What?" I shake my head, dismissing his jab.

"That smile on your face." Jimmy shrugs his shoulders as he hands me a shovel and the muddy, canvas gloves I wore last night. "Ten inches wide, two feet down, eight feet apart okay?"

Jimmy and I work side by side for hours, measuring, digging, and pouring concrete to secure the posts as a pile of empty water bottles and empty sandwich bags grows in the middle of the lawn. As the sun begins to set, the mosquitoes swarm my bare arms, and I spend more time swatting than digging. Jimmy hears me curse and tosses me the bug spray.

"It's empty." I toss it in the trash.

"We're almost done." Jimmy swings the mallet down on his post. "Another hour and we'll call it a night. You game?"

"That's cool," I squash another bloodsucker on my forearm and pick up the last post, twisting it into place.

"Tell me her name, and you can leave early." Jimmy's smirk is visible in the evening light.

"If you're a psychic at night, I'd keep my day job." I pound in my post, turning my back to Jimmy so he can't see my widened grin.

"Suit yourself." Jimmy says. "But if you need some flowers, my mom has a garden in the back, and she's always telling me, 'James, bring some pretty girl flowers. All girls love flowers,' and I tell her, 'Ma, let me find a girl first. One worth keeping, that is.' But she's getting old. She forgets I don't have a girl and watch—she'll ask me again tomorrow."

"This is your house?" The white colonial rises up into the surrounding trees, dark green trim around the big bay window and matching green shutters next to the second floor windows. "Did you always have a blue front door?"

"I painted it blue when Dad died five years ago," Jimmy said. "Blue was the color of the sky the morning his partner knocked on the door and told us he was killed in the line of duty."

"I'm. Sorry." I never thought a door could have a story to it.

"Ma asked me to paint it blue, so she and I would think about him every time we walked in or out of our house."

"Do you?" I pause, feeling stupid for thinking out loud.

"Do I what?"

"Nothing. Forget it." I go back to pounding.

"I did. In the beginning, I thought about my dad every second, wishing I could have just one more day with him, ya know?" Jimmy understood my question, but to his, I don't know. When I don't say anything, he continues talking. "Now, only once in a while. But other things remind me of him more. Like police sirens. Always think of my dad when a squad car passes by."

Police sirens make me jump as I think of the gun that still sits in the desk drawer back in my room.

"Ma still lives on her own." Jimmy walks over and hands me pair of clippers. "Help yourself. The pink roses are budding outta control, and whatever you take is that much less I have to trim back."

I'm holding a mallet in one hand and flower clippers in the other. Laying the scissors aside, I scoop concrete into the final hole, scraping the last of it out of Jimmy's wheelbarrow.

"Umm." I look off in the direction of the backyard. "Would it be okay to swing by next week?"

"Of course. Just tell Ma, Jimmy sent you, so she won't panic if she sees you in the back. Or ask her to help you. It's one of the few things she comes outside to do, and it's good for her to get out. So thanks for that." Jimmy grins and nods.

We shuttle the tools back into the shed and Jimmy tugs on the fence. It doesn't budge. "Not bad." He pulls out cash to count out my earnings.

"Thanks," I say, folding the bills and pushing them into my jeans' pocket. "For everything."

"Sure." Jimmy. "See ya."

I swing the gate open and two steps away, I turn. Jimmy's still standing in the yard admiring the fence, dark, strong arms folded over his chest.

"Summer," I call out, then keep walking. "Her name's Summer."

17
~ Talia ~

May 3rd

The art therapy session starts in ten minutes, and Nahida coaxes me out of my room to give it a try. As I leave my room, I tell Nahida, "Go on. I'll catch up." And peel off another Post-it off the question mark. When I join the others in the living room, the group counselors are introducing themselves. The tall male wears a beige vest over jeans, Eli's black widow's peak visible under the brim of his matching beige fedora. Rebecca's dark brows don't match her blond, straightened hair, and when she pulls it back into a side pony, dark roots peek out, making me wonder if I dyed my hair too, would Dad fail to recognize me? As the couple passes around papers and boxes of Crayola markers, I note that the peach of Rebecca's summer dress matches the middle stripe on Eli's fedora.

Nahida sits next to me on the couch in the living room. Some sit on chairs and others sit at the table on the opposite wall from Rebecca and Eli, who stand in front of the fireplace.

"We'll call today's session, card of houses," says Eli. "Unlike a poker game, you get to decide and draw in what your houses look like, one for each season of life. Three houses, one each to represent the past, present and future."

Rebecca hugs the stack of extra house pictures to her chest and says, "But like a poker game, you get to choose whether you'll lay your cards, or in this case, houses, down."

I flip through the three pages, each with a simple outline of a house on it. The rest is blank. I glance around and no one's watching me. They're too busy working on their pictures. I huddle over my pages, pull out a black marker, and remove the top. My first house comes easily. Although I walked on eggshells around Dad no matter where I was in the house, the one place that I feared the most was the place he burned me. The kitchen. I draw a room where I think best places the kitchen, then color the room in black.

Rebecca catches me looking around and says, "If you're finished with the first house, please take a breather, get some tea and cookies, and when you're ready, choose a different color and give the safe house you reside in some color. And after that, paint your dream house. The one you see in your future. And we'll leave the last twenty minutes for sharing. And as always, sharing is optional."

Everyone rises to get a snack. Everyone that is, besides Jaya. Jaya's picture isn't finished. She's taking her time, her body hunched over her pages, which is nice. Since it's the first time she's not shooting her laser eyes into my forehead.

I take the second house and stare at it for a while. Then I decide to draw squares on the rooms where I've found happy moments and connected with the women. Little yellow squares. My miniature Post-its fall on my bedroom wall, on the kitchen island, and in the computer room. And I add one more to the living room, the place we sit now.

When I flip the last house picture on top, I choose the blue marker. Because blue has always been and will always be the color I associate with hope. But instead of shading in the house, I shade in the area all around the house. Until not a spot is left on the right, the left, or above the house. A perfectly blue sky. With no room for clouds.

"I want to start by saying that we can all share a picture, even if we don't want to talk about it," Eli says, "And if you're not sure we'll know which house you're holding up, you can always caption it with one word like, yesterday, today, or tomorrow."

"And as always, respect first, opinions later. We're not here to decide whose artwork belongs in a museum, because no one's story is any less courageous than the next, each of you a living, breathing, symbol of beauty, hope, and freedom. More than anything else, we want you to know this. And believe it." Rebecca waits a beat. Then says, "Sunny, would you like to go first?"

Sunny holds up two pages, one with today written on it, and the house is green. All of it. "Because I've grown so much by being here." The second is the one labeled tomorrow, and a rainbow covers the page, streaming into and out of the house. "I think this one speaks for itself."

"Thanks for sharing, Sunila." Eli says, nodding and smiling in her direction. "Nahida, you're next."

Nahida holds up only one page. I know it's her today's page, because the house is full of bookshelves, more like a library than a home. She colored it all different colors. Makes me happy she met a nice guy surrounded by the world of stories. Books were my only friends until I met Lagan.

Rebecca thanks her, and with a nod, Addison rises to share her yesterday picture and I already know the room the black marker will blot out. A dark box lies in the basement of the house, where the bathroom her husband locked her in was. But the strange thing is, she drew a thick yellow trace around the black box. "Because if it weren't for this room, I might never have found my way out of that house. That life. And come here."

Eli asks, "Do you want to share your other pictures?" and she responds with a head-shaking no.

"Talia. It's your turn." I was so anxious to see Addison's today and tomorrow houses, I didn't have time to panic about being next. I'm panicking. Now. Fiddling with the papers in my lap, my eyes on the top page, the one with the blue sky.

"Take your time. And if you want to pass—"

"Blue." I blurt out, not holding the page up right away. Then I raise it, but cover my face so I can speak behind it. "Blue reminds me of my mother, and blue makes me happy. I guess I hope to see a lot more blue in my tomorrows." I put my sheet back down on my lap and wait for Eli or Rebecca's response.

Instead, Jaya answers. "Blue is my favorite color."

It's the first time I've heard her speak, and the room falls silent after Rebecca says, "Thanks for sharing that Jaya. Would you like to go next?"

Jaya rises and leaves the room, never answering Rebecca's question, leaving her drawings on the table. And Eli exhales before asking, "Ava. Would you like to share next?" but no one's listening, because Jaya left her yesterday, today, and tomorrow houses all faced up, for us to see in plain sight. Each looks identical. Colored in entirely, every corner of every house is the same. Completely black.

18
~ Jesse ~

May 4th

I'm knocking on Jimmy's mom's door, but my head is turned as I admire the fence. Looking down at my hands, I never imagined they were capable of anything, really. The door opens slowly, but the screen door stays closed. "Yes?" A tiny-framed, Caucasian woman with thinning grey hair to her shoulders smiles, and asks, "Can I help you?"

I return the smile. "Hi," I say. "Jimmy, your son, I've been helping him with things."

"Yes," she nods. "I recognize you. I watched you and Jimmy through the window. You helped my boy build my new fence, isn't that right?"

I nod back, "That would be me." I peer to the corner of the house in the direction of the backyard. "I was wondering if I could, um, have a few flowers from your garden?"

"Jimmy mentioned you might be coming 'round for some roses." She unlocks the blue door and opens it for me. "And the answer is yes, of course. Would you like to come in for some coffee or tea? Or are you in a hurry? I could just meet you around back."

"I'll just come around to the back," I say.

She nods and says, "Well then, give me a few minutes to put on some old clothes and find my gardening gloves."

"Okay. Great." I step off the porch and turn to see her watching me. "I'll, uh, wait in the back for you."

I turn the corner into the backyard, scan the property and find the bushes of pink roses bordering the side of a vegetable garden with rows of various-sized, green buds just starting to sprout above the dirt. Finding a seat on the bench that graces the cement patio, I close my eyes and see Summer—throwing her arms around me and planting a kiss on my lips as she knocks the roses out of my hand, her leaf necklace snagging on my shirt, making the moment last just a little longer. The picture dissolves as I chuckle to myself at the likelihood that it'll go down like that. Most probably not. But the hug...now that's a possibility.

"Hope she likes pink," a voice from behind says. Wearing baggy jean overalls and green Crocs, Jimmy's mom's approaches and hands me a pair of brown gloves.

"I think I'll be okay?" I say. "I can just use my hands."

"Suit yourself, son, but roses are as pretty as they are sharp, and the gloves will help you from showing up without blood dripping all over your bouquet." She's holding her hand back out to me, the gloves bouncing in her grip.

Well if you put it like that... I take the gloves and say, "Thanks."

"How 'bout we start by telling each other our names? My name's Amanda." She smiles as she watches me pulling on my gloves.

Without thinking, I say, "Justice, but everyone calls me, Jesse. I mean John." It's too late. Panicked, I start to say, "I mean..." but the truth is, I don't know what I mean. Or who I mean to be.

Amanda puts her gloved hand on my shoulder and says, "What are you running from, son? Only people I ever met that didn't know their names were the folks who didn't know where they were going either."

I swallow and say, "I'll just take a few roses and be outta

your way."

"Suit yourself, Jesse," Amanda peers at me to see if I approve her name choice as she leans behind the bench to fetch a vase and two pairs of scissors.

"Jesse's good. Jesse's what my sister calls me." I swallow and follow Amanda toward the rose bushes. Did I just tell her I had a sister on top of telling her my real name? What's gotten into me?

As she guides me on how to carefully snip the roses at the correct spot on their stems, angling the scissors and cradling each petaled flower to keep it from falling apart, I find myself thinking about Mom shortly before we buried her. By the time Talia and I realized how deep Dad cut, it was too late to cradle her fall. Dad decided Mom's hair would be the cost of trying to befriend a neighbor, and the image of her bald head, her mouth taped, and her hands tied raked across my mind every time I saw a chemo patient on a TV talk show all those months I laid in bed with the remote under my hand. And I forced myself to watch, never changing the channel, because I knew like I know Mom is dead. Dad was the cancer. *Is*. Still is.

What am I doing here? Having the sudden urge to grab the scissors from Amanda's hands and beeline to Dad's office and stab him in the heart, I step back and stare at the fence, afraid my eyes will betray me, and Amanda will ask what's wrong.

I suddenly feel stupid for being here, gathering flowers for a girl I hardly know when I should be bringing a shovel to a forest. So I can scout out where I'll hide Dad's body after he bleeds to death.

"If it's okay, you can have this here vase." Amanda fills the clear, glass cylinder with a little water from the garden hose. "God knows I have ten more inside taking up too much room as it is."

"If you're sure you don't need it?" I ask, brushing away images of hurting Dad so I can focus on what's happening in the here and now.

"I'm sure." Amanda smiles, then adds, "As sure as your name is Jesse."

I act like I didn't hear that and grab a stem full of budded roses so she can cut it, but a thorn pricks my hand through the glove. I dismiss the pain and help Jimmy's mom file the roses into a vase, one by one. When they quickly crowd the space, I start to shove one more in, but Amanda's hand gently pulls the last rose from my hands, and shifts the stems around, removing some leaves before replacing the flower.

"You're bleeding," she says when I remove my gloves.

Jimmy's mom places the vase of flowers on the ground, and pulls off her gloves, one at a time. "Here, let me see that." She then takes a Kleenex from her pocket, cradles my hand, and applies pressure to my bleeding finger, and within seconds, the color red seeps through, but she folds the Kleenex over several times, and presses in again. "Should take a minute to stop the bleeding, and I'll fetch you a Band-Aid. I know girls like flowers. Blood, not so much."

"Thank you." Picking up the vase with my good hand, I turn to walk away. "I'll be fine."

I want to say, thank you for holding my hand. And I wish I could tell Talia that somewhere inside me stopped bleeding, if only for a minute. As I clear the corner, I glance back to see Jimmy's mom waving, and my eyes blur like a camera unable to focus. *Mom?*

I stop in my tracks, face forward, shut my eyes tightly and then turn and look back again. She's gone.

19
~ Jesse ~

May 4th

She's wearing a blue skirt and pink top. No. A green t-shirt and brown skirt. No. A red top with jeans. Not that either. I've mistaken three girls for Summer as I sit on the Art Institute steps. I'm a half an hour early, but I didn't know how long it would take to cut flowers. I hold the flowers in my hands. Set them by my side. Pick them up again.

"I got these for you. Hope you like pink?" I say under my breath.

How 'bout, "Just a little something I picked up for no reason. I mean, they could be for Diwali. Or the fourth of July. Or an early Memorial Day thing." That's coming up in a couple weeks, but I shake my head at how dumb that sounded.

What if she's allergic? I'm looking behind me to see if I can find a trashcan. I could just forget this whole thing, run into the library and pump out my last letter to Dad. What's the point of trying to live a normal life when I don't feel safe to live my life yet?

She's walking toward me, and I'm back in the hospital, unable to find my voice. Only thing is, this is a different kind of fall.

"For me?" Summer sits down next to me, the flowers between us. "You shouldn't have! But I love' em."

"Uh...You're welcome." My hand runs over my head and down my neck. "Hungry?" I'm looking toward the Churro Guy behind his stand who hasn't stood still for a second, the line of customers the shortest it's been all hour.

"Sure! Wait." Summer puts her hand on my knee. "Let me treat this time. You're so sweet to get me flowers, and you didn't even know it's my birthday."

"It's your birthday?" I say, staring at her hand. The one on my knee.

"Gotcha!" Summer's hand pushes off my knee like a cord pulled out of an outlet—the current drops, and I can breathe again. She stands and picks up the vase. "But it will be at the end of this month, so I declare May my birthday month, and this—my first present." Summer hugs the vase to herself.

Purple shirt. Grey skirt. And purple toenails on her feet slipped in black flip-flops.

"I was about to get you the purple roses," I say, fishing for a comeback to her birthday tease, thankful my vocal cords woke up. "But then you'd know I...umm...googled you to find out your favorite color."

"You actually googled me?" Summer moves her face closer to the roses and inhales, her eyes closed. "Tell me you didn't."

I grin and shake my head no. But I do need to google five best ways to ruin someone's career, and set them sailing across the ocean in a boat destined to sink. Because scaring Dad, assuming the letters are actually working, isn't enough when I stand across from Summer. I'm still checking over my shoulder for the man I hate.

The little bugger of a cut smarts when I put my hands in my front pockets, making me pull my finger to my mouth. It stopped bleeding, but it stings somewhere inside.

"Wait a second," Summer puts one hand up to her face, cradling her chin, and tips her head sideways ever so slightly before saying, "I bet you just got a bunch of sites that talked about the season. You don't even know my last name."

I chuckle prematurely. *And you think you know my first name.*

"Let's share last names over churros, cool?" How can I say no to those blue eyes of hers?

I shrug my shoulders, "Sure." I made up a first name. I can easily make up a last. "But I do have to google a few things when we're done. Like what I need to do to get into pilot's school." And where's the best place to hide a dead body. And a gun. Plan B keeps knocking on my door, because deep down, I don't know if I'll be able to move on until Dad takes his final breath.

Summer nods, and we walk down the steps and get in line to buy churros. "And when you're done, promise me you'll fly me to Paris?" Summer looks at me for a yes. "I hear the purple roses over there are epic."

"I suppose for some *epic* purple roses, I could schedule you in." I'm finding it hard to tame my grin around this girl. "Fly across the ocean. Pluck some flowers. I'll have you back in time for dinner." Words roll off my tongue like an open faucet. Starting to wonder if Summer is contagious.

"Are you asking me out to dinner?" Summer asks, and my gaze drops to the floor as my hand slides over the back of my neck like I'm searching for an answer behind there. The faucet's off again, and I can't remember which knob is hot and which is cold.

"And a chocolate churro for the lady, again?" Churro Guy saves me.

"You remembered!" Summer says, then pokes my side with her elbow. "And one for this guy."

Summer makes to hand me the vase but I pull out a few singles to pay. "Not again!" she says, when the vendor takes my money. "Okay, fine. Thank you."

"Two down," I retrieve the bag of churros, and we make our way back to the museum steps. "Eight to go."

"You make it sound like you can't wait to pay it off, and get rid of me." Summer pretends to pout.

How do I tell her she's the one who will want to get rid of me when she finds out I'm a murderer? "Now why would I want to get rid of the happiest person I know? You know, I've never met anyone who gets so excited about little things." We sit back down, side by side on the steps, and I open the bag so she can take a churro.

"Churros. Flowers." Summer rustles my hair on top of my head with her hand. "What more does a girl need?"

"Can't really mess it up," I say. I put my hand on my head and brush my short hair forward. It hasn't grown much in the last ten days.

"So you're giving me permission to touch your hair, whenever?" Summer asks, her gaze squinting with mischief.

Not what I was thinking, but we can certainly go with that. "Sure. As long as you use the hand not holding a churro."

"Well in that case." Summer reaches to touch my hair again, but I grasp her wrist, open her palm and lay down my untouched churro from the bag.

"I should probably tell you that I'm not really into churros." I clear my throat. She laughs. "And now that both your hands have churros in them."

"So..." Summer places both churros into the paper bag, sets it aside, and brushes the powdered dust off her shirt with the back of her hand. "What are you into?"

Thinking of how to escape my evil dad every waking and sleeping moment. But besides that, I realize I've given this question about as much thought as what I want to be when I grow up. "I don't know, really. What about you? Besides churros and becoming a brain surgeon? Oh, and leaves, of course."

"I could help you think of something. I mean, you could start by being into one thing. See if you like it. And then try something else."

"Want to try something?" I ask, steadying my breathing. "Together?"

"Like flying planes!" Summer says like she just guessed Double Jeopardy.

I can't fly with you anywhere until I see my dad leave on a one-way plane—boat or submarine works too—to South

Africa. Or hell.

"On that note." I rise to start down the steps, toward the library. Time to write Dad that third email and make Africa or hell come true. Either one will do. "I'm thinking you should hit the books if you plan to get into med school."

"John," Summer stops me at the door when we reach the library with her hand on my arm. "Thanks for telling me the truth. About the churros."

"Sure." I look away from Summer as we walk in, kicking myself for lying about my name. "Heading to the computer lab, I'll catch up with you in a bit, okay?"

Summer says, "Okay. Maybe I'll take you up on that dinner offer, and we'll find something you like to eat besides churros."

"Sounds like a plan," I say, walking up a flight of stairs and turning to watch Summer settle in behind an empty cubicle. She pulls out a textbook, but instead of opening it, she plucks from the rose and strokes a single pink petal on her palm while gazing at the vase of flowers in front of her. Then she raises the petal to her lips and holds it in place with her index finger, and I swallow, tightening my grip on the railing. A patron bumps past me, and I'm reminded I have one last letter to send to Dad.

As I follow the woman in burgundy shorts up the steps into the room with public computers, I hear his voice before I see him. "Have you seen this young man around here?"

Spinning a one-eighty, I turn and inch toward the bookshelves nearest me, peering at Dad through the stacks of books. Dad's back is to me as he holds up a flyer, I'm sure with my picture on it, to the staff person sitting at the info desk. As he turns and looks around, I duck down lower, but I can see dark circles under his eyes and stubble on his face for the first time, like he hasn't shaved for days.

"I know he was here. Don't you people have security cameras set up?" Dad says loudly, several heads turned toward the commotion of the man in the three-piece suit who has no regard for library etiquette. "Where is all my tax money going, anyway?"

"One moment, sir. Let me check the log in sheets from last week, and see if we can't find his name." Thankful for the delay, I don't wait around for Dad to find out that his son's name isn't on those lists. For all I know, he might recognize my handwriting.

I zip back down the steps and push on the exit door, race down the street, and stop in my tracks just as I pass the churro stand. Summer.

"I know this sounds crazy," I say to the churro vendor, fumbling for what to ask. "But you know the girl that was with me? The one who likes chocolate churros?"

"Not easy to forget a girl that hot." A cloud of powdered sugar rises from the new batch he coats with the metal shaker. "Want me to save one for her?"

"Yes. Perfect." I'm pulling out a couple singles, my gaze glued to the library doors. "Could you tell her something for me when she comes to get it? Tell her that her next churro is on me. And, and..."

"You really expect me to deliver a personal message for two bucks, pal?" the Churro Guy says. "Drop me a twenty, and I could throw in a singing telegram."

Jimmy just paid me, but I owe Fred the rent in a couple of weeks. I fish out a twenty-dollar bill and slide it across. "Tell her one other thing, will you?"

"Now we're talking." He holds the cash up, like someone trying to block the sun in his eyes.

"I don't have much time, but could you tell her I know one thing I'm into." I look across the street at the library doors, shake my head left to right, take a deep breath, and say it. "Her. Tell her I'm into her, will you?"

"Sure dude. Who should I say left the message?"

"Jes—John. My name's John," I say, then take off running.

And I can hear him yelling from behind, "Take care, John. And don't you worry. I'll tell her, okay. I'll tell her you like her."

20
~ Jesse ~

May 4th

Even as I approach the hostel, I imagine my few belongings strewn around the room like the aftermath of a hurricane. *Dad, add Chicago's Master of Natural Disaster to your resume.* I linger a few buildings down the street and watch the entrance to Fred's office, the broken gate swinging open and shut with the breeze, the sun lowering behind the high-rises. Head turned, I check over my shoulder before speed walking through the door and running up two flights to my room.

A note sticks to the door from the landlord.

Jimmy says he needs you all week for a big job if you're free. Meet him at his mother's place at 8:00AM. Says he hopes she liked the flowers.

I rip off the note and peer out the stairwell window to the streets below as I picture Summer walking around the library, vase in tow, wondering where I disappeared to. With my luck, the Churro Guy runs out of sweets and packs up for the day long before Summer ever leaves the library. I run my fingers through my hair, realizing I was only partially right. I found a way to mess it up, Summer.

As I slowly unlock my door, turn the knob and stand in the

doorway, the room appears untouched. The bed covers remain neatly tucked under the mattress like I left them, and the canvas above the bed still shows the beach, the mother hidden under the envelope.

I step inside and lock the door, walking over to the window to look outside. Wonder what my sister's doing right now in that safe house. Does she feel as safe as Lagan promised? Rubbing my t-shirt under my chin, I feel the blue heart under there and wonder when I'll see her to give it to her.

After sliding the table and chair up against my door, I tear open up a pack of Saltines and down some peanut butter-covered dinner while seated on the window ledge to keep watch.

And I open the desk drawer, pull out the gun and lean it against my temple, but the cold of the metal does nothing to drum down the headache that pounds between my ears. I lower the weapon, running one palm over the barrel, and place the revolver carefully under the bed, out of sight, but close enough for me to reach in the event of an intruder.

Hours pass, while I sit by the window, the sun setting somewhere behind the brownstone. When it grows dark outside, I convince myself that Dad probably won't bust down my door today. I leave the window to pull out a pen and paper from the desk drawer, number down the page one to ten, and handwrite my last note to Dad, slipping it into an envelope with a book of matches. On the outside of the envelope I print the words, "Or Else." For all the lists Dad gave me, Talia and Mom, I think it's about time I give him one back. I lick the envelope rim and press it closed with pinched fingers, then place it under my pillow.

That night, I fall asleep on my chest in my clothes, not bothering to change, and in the middle of the night, I wake up in cold sweats, swatting my mattress with open palms. My face hits the pillow in disbelief. No flames in sight. No scent of fire like I imagined I smelled. The only thing to extinguish is how stupid I feel.

I turn to face the doorway, still blocked by my desk, and

realize the envelope for Dad slipped out from under my pillow to the floor. When I reach to retrieve it, I catch sight of the gun under the bed where I placed it.

I kept my list for him simple, staring at the envelope like I can see right through it to the letter. Ten words. One request.

You have one choice—to move out of my life.

A snicker escapes as I lie on my back and stare up, slapping the envelope onto my open palm. In the dark, the ceiling becomes a screen where the past rolls out like a black and white, silent movie. I slip the envelope under the small of my back, close my eyes, and step back in time.

***

"Move. Justice."

I heard Dad's voice. He said the same words he said to me every day around noon. But the first time, it wasn't a memory yet. The first time hurt the most.

"Move. Now."

Try 'abracadabra,' Dad. Couldn't he see his son was a vegetable? I closed my eyes, hoping he'd disappear. Walk away. Before a third—

"Move!" Dad screamed. If only anger could push me out of bed. To move. But I didn't. Because I couldn't. The scent of a lit match swooshed into my nose. Dad lit the incense stick by my bedside.

After Dad lifted me to the bed, instead of landing on my back, the momentum of his shove pushed me further, and I fell flat on my face, chest down. I could feel the cool rush of air hit my back where my shirt hadn't been pulled down all the way.

Dad cursed me out like I did it on purpose. And instead of adjusting me to my back, I saw him walk to the shelf out of the corner of my eye. The shelf where the incense burned, the swirl of spicy smoke writing the future in the air.

Dad picked up the box of matches and walked back to my bedside. Then he lit a single match, held it dangerously close to my face, and said calmly, "Move."

I thought "moving" thoughts. But the only place I moved

was in my mind. I imagined moving over so I couldn't see his anger or disappointment.

He moved the burning match behind me and said again, "Move." I felt the sensation of heat on my back. If heat could move, I'd be halfway to Paris. And as he waved the tiny stick aflame behind me, I imagined he thought it was a magic wand, capable of bending my legs, loosening my vocal cords, and making me normal.

The third time he screamed the word, "Move!" as if his sheer volume could undo my brain injury. I couldn't. I didn't. Then he simply dropped the lit match. Onto my back. I knew. Because it burned. For two seconds, I burned. Right before his eyes, I burned.

He cursed some more, shook his head side to side, tossed the match in the closest waste basket, and rose to leave. But not before flipping me to my back, looking me in the eye, and reminding me of what he thought of his efforts. My situation. Me.

"Useless."

21

~ Talia ~

May 6th

The weekend came and left. A few of the women left to meet friends, go to the movies or take walks in the park. I heard them talking restaurants, shows, and fun, and decided I'd stick to my books and my one string of lightning. After asking Nahida for some Scotch tape, I formed a wannabe letter Z above the closest outlet. I've been sleeping with the Christmas lights on every night. When I wake up from a nightmare, they greet my squinting eyes like a puddle of fallen stars. Then I get up and stick them back on the wall, reinforcing the tape. I've done this three times now, running out of tape.

Today's Group session is called "Mirror, Mirror," and, according to Addison, we will focus on our bodies. Healing and learning to love ourselves again. Addison tells me at breakfast that it'll be much better than any fairy tale. She's studied up on this exercise online.

"Here are three sheets," Rebecca says. "Once again, they represent where you've been hurt in the past, where you're hurting now, and where you long for healing in the future."

Eli, not sporting a fedora today, exposes a balding spot on the back of his head when he turns and adds, "We're not sharing these with the group today, because we want you to do this for you. If you want either Rebecca or myself to look at your drawings, we can schedule a one on one session this coming week. This time, it's really about you and facing yesterday's hurts so you can, at least visually, begin to consider what it might be like for you to tell others. But before you show others, you have to show yourself you. You have to look in the mirror."

Thinking about the last session, I whisper to Nahida, "Where's Jaya?"

Nahida shrugs her shoulders, waits a beat, then leans in and whispers. "Someone mentioned she cabbed it downtown. Something about talking to the lawyers about her case. Maybe she's not back yet."

About halfway through the session, a soft knocking is heard at the front door. Eli rises to answer it and Jaya's standing there, dressed from head to toe in black, holding a folder.

"Come in. Join us. We're doing a new session today." Eli moves aside so she can walk in. "Rebecca, can you show her the basics so the others can keep working?"

"Of course," Rebecca gets up and counts three pages, but as she hands them to Jaya, Jaya says, "No thanks. I came to share my houses. If that's okay."

"Sure." Everyone stops working on their pages now and without saying a word to each other, we all direct our attention to Jaya as Eli pulls up a chair for Jaya to sit in.

"I was tempted to color the entire page called yesterday black." Jaya opens with this.

But I thought it was all black. By the look on the faces of the other women, I'm not the only one who's confused.

Jaya holds up her yesterday picture and it is entirely black. Save one teeny-tiny square spot in the house. I see it now.

She touches the spot, covering it, and speaks. "Every second of every moment of every day of my life, I've only known darkness. I don't know if I ever nursed at my mother's breast. I do know that before I was old enough to have much of anything that made me look like a woman, my mother sold me to men, who took me to dark rooms and…all I remember is the dark. Hands. Taking. Pain. Darkness."

A lump forms in my throat. Jaya continues talking.

"Then one day, I got my monthly enemy. Some women call it friend, but for me, the day I began my menses was the day my father first beat me for hours on end, all I remember is everything grew dark. Then before the week was over, my parents sold me to a man who promised to take me across the ocean to a palace made of gold. He lied. The palace was black. I was blindfolded and shipped in car trunks from one dark place to another. Until one day, I turned sixteen, and the man who bought me told me he had no use for me any longer. It was the first week in America when no one beat me. Then one morning a woman came, stripped me, and pasted makeup all over my face. Then she dressed me up in glittery cloth, stuck a bindi on my head and bangles on my wrists. I was married off to a stranger who smiled and told me that he loved me."

Jaya rubs the back of her hand, like she's trying to clean it, while I wonder if she looked like one of the beautiful women in Mom's magazine, the catalog where Mom let me see her in a blue sari, all shiny and beautiful. I was in third grade, and it was our little secret. Mom only showed it to me once.

"But the moment he pushed me into his home, he told me he had to pay for me. And now it was time for me to start paying off the debt. I lived in darkness for two years until one Monday night, he took me back to the place I dreaded most, the rooms countless men raped and beat me—a hotel with a neon moon on its sign. The sign should have read Hell."

Jaya looks right at me and says, "The lawyer with the eyes that change color tells me to forget anything ever happened, and it will all go away. I don't believe him. And how will I ever forget what happened that night?"

Jaya turns her gaze back to the paper she's holding, and uncovers the small, uncolored square on her drawing. "This is the hotel room where he lay in bed. That was the last night he ever beat me."

I'm not following. Unless… The squeak of shifting on

couches is the only sound I hear during the short pause.

"He came to watch Monday Night football at the hotel bar with his buddies, but he wanted me to be ready for him in bed when the game ended. He locked me in the suite, warned me Security guarded all exits, and came up at half-time with a steak and salad to let me know his team was winning. If the Bears pulled it off, he might not even beat me that night. I ate steak for the first time in my life, and I savored each bite, doubting I'd ever eat like a queen again. Then I showered and waited in bed, but by the time the game finished, he barely managed to unlock the hotel door, stumbled into the room, cursing the Bears, then fumbled into bed and passed out on his back, his shoes still on. I rolled over, got out of bed, and checked the door. It was still open. All I had to do was run, but I feared he'd find me even if I managed to get past Security, so I shut the door and locked it."

I was so hoping she had said she ran away.

Jaya takes a deep breath, and I sense the story's almost over. "I went to the kitchenette to drown my foolish escape plan with a glass of water when the steak knife came into sight. And right there and then I decided one of us would die that night, and I was fine either way. So I took the knife, walked up to the edge of the bed, closed my eyes and began blindly stabbing. And the crazy thing is, he never screamed. He never even cried. And then I fell back on the carpet, blood splattered on my nightgown, dropping the knife on the floor, crying, 'Oh God Oh God. He was already dead. And now they'll think I killed him.'"

Jaya drops the pages on the floor, and looks up and right into my eyes when she says, "I just needed to tell someone," and leaves the room. Again.

There's not a dry eye in the room. And the other two houses are still dark. All black. According to Eli, the newspapers report that there's an ongoing investigation, and the hotel wants to pin charges of first-degree murder on someone. That someone is Jaya. And the outcome's looking, as the pictures suggest, not good. Not good at all.

22
~ Talia ~

May 7th

"Peppermint?" Nahida asks at the dining room table. She's sitting next to me this first day of my second week at Hope Now's, Westside safe house.

Thankful for whoever approved my tiny addition to this week's grocery list, I fold my gum into my napkin before saying, "Yes." Look down at my lap and softly add, "Reminds me of the guy I sort of mentioned."

Nahida's smile widens in my peripheral vision. "The little things."

Addison passes a plate of steaming French toast. Not sure if the French invented ballet, but Ava insisted on toes and twirls this morning to a famous piece she informed us was called, "Dance of the Hours." I suppose watching Ava and Nahida prance around the kitchen helps minutes pass if not hours.

"Anyone want to help plant a garden out back this afternoon?" Addison asks as we finish up clearing breakfast dishes, my turn to soap and rinse.

Several women chime in "sures" and "I cans" while I stare down at my hands. The cuts are healed, but I'm still on the fence. Gardening reminds me of the gardener, and I'm still mourning the loss of the willow. I still think Dad had something to do with the fire at the garden, his attempt to steal one more thing that matters to me. When I think about all that Dad's stolen from me, the thing that eats away at me most is time. Time I'm stuck in here. Time away from Lagan. Time I know nothing about Jesse and what he's doing. Time I can't get back.

"Talia." Sunny's looking right at me, and I'm gearing up to say, "No, thank you," but she continues talking. "Nahida tells me someone sent you a beautiful bouquet of flowers. Wanna tell us his name?"

Warmth spreads across my cheeks as I feel the gaze of all eyes on me. "Umm."

"Kidding, honey." Sunila giggles. "It's none of our business. Unless, of course, you feel like sharing."

I stab a blueberry with my fork and pop it in my mouth, keeping my gaze downward. I've only ever told Jesse about Lagan. And Jason knew once Lagan started venturing to the garden for our willow dates. I scarf down one slice of toast and politely excuse myself from the table.

The floral arrangement sits on my desk with a small card taped to the glass vase. Orange tiger lilies, white daisies, purple irises. I can name them all from my days working at the garden. I lean in to breathe in the scent of outdoors before removing the card, pulling out the chair, and sitting down at the table to read my third little note from Lagan.

This time the envelope reads my name spelled correctly. Talia. I trace the print with my fingertip, then drop the letter like it's on fire, knocking the vase over with my swinging arms. The fallen vase tips off the edge, and I hear the kshsh of shattered glass when it hits the floor. Water spreads across the floor under scattered petals and broken stems pierced by glass shards.

I rip open the envelope, pull out the letter and devour the words.

Dear Talia,

If you're reading this letter, I know where you are. [I bite down on my lip. Hard.]

I had flowers delivered to every hospital, shelter and girls' home around Chicago, and they were all returned. But not this one. [The taste of blood trickles past my lips, down my throat.]

Come home. Whatever the misunderstanding, I'm sure we can work it out. I'll see you soon.

Dad.

I fumble to refold the letter—my hands are trembling—when someone knocks at the door. The note sails from my fingertips to the floor and I fall to my knees, my heart pounding against my chest like a punching bag. Afraid to hide in the closet, I turn and crawl under the desk, the opening where the chair slides in. Pulling the chair to me, I count to ten over and over again. Practicing, because I know what I'm returning to. I pick up the triangular glass chunk closest to my shoe and trace a fading line across my wrist. I cannot go back. I just can't.

"Talia." Nahida says, "I just came to apologize. Woah! O.M.G, this here is a mess. Let me fetch some paper towels."

I pull my knees to my chest and lean back against the desk wall. My mind is a tornado—I'm cornered, tossed, and flattened. Nahida returns, squats down, and I can hear her sweeping up the broken vase into a dustpan.

"It's safe to come out, ya know." The sound of glass on glass grates my senses as Nahida drops the contents into a waste basket. "Want me to call Diana?"

"Yes. Please." I bite down on my lip again.

"K. Be right back." Nahida's footsteps fade, but the sound of Dad's voice, reading the letter to me, crescendos between my ears.

Nahida and Diana return, but I have no concept of time. It feels like hours later, but it also feels like minutes after the vase crashed to the floor. Diana speaks, but I can't see her from where I'm crouched. "Hmm. Okay. First things first. We have to get her out of here. Text headquarters so they can begin making arrangements. The letter doesn't give us much to go on, but security will be on high alert for any trespassers."

I can see Nahida's pink flip-flops from under the table now. They turn and exit the doorway. Diana squats down on the ground in front of me, pulls the chair out, and reaches forward to gently remove the glass from my grip. "If you don't want to come out, we can talk right here?" Her slowly-delivered words do not match the hurry in her eyes.

"He knows." My knees knock together, over and over again. "I told you he'd find me."

"Let's not jump to conclusions." Diana's eyes look away from me. "But to be on the safe side. Just in case somehow he followed our mail delivery guy from the main branch to this safe house, we have to move you." Diana offers me her hand.

"I could stay here." I push my back further into the backing of the desk. "I'm fine. Here."

"I'm sorry, hon. That isn't an option." Diana offers me both her hands now.

I let my wrist flop into her grasp and scoot out from under the desk slowly, stand up and grip the table to steady myself. "Where?" And how will I get in touch with Lagan and Jesse? Why can't I just run away and be with one of them?

"As soon as the main office finds an opening at another shelter, we'll accompany you over. Should be no later than this evening." Diana's gaze darkens. "This is no light matter. We're committed to your safety and the safety of all who live here, okay. We'll make it happen ASAP."

"And when he finds me again." My arm slips off the desk and falls limply to my side. "Then what happens?"

"Talia." Diana raises my chin to look in my eyes. "That's up to you. We talked about options. Ways you can stop running. A restraining order to make it illegal for your dad to come near you. Pressing charges. The choice has always been yours."

I swallow her words, letting one linger on my palette. *Choice.*

23
~ Talia ~

May 7th

I fix my eyes on the white lights in the loose shape of a Z on the wall. The lights are off. They'll have to come down.

Diana's phone chirps and she says, "Excuse me a moment," and steps out of the room to take the call.

Flowers fill the trashcan. My blue nail polish is chipping. The Post-it's on the wall mock me with their questions at a time when I need answers. And the Z shape made of lights— it's all wrong.

I walk over to the wall and yank the string of lights off the wall. They fall to the floor, and I spread them out with a kick, then two, making an S-shape instead of a Z. S for sorry.

Sorry my life is a broken mess. Sorry you thought you could fix it. Sorry it's going to take *forever* before we see each other again.

When Diana hangs up, she faces me again and clasps her hands, taking a deep breath. "There's an opening on the other side of town at a place called, Casa de Manana." I'm sitting on my bed, and Diana moves one step closer. "Jody runs it, and she's so great. She said one bed just opened up, but the woman won't be moved out until tomorrow. Said you can come first thing in the morning or crash on the couch-bed there tonight if you don't want to wait till then. She says that we can make it work."

"Thank you, Diana." I pause to choose my next words. "Thank you for everything, but respectfully, I have to say no."

"I understand you want to stay here?" Diana asks. "But shelter policy—"

"No. That's not what I mean." Dad set the garden on fire. What would stop him from lighting a match to this safe house? "What I'm saying is I think it's time for me to go. But not to another home where I can put another group of ladies in danger."

"And where will you go? What's your plan?" Diana's shaking her head, her hands on her hips.

"I'm not sure. I just know this isn't working out for me like I thought it would." I sit back down, my gaze fixed on my open palms lying on my lap. "Maybe I'll change my identity, go back to Benton Harbor, where I was born, get a job waiting tables. Save up for school." If I cut my hair and dye it blond, no one would recognize me. I just need to find some place I can hide where Dad can't hurt the people I care about.

Diana exhales a deep breath, her hands falling to her side, then walks over and sits next to me on the bed. "And if your dad follows you there, who will you turn to? Are you telling me you're giving up before you've even put on your boxing gloves? You haven't thought this through, Talia. How long will you keep running? You have options."

I've spent my whole life worried about running into Dad's wrath at every corner turned. "I can't go on like this."

"Well, apparently you can." Diana's words sting.

"I just. I feel. I'm—" I beat the mattress by my hips.

"You're only stuck if you refuse to move." Diana rises from the bed and walks to the doorway before turning and saying, "Talia. If there's one thing I've learned about this life is you get very little say in what happens tomorrow, but you have some influence on how this day will end. I'll stop by in the morning. We've already told the florist to tell the sender that there was a mistake, and we'll cover the cost of the damaged goods. But according to the cashier who posted the transaction, the buyer paid for the flowers in cash. There's no way to trace who exactly sent the flowers."

I don't say a word. Because nothing about Dad surprises me. Of course he would cover his tracks.

"Doesn't mean we can't prove your dad's harassing you with the note. And there's always…" Diana softly touches my sleeve, then lets go. "I hate to see you take two steps back, but you're not a child. You have every right to decide your next step yourself. First things first, you have a few hours while I make some more calls. We'll chat this evening. Call me at my office if you know sooner what you want to do. Either way, I'll see you tonight, and you decide, okay?"

I nod okay, and Diana leaves. I am the furthest thing from okay right now.

Countless minutes pass as I seesaw between my nomadic half-plan and Diana's words. Holding onto the broken string of possibility that Dad might not know my whereabouts, I walk over to the waste basket and kneel down to pick out flowers. White. Orange. Purple. One by one, I pluck out the wilted and torn petals from the broken glass, gathering them in my t-shirt-cupped basket.

Can't I just pretend I'm a little girl who has a daddy who sent her flowers? A daddy who wrote her a note with hearts on it. A daddy who loves her.

Memories of my time in the garden flood me, and I see flowers blooming all around, petals caught in midair, as if with invisible hands. The gardener's reaching down, gently lifting my chin to see the flowers that used to surround me. Lilies and tulips. Hydrangeas and mums. Lilacs and daisies. And the tiny yellow and pink blossoms that once draped a willow tree.

As the petals tumble off my shirt to the floor, a message tickertapes across my mind, streaming its way down into my heart:

For you. They were all for you.

Wanting company, I take *The Beautiful Fight*, the book Lagan gave me, from the top of my books on the desk, and put it next to my pillow and lay on my side, leaving the lights on. Miss Jesse more than ever when I think about all the nights we snuck into each other's rooms at night just so we wouldn't have to be alone. As I turn Post-it marked pages, I search for the single thing I have left from my mother. I reach the last page of the book and start over, sitting up in bed now, this time turning one page at a time. But it's no use. The single strand of Mom's hair that I saved is gone. *Gone.*

How could I have been so careless? I skirt off the bed and dump out the contents of my dresser on the floor, pushing through clothes, my textbooks, and my few toiletries, shaking my backpack upside down, but it's lost. *She's. Lost.*

The single strand was my last link to her. My memories of her. Her story. What if I forget the details? What if I lose that too?

I push everything aside and climb back into bed, flip to a random part, and start to tear pages out of *The Beautiful Fight*, like it's the book's fault, the Post-its all out of place now— Lagan's favorite parts. Lost, too.

Exhausted from my tantrum, I lay back on my bed, surrounded by ripped paper, and stare at the ceiling. Maybe, I'm supposed to find my own stories. And decide which are my favorites. The woman who followed the gardener, whose bleeding stopped when she touched his back, was a favorite until I couldn't understand why the gardener left. Kept walking. Walked away.

But the same story draws me back, like I can't move on until I find answers. Because I love that the gardener showered me with flowers while I worked. I see that now. But I'm not there anymore. At the garden. I guess *I* walked away. And now the garden is burned. Just like my arm. Did the gardener walk away when Dad set it on fire? And where did he go? And can I follow him to a place Dad can't find me? Like my worries about Jesse and Lagan, the questions pile on.

I close my eyes and I'm back in the garden, flames rising all around, and I hear him calling. *Follow me. I know the way out of here.*

The smoke blinds me, but I strive to hear his voice, and burns lick my scars, but I push ahead, gritting my teeth, determined not to die here. But the entrance is blocked by a fallen tree. The willow. It's weeping tears of orange and red, my tree of hope too hot to hold and too dangerous to pass over.

I cry out for help, straining to hear his voice. Maybe the gardener knows another way out. He built this place after all and maybe he made a secret passageway for such a day as this. Nothing. Only the crackle of fire breaks the silence of the night, as embers float to the sky, gating off the only escape.

If I stay I burn and die. If I walk over the tree, I still burn, but I might live to see another day. And see what's on the other side. Pulling my shirt up over my mouth, I take one step into the flames, expecting my feet to burn before they touch ground, but instead I'm walking over what feels like rocks. A bridge made of stones. I take another step. No burn. Another and another, all the while, the flames licking my body, pain I despise for being familiar. When I pass over the burning willow, I stumble into the parking lot, surrounded by strangers carrying potted plants. And flowers bulbs. And tree saplings. I rub my eyes and look back to where I just escaped. The image startles me awake.

Sitting up in bed, the pages of *The Beautiful Fight* lay all around me in a not-so-beautiful mess. The words in my lap swim across my eyes, mirroring the last image in my dream. "A man lay on the fallen trunk of a tree, his body covered with cuts and bruises, his heart no longer beating. Stones lay all around. He's buried. They buried him under stones. That man was the gardener."

24
~ Jesse ~

May 7ᵗʰ Morning

I come home after working with Jimmy till past dark for the third day in a row. We've been digging a new foundation for an extension on his buddy's house. With every lifted shovel, I envision myself digging a grave. For Dad.

Like learning how to walk again, my courage returns slowly. Maybe because, although he didn't realize it, Dad found me first, and now I'm ready to pay him a visit. When morning comes, I clean up, retrieve the gun, and grab my money and the envelope for Dad, tucking everything into my pockets, and pull on my black hoodie sweatshirt. As I pass the bathroom on the first floor, I step in to do a mirror check. In two weeks, the only notable change in my appearance is facial hair. Turn my cheek to the mirror, one way, then the other, to admire my sideburns that Dad never let me grow out. Ever. I stroke my chin with thumb and index finger at the stubble that forms a thin black goatee, making me look eighteen-ish. Only three days till my birthday and the number will match the face.

Pulling my hood over my head, I pat my pocket to feel for the cash. The gun needs no reminding. As I pass the gate my hand lingers on the post. Turn right and I can jump on a train, transfer, walk three blocks and be standing in front of Dad's office. Turn left, and I can jump on just one train, step off the train, walk one block and check if the Churro Guy ever gave Summer the message. I could consider taking back the twenty if he forgot to.

My eyes look left, but my feet turn right, and I head toward the law offices of Gerard Vanderbilt.

The girl standing to the left of me on the El wears a red, polka-dot backpack over her shoulder, but it's her long, straight, brown hair and green long sleeve that causes me to hallucinate. Talia?

She turns and her perfectly, red-painted lips kiss my illusion away. Leaving me with the bittersweet taste of my sister's name in my mouth.

Three exits from my stop, and I find myself reading all the ads lining the subway ceiling. Then I lean back, the back of my head meeting glass, and skim the billboard above me upside down. "Dream a new dream" in boldface white letters peppers a cloudless, blue sky—a blond beauty laying on her back in a grassy field, her hands clasped behind her head.

I run my thumb along the trigger of the gun in my pocket. I'm done running. It's Dad's turn to watch his back, fear every corner turned, and agonize over where he should hide.

The train comes to a jarring halt, and I move through the crowd, pole to pole, and step over the gap into the crowds of people, men wearing suits, carrying laptop bags, women in heels, talking on their phones, and tourists wearing I heart Chicago shirts, doing what tourists do best—looking lost. Even I'm wearing my Chicago skyline tee, but that's about to change.

The department store opens at 10:00AM sharp, just like the website said and across the street, catty-corner to the coffee shop lies Dad's office. Pushing through the heavy door, I walk past aisles of perfumes and shoes before spotting the men's section, and beeline to the dress clothes.

"Excuse me, Sir." The short gentleman with a receding hairline wears a three-piece suit with an employee tag that reads, Thiel. "Can I assist you with anything today?"

"Umm." I've never shopped for these kinds of clothes. Heck, buying the few t-shirts was the first time I ever shopped for anything, but I don't mention this. "I need a business suit. A tie. And a dress shirt. And…Uh…I have no idea which size I should choose."

"No problem. Come with me." Thiel says, and I follow him to an opening in front of the fitting rooms.

When he pulls out a measuring tape, I turn to walk away, saying, "No worries," because my clothes stay on. Especially my shirt.

"This will only take a minute," and like he can read my mind, he adds, "You don't have to take anything off. And if you want, I'll pull a few suits off the racks for you." I return to stand next to him, and he stretches the tape between his hands. "Lift your arms. Sure. Just like that. So, what's your price range?"

And as he runs the tape across my chest, panic seizes me when the measuring tape bumps my hip, right below my pocket. The pocket with the gun in it. "I changed my mind." This time for sure. "But thanks. I have to go."

I leave without waiting for his response, and as I pass the racks of dress suits, I catch a price tag by the hand just to know. *Woah.* $750.00. The disguise would have wiped out my last penny. So not worth it. Dad's not worth it. Not like I was planning to wear a mask so with or without a dress suit, not like he wouldn't recognize me. I just worry I need to look the part before someone lets me into his office. At this point, I'll take my chances.

Out on the street, as I walk in the direction away from Dad's office, my heart races like I've been running uphill for hours. I've rehearsed this moment a hundred times since the day I woke up in the hospital. Why then does my throat tighten, and the list of ten dictated words leave my lips in a continuous stutter. "I'm, umm, looking for a, uh, lawyer to represent me, because, my, umm, I want to sue my father for… yeah…. irreparable damages… and…"

"What'd ya say, son?" A bearded, elderly man walking behind me wearing a stained trench coat bearing the sour stench of urine speeds up until he's in step with me. I ignore his question and turn left at the corner. Dad's office is three blocks in the other direction, but I need to shake this guy first.

"Got any change to spare for this hungry ol' man?" The dude follows me down Wacker Drive.

I shake my head no, and say, "Sorry, man," and pick up my pace, but the scent alone tells me he's still behind me.

"You know I used to hate my dad." Homeless-looking guy is still chatting, but his words sting more than his body odor. "He was a two-timing, womanizing alcoholic. Yep, best example for a young man growing up, he was."

Not exactly sure why, but I slow my stride and let him fall closer in behind.

"One day, I decided to show him." He stops talking a second and sputters out a raspy cough. "That's right. When I turned twenty-one, I maxed out Dad's credit card during my freshman year in college, bought myself a ticket to Vegas, got me some beauties at the casino and found my drink. Got so drunk that weekend, missed my flight home. Then when I tried to buy a new ticket, found out my boozing dad had canceled the credit card. So I had to hitchhike home, but by the time I arrived back to campus, my tuition was canceled, my bills were unpaid, and they kicked me out of school for disorderly conduct. So I found a girl who'd buy me drinks and moved around until the last girl booted me. That's right. I showed my dad all right."

I turn for a moment and look into those deep-set eyes and then turn back and resume walking.

Dude keeps talking. "My dad died last week, and would you believe he left me nothing. Well, he left me one thing. A note that said he was sorry. Can you believe it? He died in a hospital. Alone. But that's not the worst part." Old man stopped walking when I turn to hear him out. He's shaking his head, his gaze on his ripped boots, his toes poking through. "I look at myself in the mirror, in the public bathroom, and you know who I see?"

But before he answers his own question, another shaggy dressed fellow comes at me from the other direction with an unlit cigarette dangling from his lips. "Gotta light for a friend?"

First dude with the story pulls out a lighter from his trench coat and reaches across me, the fire flickering inches from my face. The scent of fire shoves me back and I lose my footing and fall to the sidewalk, my hands catching my fall behind me, the gun slipping to the edge of my sweatshirt pocket.

"Dude's packed!" Cigarette-smoking guy says. "Run! Before he shoots us."

I put my hand in my pocket to push the revolver back in and the story teller, hands in the air and backing away, says, "Don't shoot. Don't shoot." And the two take off running, stumbling down into Lower Wacker Drive, leaving me on the sidewalk, shaken up by how affected I still am by fire, memories…Dad. The gun against my gut suddenly feels like a vial of poison, seeping in, transforming me into the very thing I loathe. And I don't want to say his name.

I get up and take off running. I run so hard, the weight of the gun shifts, and I feel it slipping out of my pocket again. Shoving it in deeper and checking my shoulder, I run through a red light and begin backtracking toward the train station. Jump on at the next stop and race down the steps to climb up onto the other side of the platform. *Summer.* Hope it's not too late to find you.

Twenty-five minutes later, I'm standing across the street from the churro stand, feeling exposed even with my hood pulled tightly around my face. The light turns green. Yellow. And red again. I turn to walk back toward the El, five steps back, and then spin on my heels and return to the corner. Another green light turns yellow and back to red as I tug the hoodie already over my head one more time and shove my hands in my pockets. The sidewalk offers little wisdom as do the pedestrians bumping past me. For all I know Summer never got the message, thinks I ditched her, came looking for me and recognized my face on Dad's flyer. Reading the name, she'd hate me all the more for lying to her.

Light blinks to green. Ten, nine, eight...the walking symbol mocks me with her blinking countdown.

Seven, six, five...Don't have it in you, do ya?

Four, three...What's the point, anyway?

Two. One. Like a punch in the gut, the traffic light turns yellow and the orange palm blinks *No*. Over and over again. I kick a stone into the street, and it only makes it halfway across. I take off in a run, and as I pass the spot, I scoop up the rock and keep running till I reach the other side of the street, now only a few feet from the churro stand, heart-pounding in my throat.

As I wait for the line to move forward, the woman in front of me has two little kids, a boy and girl. When it's their turn, the boy cannot make up his mind, and the little girl starts crying, because she wants two and the mother told her, "Only one." She turns and tells me, "I'm sorry."

I give her a no worries wave, and she smiles back before crouching down to her children's level and whispering something to her daughter.

I look off to the library door.

The woman pays the vendor, a forced laugh leaving her lips as she ushers her kids away. I watch them walk off when the dude behind me says, "So are you gonna order or what?"

"Umm. Go ahead." I step aside to let him place his order. "I'm still deciding."

When he leaves with a bag of churros for the guys at the office, no one's waiting in line anymore.

"What can I get you, sir?" Churro Guy asks, his head lowered as he pulls out a clean tray from beneath to organize the freshly baked batch.

"Yeah. I was wondering if you...remember me?" I scan all around but no one I know is within sight.

He puts the tray, only partially covered, down on the counter, and peers at me, shaking his head no. I pull my hood off and say, "You know, the guy who gave you a twenty dollar bill last week for the girl who loves chocolate—"

"John!" His eyes brighten. "How ya doin', my man? Where ya been hidin'?"

Another look over my shoulders and a deep breath before I ask, "Didja tell her?"

"Man, I am so sorry." My insides contract at this words. "Your girl never came by since then. Just haven't seen her 'round." He fiddles with his cash box, "Want your money back?"

I shake my head, no. "Thanks. I guess if she comes by..."

"Yeah, yeah. Of course. I gotchu." He clicks the metal box shut and tucks it back under the counter. "I'm supposed to tell her John wants to ask her to dance. And he's sealed his request with a month's supply of churros, correcto?" Churro Guy punctuates his words with an air-peck to his tray.

I walk away, not bothering to acknowledge his question. I step around the stand, cross the street again and approach the library—pulling my hood over my head before pushing through the entrance. Fiddling with the bindings on shelves, I scan the cubicles with my peripheral vision. Nothing. And as I see a portrait of the fighter planes on the wall, I wonder what it will take for my pilot dream to take off.

U-turning for the third time today, I scan the shelves and two over, on the bottom row, I spot a bunch of books with titles that include the words Air Force, pilot, or sky. Pulling several titles off, I carry the books to a corner behind the stacks and sit on the floor, secluded from traffic and begin to read. I read and read, all day long, scouring pages and pics, diagrams and charts. And as I read the stories on heroes of the sky, training and emergency tactics in a combat situation, one photo strikes me, and I stop flipping pages to read the caption. It's a picture of men in uniforms chucking items from the open cavity of the camouflage-painted plane. The soldiers were fighting back guerrilla thugs in order to deliver food and medical supplies to refugees in danger. The caption reads, "When the fuel ran dangerously low and refueling was not an option, Air Force G46, Unit 932, decided to lighten their load in order to buy minutes in the air and stay in the fight."

I close the book, leave the pile on the side neatly stacked, and exit the library, keeping my head low as I pass the circulation desk and spot a taped flyer with my picture on it. Picking up my pace, I head to the streets, doubting whether I'll ever set foot in this library again. I do know one thing. I've been fighting this war far too long, my fuel to stay in the battle is running low. And my sister needs me like I need her. Patting the gun on my waist, I nod to myself. It's time to lighten my load.

25
~ Talia ~

May 7ᵗʰ Evening

As I remove the sheets from my bed, a single Post-it sails up off the wall and lands by my feet, and I imagine it turning into a magic carpet, inviting to whisk me away to meet Lagan on the moon. Alaska would do.

Diana told me to leave everything in the room, since Security needs to examine all packages I've received since I arrived to determine if Dad has tampered with anything else since my first day at Hope Now. There's no point in trying to convince her that the other items are from Lagan. I'm used to leaving things behind. Walking away from people is what I can't get used to. I decide one Post-it from Lagan is something I came here with so this one thing I'll keep. The me-plus-you-equals-us-three one. I get it now—in a perfect world, it would be Lagan, the gardener, and me.

I file it into my back pocket, stand in the doorway to my first home away from home, read the Post-it message from Lagan on the wall one last time, half the question mark gone. I guess some answers seem clearer while other questions still remain. Like where is Jesse and when will I see my Post-it friend again. Flipping the light switch to off, I make my way to the phone room to call Diana and tell her I'll try the new shelter.

Nahida intercepts me in the hallway and asks if I might not join the ladies for one last group session.

"No, thank you."

As I turn to keep walking, Diana surprises me, touching my upper arm. "Talia. We just want to say goodbye. It's sort of a tradition." With her pressed lips and nodding face, I gather she's not going to take no for an answer.

Together, we walk over to the dining room, but the table has been moved to one wall while the seats all form a circle surrounding one empty one.

"So..." I'm biting my inner cheek and staring at my shoes. "Does this mean I'm the main dish for dinner?"

Diana laughs first. Then everyone follows, giggles surrounding me. I find myself smiling while the ache in me grows by the second. In only a couple of weeks, I grew to love these ladies around me. Just as I feel loved by them. Even Jaya has slightly warmed up to me since she declared our common favorite color.

Diana clasps her hands together and her chest rises and falls. "Each of us comes here alone, on our own, and the journey to get here is never easy. But it's something we all have in common. We made it. This far. And when one of us leaves, we want you to take a little part of us with you. We want you to remember a few things."

With that short intro, Diana rises from her chair, walks up to me, forms an arch with her arm above my head, and says, "Talia, you are lovely," and my hand rushes to cover my mouth as a whimper escapes my throat. She sees past my broken lips.

Nahida walks over next, places her arm over my head and links hands with Diana. "You are courageous, Talia. Yes, you are."

I suck in my breath, and my lips begin to tremble.

Sunila pushes back her chair and slowly makes her way toward me, reaching over me like the others. "Baby girl, you are strong." She cups my chin with her free hand to look me in the eye, nodding to me, her eyes searching for agreement.

Jaya stands next, but instead of speaking, she walks toward me, and places a paper in my lap. It's colored in to every corner in one shade. The color blue.

And the tears stream down my face, because I wonder if her future has blue in it too. The trial is a few weeks. I won't be here to find out what happens.

Addison comes next, her beautiful bare arms smooth to the touch as she wipes my face with the back of her hands. "You are not done, nor is life done with you."

And the others just keep on coming. Some with words. Some with pictures. Some with nothing but their smiles.

Until each woman surrounds me, a canopy of hugs descending on me like morning dew.

Diana lifts my head with her free hand and looks me in the eye. "You will find your voice. And one day, when you're ready, you will tell your story."

26
~ Jesse ~

May 7th Evening

With no one nearby on the beach and darkness setting in, I begin walking along the shore, waiting for pitch blackness. As I head north, eventually the beach wanes and piled boulders line the shore, the waves splashing my side closest to the water. Steadying myself with one arm stretched out, my shoes slide several times on puddles that look like black paint in the dark. Finding a gap in the rocks, I jump down onto the sand, and the boulders behind me make a wall high enough I can't see the grassy park behind me that runs up to Lakeshore Drive. Perfect.

I set the gun next to me on the sand and pull off my shoes, and socks and lay them neatly on the highest rocks. Hesitant, but aware that dry clothes will greet me like a hug, I strip down to my boxers, laying my jeans and t-shirt on top of my sweatshirt on the highest, driest rocks. Stepping forward and dipping my right toe into the water, the tide sweeps forward, splashing ice-cold water up to my knees. Shuffling backward in the dark, something sharp jabs my skin, and I turn, fists poised to fight. *Rocks.* They're just rocks.

Searching the sand, I see the gun slipping away with the tide and step on it just in time. The sand, the beach, the water and the rocks all symbolize moments and memories weighing me down. I came to bury much more than the gun. Mom never finished teaching me to swim, deep water always a place I avoided. I have no plans on trying to swim. Just stepping into the water and finishing what I came here to do. Walking toward the water, I count my steps into the lake to calm my pounding heart.

"One. For the time you locked Mom in the closet. Two. For the times you burned Talia, and I was stuck in the wheelchair."

White foamy waves reach my waist, and I still feel the sand below my toes, my skin prickled with goose bumps.

"Three. For the time you caught us when we tried to run away with Mom. Four. For my N.E. Where airplane drawing I threw away."

The tide surges toward me, and my feet no longer touch the ground. As I push my head above water and spread my arms side to side to tread water, the rest of the numbers come out like gurgles, but I need to say them. "Five, six, seven...Eight, nine, ten. For all the times you told me to move. For all the lists you laid out for me. For all the burns. And the minutes stolen from me. For the time I can never get—" and as my head goes under, I hold my breath and dive to the sandy bottom and begin to dig a hole as fast as I can, the waves pushing my body to and fro so harshly, I restart a different hole, my chest tightening by the second.

I'll bury my regrets, disappointments and anger with the gun, and hope they won't follow me out of the water. I push Dad's gun into the second hole and cover it up with sand, pounding it deeper with a softball-sized rock my hands fumble across, and just as I turn around to push off the bottom and return to shore, the tide flips me forward and pulls me out so fast, between swallowing water and the disorienting darkness, when my head finally breaks through the surface, I can't tell which way the shore is. And my feet no longer touch a sandy floor as a fresh set of waves arches over my head and gulps of water push past my mouth as I attempt to get a breath in. My flailing arms and legs search for something solid, but the receding tide pulls me out again like hungry hands with unquenchable thirst. I'm further out into the water, and I can't stop coughing and sputtering, the dark world underwater brightens as plankton light up like stars in the waters around me. I reach for them, because I wanna live. I just want to hold one star. Just. Need. One. Star. But they disappear the moment my fist closes. Darkness envelops me as I sink lower and lower—the last thing I recall feeling is a stab of pain against the back of my head.

27
~ Jesse ~

May 8th

The splash of a single raindrop lands on one eyelid. Then the other, forcing me to wake up from one dream. And swim into another. I see the rainbow-striped umbrella in a pretty girl's hand, open and propped as she skips across a field. Another droplet falls and lands smack-dab in the middle of my forehead, trickling off onto my pillow. I open my mouth to ask her to share her umbrella, but no sound comes out.

I've been warned. The rain is coming. I just need to reach for the—. Floodgates open and a tornado descends upon me, whipping the curtains side to side, window pane rattling with the force of high winds. And the umbrella lifts, high, higher and sails toward me, the curve of the handle runs over my palm, teasing me with a taste of rescue just before taking flight and twirling out the window. Taking the girl with her. Taking Summer away. I wake up drenched, feeling exposed, but strangely comfortable. The metal bars of the bed, the scratchy feel of scrubs, and the scents of cleaning products grant me the familiar. I've been in a hospital before.

"Oh Lawd, your face is one wet mess, sweetie. No worries. We'll get you cleaned up before they take you for treatment," says a nurse in pink floral scrubs who just entered my room. Her tag reads, Sheela Myers. Like deja vu, she dries my face, takes my temp, checks my pressure and charts all her findings. But unlike my first trip to the ER, she says, "Today's the day you go in for your first round of kidney dialysis. Doc came by and explained this to you, right?"

Kidney what? I shake my head no.

"Honey, you took one crazy swim the other night, and if that couple hadn't seen you drowning, you might have died out there with acute renal failure from the lack of oxygen and all the water you swallowed. Might take a few rounds before we can assess if the damage is temporary or permanent."

My chapped lips part but I don't respond, trying to think back if I ever finished burying the gun. If my voice is gone. Again.

"Don't worry, son. There'll be plenty of time to explain why you were skinny-dipping in the middle of the night, and teenagers nowadays do crazy things, but I still want to know. For now, it's time to clear up your pretty little head and get your strength back."

I reach up to touch my forehead where a Band-Aid covers my right brow, and Nurse Sheela says, "Probably hit the rocks when the tide brought you back in. It happens. That's nothing like the mess of scars you have on your back."

The mention of Dad's burns makes me avert my eyes.

"It'll be aw-right, but I'd promise your Mom you'll never again swim alone. She must be worried out of her mind."

I look over to the hospital room window, and say my first words. "My mom is dead."

"Oh." Sheela's dark-skinned hand stops writing in her chart again, and she moves to eye the levels in the plastic bag apparatus dispensing some kind of fluid into me. "I didn't know. Your dad?"

"He's dead, too." He should be.

"Without any ID on you, the E.R. staff assumed you were a college student who left his wallet in the dorms or something. I told them I'd ask you when you woke up." Sheela peers at me, her eyes soft with concern. "Do you have any family?"

"No," I start saying, "but my cousin, his name is Lagan. Can I call him to come get me?"

"You're not going anywhere for a couple of weeks. Not if you want to live, young man. Kidney failure, even temporary shutdown, can lead to an early arrival at the pearly gates, and by the looks of your age, you got some living left to do."

I shift in my bed to my side. "Youch!" The jab of pain in my back that rushes in forces me to lie down again.

"Limit your movements till physical therapy comes in and gives you some pointers, you understand?" A lock of her wavy, black hair falls over her face as Sheela adjusts the pillows to help prop my back.

"Looks like May showers could bring in some May flowers." Sheela's gazing at the rain outside the window. "Thank ya, Lawd. Cuz we all know—nothing grows without the rain."

One thing that grows inside me is the need to talk to my sister. When Nurse Sheela leaves, I stare at the phone and do the next best thing, dialing the only number I know by heart. Talia used to sing the digits around the house during chores with such enthusiasm, someone might have thought she had the inside scoop to the Mega Lotto. Enough circuits and the tune got stuck in my head. Along with the numbers.

"Hello." A woman's voice answers on the other end.

"Hi. Yes, is...Lagan home?"

The woman covers the mouthpiece but screams loud enough, I hear every word she says. "Urr-ray, Lagan-beta. Von of your buddies is on the phone."

"Got it, Mom." Lagan's voice streams through the phone.

I hear a click of one phone being put down. "Reg?" Lagan says.

"No," I say. "It's—"

"Jesse!" Lagan says. "Great to hear from you. Dude, you're doing okay?"

"Never been better." I rub my side where my abdomen feels more tender than on the other side. "How's Talia? Have you seen her?"

"I wish." Lagan sighs into the phone. "I do know she's good. Safe as far as I know. Man, not a day goes by that I wonder if you're still alive? If I shouldn'ta just left you like that. Where you at these days? You need more cash? A place to crash?"

"Still downtown." I shift in bed, slowly to keep from setting off the pain buzzer that seems to be located on the left side of my lower back, deciding to keep the conversation short. "I'm at Northwestern Hospital."

"You got a job at the hospital. That's—"

"Lagan." I cut him off because it hurts to talk. "I need a favor."

"Shoot. Whatever you want—"

"I want to see Talia."

"Except that." Lagan's voice falls flat. "I mean, I want to see her too. I just don't know with your Dad's history if it would be safe to get in touch with her. I don't think it's wise for me to be seen with you right now, either, not when your Dad's been breathing down my parents' necks with his own version of the law."

I bang the receiver on the bed next to me, curses leaving my lips. When I put it back to my ear, Lagan says, "Sorry, man. Believe me, I know how much it sucks to have to keep waiting. I wish I had something else to tell you."

"Can I write her a letter? Send her a note? There's something I need to tell her." I'm ready to start over. Leave Chicago. Use the cash I've made to head down to Texas. Find out if I can join the Air Force, complete the basic training, and make this Pilot dream a reality. And I can't leave without saying goodbye.

"I wrote her a letter. Two actually. Just mailed them to the main headquarters, and I hope they brought it to her at the shelter." Lagan pauses, and I can hear my own breathing. "I don't know for sure, but it's worth a shot."

"Forget it." I'm determined to see Talia. "When I get out of here, I'll find her myself. I don't care if I break the rules, give me the name of the shelter, and I'll tell them I have to see her. She's my sister. I can't just leave without—"

"You're leaving?" Lagan asks. "To where? When?"

"Nowhere yet. I'll be here for a few days. Probably for two more weeks."

"Wait. You're admitted?" He didn't ask. I didn't mention it. "What happened?"

"I'm fine. I'll tell you more later."

"Whatdya mean you're fine? You're hurt? Did your... Dad find you?"

"No. Well, yes and no. Long story."

"I got time. I want to know. And I need to know, because I promised Talia you'd be fine. What happened?"

"Fine," I take a deep breath and decide to tell him the two-sentence version. "I nearly drowned in Lake Michigan last night. Two people got me out of the water. Now I'm recovering. Like I said, I'll be fine."

"What do you mean by nearly drowned?" Lagan pauses a beat. "I'm not gonna even ask you why you'd go swimming in the lake at night. But tell me you know how to swim and it was just a fluke."

I don't say anything.

"Look man, I'm sorry for giving you a hard time. Glad you're okay. I'll tell Talia if I talk to her, okay?"

"And tell her the number here so I can talk to her. Oh. I almost forgot." I lower my voice. "I told them my name is John."

"Uh. Okay, John." Lagan says. "We'll talk more soon."

28
~ Talia ~

May 8th Past midnight

An hour plus drive leads to a post-midnight arrival at Casa de Manana, a home for DV survivors just outside of Zion, Illinois. DV is the fancy way of saying domestic violence without having to say it, as if even the words want to hide like the women in the shelter.

And after the flowers incident, like a dagger in a wound that never stopped bleeding, Diana asks me to wait a bit before contacting Lagan in case his limited interactions lead Dad to me. Jody, the in-house supervisor, greets me at the door the night I arrive at Casa de Manana, her blond waves pulled back in one of those springy-teeth, hair clips. She wears a soft pink house robe, her flawless skin making her look like she's in her twenties.

"All the other ladies are sleeping," she says, keeping her voice soft like her footsteps. "But the woman I mentioned earlier, she was able to move into her new place after all." Jody motions Diana and me to follow her. "So you can settle into your room, and we'll talk paperwork and logistics tomorrow, okay?"

Jody opens the doorway to my bedroom, similar to the one

from Hope Now in terms of furnishings, with its twin mattress and table, although the desk has circular knobs and the dresser has a semi-circled mirror on top. Clean sheets and towels sit on top of the bed. There's also a window, which the first room didn't have.

Jody smiles and says, "You need anything, my room's just two doors down."

I nod and plop my bag on the desk, relieved to see there were no locks on the closet door. "Thanks. I'll be fine."

Diana thanks Jody who leaves for her room, and then Diana turns to me and says, "Try and get some rest. Things tend to look clearer when the sun rises." She rests her hand on my shoulder, and says, "Call me if you need to talk, okay? I'll be in my office tomorrow morning."

Her hand slides to my back as she hugs me goodbye.

"Thank you," I say. "I miss the ladies at Hope Now already." Change is hard.

"Talia," Diana pulls back so we can see each other face to face. "Change is inevitable. And some of life's best changes begin with choice."

I nod, letting the words push past my walls. Change is all I've ever wanted. Dad to change how he treated me. Mom to change her tune to a song that I could still hear. Jesse to change his anger to dreaming.

Even as I close my bedroom door, I watch my wishes sink to the bottom of a well. They were never within reach. Because they weren't mine to wish. Changes I could not choose. I see that now.

The mint green curtains on the window glow in the dark, and as I part them to look outside, the half moon lights up the yard, two trees towering above the house. One looks like a maple and the other an oak, but in the dark, it's hard to know for sure. What I do know is there's no willow.

I let the curtains fall back in place, and as I begin to spread the sheets over the mattress, each corner feels heavier than the last as I wonder how many places I'll sleep before I'll stop having nightmares. The vase of flowers. Dad's note, more so, play on repeat in my head. He could have followed us here. He could be hiding outside my window.

I fall asleep and my pillow turns into a time travel machine, blurring me between two worlds. One moment, I'm nursing my mother's back, plucking out broken glass and dabbing her cuts, and the next, I'm picking up stones off the gardener's body, begging him not to die. Before sunrise, the sound of a door shutting stirs me and I jump out of bed. *Dad? Has he found me?* Heart pounding, I peer through a crack in my doorway and exhale relief. Jody's crouching down, tying her runners.

"Sorry. Did I wake you?" she says, smiling. "Just going for a morning jog before breakfast. Wanna join me?"

"Umm. I…" When will I know what I want, exactly?

"Cool breeze on the beach helps me clear my head while I chase away yesterday's worries so I can face a new day." Jody rises to her feet. "I highly recommend it. And I still need to stretch and down a cup of juice, so if you want to join me, meet me by the front door in, say, ten minutes."

I nod and shut my door, leaning against the back, eyeing my sneakers on the floor. The most time I've spent outdoors since I left home was the drive between the two safe houses. I walk over and peer out the window, the moon setting behind the trees as the deep blues of dawn push back the black of night.

Reasoning that Dad wouldn't try and hurt me if I was with someone, I slip into my sneakers, clean up quickly in the closest bathroom, and meet Jody in the kitchen.

"Here." Jody's blue eyes blink, as she passes me a cup of O.J. "Glad you made it. Bottom's up."

I drain the cup and follow Jody outside where she leans against the siding to stretch her quads and calves. I imitate her as I inhale the familiar scent of damp earth, the dew on the grass making a dark outline around my runners. The sky is lighter already, and as we begin to jog down residential streets, streaks of red and pink move across the morning sky.

"It takes about fifteen minutes to hit the beach. You up for three miles?" She glances over to me as we continue to jog ahead.

"Umm. I think so." I'm sure I ran that far in high school gym class, although that was over a year ago.

"Great." And Jody picks up her pace, and I do too, drinking deep of the cool morning air, trying to steady my breathing and keep up with her.

When the houses begin to thin, Jody turns down one more street, and the space widens up to a mostly empty parking lot. Beyond the concrete lies the beach and the lake ahead, the sky a water color painting before me.

Easily mistaken for an illusion. The sun begins to ascend out of the water. Like a humpback whale coming to the surface to take a breath, the sun rises and streaks of orange and pink and more red, spray across the dawn canvas in slow motion. The red ball of fire pierces the darkness and mesmerizes me. I cannot look away.

When the crimson sphere is fully unveiled, I see a line over the water, like someone took a waterproof Crayola marker, and drew on top of the lake. It starts from the sun, and it comes straight to me. As we continue jogging along the shoreline, the line moves with me, like the sun means to lasso me, and I fall behind Jody's pace, captivated.

"Come on! I'll race you back to the parking lot." Jody passes me running in the opposite direction, and I'm shaken from my digression. I turn and book it, sand flying behind me as I pump my arms to catch up to her, but she's quick, and I finally meet up with her when she slows her pace to a walk to the edge of the lot. "Beat you. This time."

And I'm out of breath, trying to smile, leaning over, my hands on my knees. "Right. So…" Inhale. Exhale. "You do this…" Exhale. "Every morning?"

"Except on Sundays. One day to rest up, and back at it on Monday." Jody nudges me to walk with a playful bump of shoulders. "Wanna jog or walk back?"

"Walk," I say, still sucking in air. And we walk. In silence.

About a block from the house, Jody says, "You know I wasn't always able to leave the house so freely?"
I'm not sure what she means. "Why?

169

"I wasn't always a DV house leader, or House Supervisor as the title reads." She glances my way and keeps talking. "I came as a survivor first. It'll be ten years ago next month."

I sigh. Everyone has a story. I wonder how bad it was for her. What made her leave? I manage to say, "Oh." And wait to see if she wants to share more.

But she doesn't. We reach the doorway and as she unlocks the door for me, Jody asks, "Are you glad you came?"
I look back outside, the day bright and sunny now, and nod yes.

29
~ Jesse ~

May 9th

My first dialysis treatment redefined the word "drained," for me. The machine Dr. Singh, the physician assigned to my case, hooked me up to reminds me of a milkshake made for two at Baskin Robbins. Except for the minor detail that the dark red liquid sieving through the two tubes from my veins makes me queasy, instead of making me salivate. The whole procedure takes hours, and I finally resolve to take a nap for fear of passing out. In place of sleep, I find myself replaying my moonlit dive, wishing the rip tides hadn't stolen my assurance that the gun was buried for good.

Dr. Singh's voice returns me to shore when he tells me it's over and helps me back into a wheelchair, telling the staff, "I'll take him. We need to chat anyway." Then he turns to me and says, "Not bad for the first time. Your numbers are improving quickly. We might have you up and feeling like yourself again before the week is over if you follow Nurse Sheela's orders. Which includes no McDonalds for a little while, okay?" As Dr. Singh guides my chair into the elevator, he adds, "But let's wait to talk to the press and give you some time to rest."

"Press?" I am not talking to any newspapers.

"They keep calling, wanting to interview you about your

little swim, but I gave the front office strict orders to wait till you gain your strength back. And even then, the choice is yours."

"I can't." I catch myself. "I mean, I don't want to talk to the media. Just tell them no for me, please."

"Of course. Respecting one's privacy is a lost art in today's world." We're in front of my room now.

I smile and nod. "Thanks, Doc," I say as he opens the door.

"Looks like someone has a visitor." Doctor Singh backs me into my room before saying, "I'll leave you two alone. Just remember what I said."

As the wheelchair spins to face forward, Summer's smiling face comes into view as she rises from the chair next to my hospital bed. "It is you!" are the first words out of her mouth, and I'm just as shocked she sounds happy and that she's actually here.

"Uh. You two definitely know each other, correct?" Doc's standing in the doorway.

I chuckle, then buckle over and grab my sides. "I think he's falling for ya," Doc says, walking over and rubbing my back. "Take it slow, son. And you young lady, no more side-piercing jokes, okay?"

Summer's jaw drops open, her blue eyes wide. "But, I. I didn't even say anything?"

"Whoever said a lady needed words to make a guy's heart ache. Well, in John's case, his kidneys." Dr. Singh signs my chart, files it back under his arm, and heads to the door. "And on that note, I'll check on you in the morning. And no trying to feed your way into his heart either. He's got a strict diet plan for the next few weeks." Doc's wide grin widens as he smoothens his silver-speckled beard. And then he leaves.

I ask Summer, "How did you even find me?" even though I'm thinking, *you have no idea how thrilled I am that you did.*

You're all over the news!" Summer says, pointing to the TV on the wall. "Well, not you, exactly, but the young couple that rescued you after they saw your clothes on the rocks."

"You recognized my clothes?"

"Well," Summer looks down at her hands. "You sort of wore the same Chicago skyline t-shirt and jeans each time we met. And I hadn't heard from you. But—" Summer looks up at me, eyes searching. "I didn't know for sure. I just had a hunch. I was really hoping..."

And if I had bought a men's suit like I had planned to...Enough about me. "Did you ever get the churros I left you?"

"Yeah, but you broke our deal." The light in Summer's eyes dims when she squints. "If you must know, I've cashed in one. And thanks, but I still hope I can get the rest in person."

"I was just..." My gaze lingers on the window, the rain pelting away. "Something came up, and I didn't have time to say goodbye." I keep from looking at her when I add, "I'm sorry."

Summer sits back down in her chair and crosses her arms over her chest. "I mean, a guy needs to leave a number, a forwarding address, heck, a last name would be a great place to start if he wants a girl to follow up. Don't you think?"

Name! Did Dad watch the news? Does he suspect I'm the teen the couple rescued? "Hey, did the news reports mention my name? Or show my face?"

"Of course not!" Summer shakes her head slowly side to side. "Are you trying to change the topic? Cuz this time I'm not leaving till I know I can't lose you." Summer clears her throat. "Lose track of you. You know what I mean."

Warmth spreads to my ears, and something stirs inside me. That same kinda something I felt when Summer hugged me.

Bracing myself with the wheelchair armrests, I say, "Just one last question, I promise. Did the news reporters say they found, um, anything other than me in the water?"

"Like what? Buried treasure?" Another giggle escapes Summer's lips as she crosses her legs one way, then back, her long legs covered up to her knees in navy blue rain boots. Summer purses her lips, rises, and walks to the window to look outside.

"No, just..." I can't tell her what I'm referencing, but my heartbeat steadies knowing the gun stayed buried.

"I'm guessing the reporters will want to interview you at some point. They're calling your survival a modern day miracle. Kinda like this early summer weather, unheard of for the windy city."

"What'd you just say?" Didn't the nurse just mention something about summer coming early? And Summer found me. In more ways than one.

"Which part?" Summer turns, her hands on her hips. "And you are planning to tell me your last name or what?"

Feeling stupid that she doesn't even know my first name, I take a deep breath and say, "There's something I need to tell you." There's no point to hiding anymore. By the time Dad finds out about me, I should be halfway to Texas.

Summer quips back without hesitation. "I have something I want to ask you. You first."

"Visiting hours are over. Time to let the patient rest," Nurse Sheela enters, beelining to my chair and assisting me back into bed. "The pretty lady can always come tomorrow."

Summer looks at me with a "can I?" expression. I smile and say, "I guess now you have my address."

"Here's my number." Summer scrawls her number on a notepad by my bed stand. "So call me, maybe. Ya know, in case you think of something you need, I can drop it by. Like a new poncho, in case the roof starts leaking."

Summer and I exchange smiles, and the nurse just shakes her head. "I'll be back in a few to take your vitals," Nurse says, looking up at the ceiling for a moment before walking toward the door. "Now say your goodnights."

Silence fills the room when the door shuts as Summer gathers her purse. "So what were you gonna say?" she asks, walking up to my bed, her hands on the metal railing of my hospital bed.

"Why don't you go first?" No matter how many ways I formulate the sentence, "My name is not John. I lied," I sound like an idiot. "Ladies first, right."

"If you insist." Summer runs her fingertips over my bandage as my gaze rises to meet those blue eyes. Now there's a place I'd like to learn how to swim. Her eyes lower to my hands in my lap. "Were you?" Summer stops a beat. "I mean, why were you out there in the lake by yourself, late at night?" Her eyes squint as her gaze meets mine again, and her smile relaxes to a line. "The news anchor suggested you were trying to take your life. Is that true?"

"Long story." I say, looking at the doorway for Nurse Sheela. "But just so you know, I wasn't trying to kill myself."

I wonder if someday I'll tell her about a time I did think along those lines? Sure, right after the part about the fake name and carrying a gun to my Dad's office to threaten his life. Texas means more than just joining the Air Force. It's a chance for me to start over.

Nurse Sheela opens the door, and I clear my throat. "I guess my little news can wait till tomorrow. I'll see you tomorrow, maybe?"

Summer's smile returns as she moves to the door. "Probably" is the last thing she says before walking out.

30
~ Jesse ~

May 10th

The phone rings, and I half expect to hear Talia's voice. "Sorry I can't come by today, John." Summer's on the phone. "It is John, right?"

I panic. Did someone tell her my real name? I wanted to tell her myself. "Uhh…"

Summer laughs, "You still there? I'm just making sure this is the right hospital room, and my friend John hasn't been discharged?"

"It's me." I tell the truth without saying my name.

"Nice to know I can find you." Summer waits a beat, then says, "But I'll be by in a few days when I finish some of my finals. You doing okay?"

"Sure." I say, heart sinking a bit with the news. "Getting better."

"So I'll see you soon?" Her intonation rises, like she wants to make sure she's still welcome.

"Can't wait," I blurt out. Then add, "I mean, I can. I will. Wait. Uh…Yeah. See you soon."

I hear a giggle on the other end of the line, and we say our goodbyes.

A knock at the door, and another hospital person walks in, introducing herself as a crisis worker.

"Are you sure no one in your house smokes?"

The repeated question angers me. I already said no the first time the woman in a white lab coat asked me. I shake my head no to keep from cursing.

"Is there any history of mental illness in your family?" Ms. Dillon, as she introduced herself, asks me all the same questions the doc asked me on day one.

"My parents died when I was young, so I have no idea who had what on which side of the family." I avert my eyes and flick away at a hangnail.

"Well, the thing is, the marks on your back." Ms. Dillon waits a moment, then continues. "If you were trying to give yourself a tattoo job, the location of each mark is so perfectly placed, it's like you had eyes on the back of your head."

"Oh that." And all this time, I'm thinking she's accusing me of attempted suicide when I dove into the lake. "A few years ago, I had a...friend—"

"Friends don't burn friends, John." She taps on her clipboard and looks at me over her bifocals. "Who burned you, John? The marks are only a couple months old at best."

"Does it matter?" I ask, eyes on the window now. The sunset dips behind the other buildings outside the hospital. "No one's ever gonna burn me again. Just so you know."

"If you're involved in a gang or someone out there on the streets is hurting you, there's one way to make sure they don't burn or hurt you again." Ms. Dillon waits for me to look up, the cool grey of her eyes surrounded by a warm, light green. "Tell someone. Start by telling me."

"Thanks for your concern, Miss, but I can take care of myself." I maintain my stare until she lets out a sigh, shaking her head to herself as she jots down more notes.

"Even if you never tell the police, sometimes it helps to tell one other person. Just so you know." Ms. Dillon repeats my words with an edge to her tone.

"I appreciate the offer. Will that be all?" I swallow and adjust the pillow behind my head.

"Yep. If there's nothing to tell, then case closed." As she walks to the door, her hand lingers on the doorknob. "If you ever change your mind, the medical staff took images of the burns when you came in, nearly unconscious, because one theory was that the same person who caused you harm pushed you into the lake. We couldn't rule that out as a possible option." Her voice softens and she leaves after saying, "Just thought you should know."

Left alone, I wince at the irony of her words. I suppose whoever came up with the idea that Dad pushed me over the edge, for the second time in my life, was onto something. But telling her the truth would mean they'd find Dad. And then Dad would find me. Case closed.

31
~ *Talia* ~

May 14th

Each day, I wake up before the sunrise for a beach run with
Jody, silently jogging as I sort through my thoughts. And each
day, I meet the residents, slowly learn new names, and just like
Hope Now, I learn their stories, one at a time. Some speak up
in the group sessions, others speak through their artwork, and
some roam about silently, still in search of their voices. And
the faces are different, as are the stories. And even though the
string that links us together is loss, I'm anxious to hear the
other half of their stories. The part where they find new
beginnings. And find themselves.

One evening, a week after living at Casa, Jody knocks at
my door. "Diana's on hold for you." Jody brushes her curls
over her shoulder as she stands in the doorway of my room,
holding a phone. "When you're ready, you can take it in the
phone room, okay."

"Umm, okay." I rise from the bed, throw on a long sleeve,
and follow her to the phone room to take the receiver. Jody's
pink painted mouth presses into a smile turned down at the
edges before she leaves.

"Yes, this is Talia."

"You doing okay?" Diana waits and when I don't respond, she keeps talking. "Just thought you should know I used a secure line to call Lagan on your behalf and tell him you're safe and in a new shelter."

"So, when can I call him?"

"Any time you like." Diana exhales right into the receiver. "But you know the deal. If he or, God forbid, your Dad, exposes the location of the shelter, we'll have to move you again."

I understand. "Okay. Bye."

As I walk back to my new room, I pass a few of the new ladies sitting on couches in the common room who smile in my direction. Then I knock on Jody's door and say, "I'm turning in early tonight. Not in the mood to eat dinner, if that's okay."

"Okay, Talia," Jody brushes her hair behind one ear and looks me in the eyes, her eyes the shade of blue Mom loved. "Rest up. We can chat tomorrow about your appointment with Social Work, okay?"

"Okay." The word leaves my mouth like a reflex.

As I enter my room and spot the broken book that Lagan gave me on my table, I think of how someone took the time to compile all these stories. Memories of broken people who fought the beautiful fight of life. This was how they will be remembered. And the women I met at Hope Now are gone, but they're still fighting. Will immigration grant Sunny the paperwork she needs to leave? Will Nahida ever marry her library crush? How will the investigation on Jaya turn out? And will she choose blue someday to color in her pictures?

I open the desk drawer and pull out a notebook Jody handed to me the morning I arrived at Casa, alongside a fresh set of paperwork regarding rights and waivers. Pulling up my chair to the desk, the blank lines on the page stare up at me. As I fiddle with my pen, I realize I can't bring them here. But they didn't leave me empty-handed either. They gave me their stories. Just as the women at Casa have begun to share theirs too.

Maybe if I write them down, they won't seem so far away. Making a conscious decision to change their names, my hand flies across the book, filling page after page. I write each story, filling in the missing details as I imagine them, painting rainbows in their futures with my words. At the end of each woman's story, I draw three lines before starting the next chapter, but even after hours of non-stop writing, the ache inside fails to subside.

It's past three in the morning. I've been reading and rereading the stories I've written, editing them and drawing little doodles in the margins, moments I don't want to forget in the kitchen, the computer room and in the group sessions. Stick figures dancing around breakfast, some planting a garden, and others forming a willow over a girl during a goodbye. The girl is me.

Ripping out the pages, I fold them in half and file the ink-covered sheets into the top drawer. Once again, a blank page stares up at me. I take a deep breath, doodle a music note on the corner of the page, and start a new story.

My name is Gita.

Like a rope drawing me out of a deep well, my mother's name reaches down in an attempt to pull me out. I rewrite the first line.

My name is Gita. My name means song. All the songs I've ever sung were sad save two. One named Talia. The other Jesse. My children's cries sounded sweeter than my sadness but one day, even their cries could not drown out my pain. I left them so they wouldn't drown with me.

My story started in India. In poverty, in want. And when I left, when my parents sent me across the ocean, I trusted I would one day return. I did, but only in my dreams.

The s of dreams turns dark and thick as I retrace it over and over again. No more words come to me, as the rope breaks and I fall to the bottom of the well, crashing, punching at the imaginary dark puddle I lay in.

Even as I reread my mother's story, I question the truth of my words. *Is this how it went for you Mom, or is this just how I want to remember you?*

My head lays atop my folded arms as I try and picture my mother in an image that doesn't make me wince. I was too young to understand my mother's history. And at the end of her life, she disappeared into her own deep well, leaving me weeks before her final breath. I washed her body, clothed her wounds, held water to lips, and yet, I didn't know her.

I rip out the page, fold it several times and tuck it into my back pocket. Once again a blank page stares up at me. I place the pen on the paper and doodle a stick figure of a little girl wearing a triangular dress, with three daisies on it. I draw a teardrop-shaped loop around her.

My name is Talia. My name means dewdrop from heaven. I do not know if heaven exists. I do know that dew appears each morning, a tiny teardrop, pierced by the blade of grass atop which she balances her life. To the world she seems brave, for she shows up faithfully, regardless of the storms of yesterday. But only she knows the density of her pain, the lines under her seamless smile.

My tongue runs over my broken lips. Seamless is the last word that applies.

I do not know the beginning of my mother's nor the end of my brother's stories. I do not know the details of my father's life nor the days of the boy I love more than my own life. All I have is this: my journey, my life, my story. It's the only story I know. It is mine to hold or mine to tell.

I lay my pen down and pull my sleeve up, running my fingertips along the bumpy terrain of years of hurt. Pick up my pen, stare at my arm another beat, then begin writing again.

My name is Talia. And for as long as I can remember, I've been in pain. My father, the one who was supposed to love, hold, and protect me did none of those things. Instead...

I chew on the back of the pen, take a deep breath, and put the pen back on the paper.

He. Scares. Me.

He. Hurts. Me.

He. Burns. Me.

And I don't want...I cross out the words ~~don't want~~ and

write, can't, then cross that out too.

I refuse—. Even that is not the right word, and I cross the entire sentence out. One word sums up how I feel at this very moment. How I've felt for a long time but was too afraid to ask. To tell anyone. To say aloud.

Enough.

I shut my journal and trade places with the folded papers I put in the drawer. I flip each story open, penned side up, and line them across the desktop until every inch is covered. Then I rise from my chair, step back and continue to spread the sheets over my bed. Then the floor. Until the final sheet leaves my fingertips. Only a tiny corner of the carpet isn't covered with a story. The spot underneath my feet.

32
~ Talia ~

May 15ᵗʰ

Dawn stretches into her first yawn outside my bedroom window. After opening the shades, I tiptoe to the room down the hall to make a phone call.

"Hello." Lagan's voice sounds raspy.

"Lagan?" I keep my voice low to keep from waking the other residents.

"Talia?" His voice rises an octave.

"Can we talk?"

"Do you even need to ask? God, I missed the sound of your voice. How are you? How's everything going?"

"I mean...in person?" I wait a beat. "Are you busy?" I wonder if he has classes? Work?

"When? What? Where should I meet you? Jesse's gonna be so thrilled."

The very sound of my brother's name makes something inside me soar. "He's doing okay, then? Can you take me to see him?"

"Of course. And I know he's okay. He did have a minor situation, but as far as I know, he's going to be fine."

"Whatdya mean, minor situation?" My mind goes straight

to the fall. The night Jesse fell off the roof. "Lagan, if Jesse's hurt—"

"He called me from the hospital a few days ago."

I bite my tongue and inhale, afraid to hear more.

"Talia. He told me he's fine. But he'll be there for a few days. I'll take you to see him."

"Okay." I need to ask. I need to know. "Lagan. Can he still walk?"

"He never mentioned otherwise. Why don't we call the hospital together on the way and get the details. Just have to remember to ask for, I think he said, John. Okay?"

"Okay." I take a deep breath. *John?* I'm guessing I wasn't the only one changing names in our family to survive. "O. Kay." I repeat. I can do this. A couple more hours and I'll be reunited with the two men in the world that I love. Like a wick on ignited fireworks, I can't contain my excitement much longer.

"Hang tight, okay. Says here that visiting hours at Northwestern Hospital start at 9:00AM. That's in like three hours. Want me to come get you around eight?"

"How long will it take for you to get to the north shore of Illinois Beach State Park?"

"Umm. Hold on." I can hear mumbling in the background. "Reggie says I can borrow his car. I'm leaving now. I can be there before 6:30. Where should I meet you?"

"There's a row of green benches there. I've been jogging there in the mornings with Jody, the woman who works here. It'll take me about twenty minutes, and I'll wait till six to start walking." I think for a second. "Should I wait for you on one of the benches close to the parking lot?"

Lagan says. "Do you feel safe walking by yourself? It's still kind of dark outside. Are you sure?"

I want to say, it's not the dark that I'm scared of. I stick to answering the second question. Because I am sure. "More than ever."

"So..." Lagan waits a beat. "S.U.S. turns into S.U.N.?"

I know See You Soon. I made up S.U.S. "What's the N

for?"

"Now. A sunrise date, it is."

***

"Jody?" I knock softly on her door, feeling bad her alarm clock hasn't gone off yet.

"Talia?" Jody unlocks her bedroom door, cell phone in her hand, her blue eyes still squinting with sleep. "It can't wait…another thirty minutes?" She's holding the phone in the air and waving it.

I clear my throat, and she looks down and sees my running shoes. "If you're going for a jog, I can get my things—"

"No," I say. "I'll be fine. The sun's gonna rise soon, and I just want to walk today. Get some air." I run my fingers through my hair, pulling a lock toward my mouth, but detouring it as I tuck the hair behind my ear. "Lagan, the guy, maybe Diana told you about him. Anyway, he's going to meet me at the beach. Just wanted to let you know."

"Oh, okay. Take my cell, and call me if you need anything, okay." Jody puts the phone in my palm and, her fingers wrap my hand for a moment. "The emergency house number is speed dial one. Curfew is 10:00PM, okay? What time do you think you'll be back?"

"I dunno. I mean, I haven't seen him in over a month. And there's something I need to do. I…I want to…" I'm fumbling because I haven't mustered up the courage to say it out loud. "What I'm trying to say is I'm ready. I don't know how it all works. I don't know how long it will take. And I have no idea how it will all turn out."

Jody ushers me into her room and we sit across from each other at her little table for two, next to her bed. "Go on. I'm listening."

I take a deep breath and say, "I do know one thing. I'm I've had enough. I want to do what Diana suggested from the beginning. I'm ready to place a restraining order against my father. And press charges." I look up, greeted by Jody's ear to ear grin. "So…can we talk when I get back?"

Any hint of sleep disappears like fog lifted from a valley.

"Oh Talia!" is all she says before throwing her arms around me.

My shaking arms encircle her, and I'm sinking and swimming. Railroad tracks leading to a tunnel I can't see in lay ahead of me while the whistle of a train warns me from behind. I've made my decision: I'm moving forward. Heading through.

33
~ Talia ~

May 15th

I walk on what feels like autopilot, the same trail Jody and I have jogged all week, and when I think of Lagan, my pace quickens. Along with my heart. The colors of the sky are already changing when I reach the parking lot, the first light of dawn pushing out the black of night. I sit on a bench, lean forward, and watch seagulls arrive, peck along the shore for a meal, and fly off disappointed. Checking side to side, no sight of Lagan, I focus on the tide receding with the dawn, leaving behind her fingerprints in the sand, wavy lines speckled with shells.

Glancing to the right, I spot him. He's walking toward me, wearing a Bull's t-shirt and jeans, his hands in his pockets. I've dreamt of this moment every night since we parted, and yet now that it's here, it feels like a stranger approaches me. I exhale deeply, because the stranger is me. He doesn't know I've changed. How I've changed.

"God! It's really you," Lagan says.

I stand, my fingers reaching up, and the stubble of his goatee presses against the inside of my hands. Eyes closed, he turns his face, and his lips slide into my palms, and for a moment, time stops. The sand surrounds us as the deep blues of the new day usher out the night's blackness.

Lagan opens his eyes and begins to gently kiss each fingertip. "You're." Kiss. "Still." Kiss. "Here." Kiss. Kiss. He turns my hand over and examines my fingernails. "Blue?" Eyebrows raised and dimple dancing as he says, "This is new."

I just smile back, tickled by how he still notices the details. *And that's not the only thing that's new about me.* But that can wait. Giddy from all the attention as he takes my hand into his, I nod and say, "I got the lights. The lightning." Thankful for the squeeze of his hand—I know he's real. And I'm not dreaming.

"And the Post-its?" Lagan pulls me in closer, his dimple-accented smile alit like he already knows the answer.

"Yes, but I don't think I did it right." I look away so he won't guess I'm teasing. Then turn back and say, straight-faced, "You might have to spell it out for me."

Lagan takes the palm of my hand and traces a number four, but before he dots the question mark, I let out a squeal, pulling back my hand. "That tickles!"

"Just trying to refresh your memory."

"I remember." I say, taking his hand in mine again. "I remember everything."

Walking from the benches, we reach the water's edge and begin walking north as dawn sprays across the sky, streaks of orange, red and deep purple. Hand in hand, we step over rocks where the sand border turns to boulders.

"Careful, okay?" Lagan smiles and moves his arm to let go of my hand.

As I follow him a few more steps, he chooses a relatively flat rock to stand on and turns to face the water. I stop too, and he moves behind me and wraps his arms around my waist. A dark red streak rips the cloudy, deep blue sky in half. Even the horizon seems divided about the future. When Lagan inhales deeply into my hair, my shoulders rise to the sensation of his warm breath on my neck.

I scan the water. Then the sky. Back to the water. As I look down the beach, the jogger a faint speck in the distance, entices me to run. I turn to face Lagan, stepping closer, closing the gap. I resist fleeing, my fingers locking behind his neck—Lagan—my anchor.

"Something's different." Lagan's eyes squint with curiosity. "What is it? Everything okay? Did they treat you okay in there?"

A giggle escapes. "Yes. Yes. And yes."

"Care to elaborate?" Lagan slides his hands from behind my back to find my hands. His two hands hold mine now.

"Every day this week, I've been running."

"Yeah," Lagan nods. "You mentioned jogging with Jody, right?"

I nod, grateful for his attention to detail. "The thing is, for all these years, I've spent so much time focused on what I've been running from. I never really gave much thought to what I was running to."

Lagan nods, silently waiting for more. I take a deep breath and continue. "Until you came into my life and gave me something to look forward to. Something to run to. Something to live for."

Lagan's grin returns as he shifts his hands, but it disappears almost as quickly. "And what about your dad?"

"That's why I called you this morning." I smile, entwining my fingers in his. "I couldn't wait to tell you. I'm ready to put up a fight. The restraining order. Press charges." I stare down at my feet on the sand, standing inches from Lagan's. "I'm ready to face my dad."

"I'll be with you." Lagan inches closer. "Every step of the way, okay. That investigation I wrote you about is on the news every day. With the way it's developing, he might just sink with his own ship?"

The only investigation that's been on my mind is Jaya's. The murder. In the hotel. "Wait. Did they say my dad is going to trial on this case?"

"I think the papers said no one has been formally arrested yet. Why?"

I'm shaking my head. *Couldn't be.* "Just that the details

sound familiar. A girl I met in the first safe house—" And then I stop myself, because I signed a paper promising to keep all information I learned confidential. I say, "It would be totally coincidental if the two stories connected. It's probably just two similar situations." I stop then, because after meeting all the women, I, of all people, know that no two stories are the same.

"The papers never mention her name. The woman accused of defaming the hotel with the trafficking angle. Your dad says some people will make up anything to get away with murder." Lagan pulls me into a hug. "But he's representing the hotel more than just the big CFO who died, apparently. Every story makes him sound like a spokesperson for justice."

When Lagan says Jesse's formal name, Justice, a wave of relief washes over me. I'll see my brother soon and very soon.

"Post-it for your thoughts?" Lagan says, his lips brushing my temple.

"I have to write 'em down?"

"Not today. Not now." Lagan runs his hand along the side of my face, brushing my hair back. "I'm here. You can just tell me."

Where do I start? I take a deep breath. "Jesse. Mom. I just… How does a guy claim to fight for justice and never once stand up for his wife or kids?"

Lagan doesn't answer at first, his heavy sighs tell me what I already know—he can't change Dad any more than me. Then, with those earthy brown eyes looking into mine, Lagan repeats his vow. The one he made when we said goodbye at Buckingham Fountain weeks ago. "I'm here for you now. And I'll always fight for you."

Moments pass as we hold onto each other, and I take hold of his promise, locking it inside me.

Lagan breaks the silence with, "I'm thinking we should seal this moment with a kiss." One step forward and my lips would be on Lagan's.

I look down, ever aware of my broken lips. Not healed totally yet. But more healed than ever before.

When I hesitate, Lagan says, "You know if you had given

me a tiny bit more notice, I woulda brought you flowers."

"Yeah?" I say, my face close enough to his to feel his breath. Familiar peppermint.

"Tulips." Lagan's grin widens. "For your two...lips."

"Well in that case," I let go, hop back down the line of rocks, and start running down the beach. "I guess the kiss will have to wait!"

Lagan and his long legs catch me before I make it back to the bench, and his arms swing me around, lifting me off the sand in a playful twirl, the bright yellow sun lighting up the whole beach now.

"Okay, okay!" I say, "Put me down, and I'll consider a compromise."

"Like what?" Lagan lowers me and as soon as I kick up sand, he lifts me up off the beach again.

"Like...you can kiss me when you see lightning."

He cocks his head sideways, and says, "That's easy."

"What? You carry around Christmas lights in addition to Post-its in your back pocket these days?"

Lagan laughs, pulling me in close so we're eye to eye, his voice husky when he says, "My sky's right here," and before I change my mind, I'm falling into a kiss. Lagan's lips—sweet, so tender and sweet.

Opening my eyes and stepping back, a bit breathless, I look up at the brightened day, and suddenly flip. "Jesse!" Shaking free my hand to find out the time, I say, "It's almost eight. Let's go!"

I'm content to be moving as we pull out of the lot, and Lagan drives along Lake Michigan back toward the city. An increased traffic of joggers, bikers and moms behind strollers dot the sidewalks as we drive along the water.

"So what's it been like? In the shelters?" Lagan glances over for a second, checks over his shoulder and makes a lane change.

"Hard. And amazing." I go on to tell him about the first place, and how they took me in, befriended me, and became my family. Diana, Nahida, and each of the other women I met.

Lagan listens quietly, exhaling huge sighs when I get to the part about my dad sending me flowers. "And now there's Jody. And she's gonna call a lawyer for me to start working on my case. We'll start the paperwork when I get back."

We pull off Lakeshore Drive, and Lagan enters a parking structure after pulling a ticket from the dispenser. "Jesse asked for you when he called." Lagan says as he opens my car door and gives me his hand to step out.

Jesse.

We follow the signs pointing to the hospital entrance.

"What do you know about why he's here?" I ask.

"Your brother decided to take a dip in Lake Michigan at night. He didn't tell me why, but he did tell me he almost drowned."

My hand rises to my mouth, and I don't know whether to cry or punch my baby brother. He knows he can't swim!

Lagan pulls me in closer, his arm around my shoulders, and adds, "But when I called this morning to ask about visiting hours, the nurse told me that he'll start to feel better in a few days, and in the best case scenario, he can leave in two weeks, but to expect it could take longer." The elevator dings our arrival to the tenth floor, and the doors slide open.

When we reach his room, I peek through the crack in the door and see a girl in a yellow sundress sitting in a seat next to Jess, laughing and chatting like they're good friends.

Lagan nudges me from behind.

"Is she his...? Are they?"

Lagan shrugs his shoulders, turns the doorknob and walks in ahead of me, holding the door open.

"Talia!" Jesse says, pushing his covers off to scoot off the hospital bed, but retracts, keeling over in pain.

I beeline into my brother's arms. "Jesse." But back off quickly when I hear him moan in pain. "Sorry."

"Summer. This is my sister." Jesse lets go too, and we both turn to face the smiling brunette wearing a lemon yellow headband to match her dress. "Talia, meet, umm, my friend, Summer."

After an awkward handshake, Summer's hands move to her hips. "What did you say your name was?"

Jess sits on the end of his bed, tugging my arm to sit next to him. "Yeah. I've been meaning to tell you…"

A knock at the door and a nurse enters, pulling a rolling cart behind her.

"That's Nurse Sheela," my brother says softly. "She's cool."

And all eyes turn to the small chocolate-frosted cake with candles on it. We stopped celebrating birthdays after Mom died. Just another day to Dad.

"It's like you all started the party without me." Nurse Sheela lets out a hearty guffaw. "But it ain't a real party till a cake shows up. Nineteen, right?" Jesse and I exchange looks as she moves the cart till it reaches Jess' bedside. "And a one. A two. A one, two, three...Happy Birthday to…"

I guess now that he really is eighteen, he's legally an adult today. Everything should be easier from here on out.

And we sing. And eat cake. And chat. And laugh. And take seconds.

Except Summer. She doesn't say much. Or laugh. And she refuses seconds. Then she excuses herself. "Got a chem lab and two more finals to study for," she says as she curtly waves goodbye, picks up her backpack, umbrella and makes to leave.

Jesse shakes his head, eyes on his dish with only crumbs on it. I watch her, the way she glares at Jesse, and I can't figure out what's going on between them.

"Dude," Lagan says, as he tidies up the tray and tosses the cake plates in the trash. "If I had known, I woulda brought you something."

Jesse's hand covers my hand and squeezes. "You did." Jess eyes each person in the room, nodding thanks, and one by one they step outside, leaving me alone with my brother. The party's over. It's time to start planning.

34
~ Jesse ~

May 15th

The room grows very quiet when everyone steps out. The last time Talia and I sat together, we were talking about setting the house on fire. That seems so easy in light of what we're about to talk about.

"So...I think she's pretty mad." I can't read minds, but Summer's never been short on words.

Talia picks up a blue Dixie cup and pours some water from the jug next to it. "What did you tell her your name was, anyway?"

"John. I dunno. It seemed like a good idea at the time. In case Dad had police looking for us." Jesse punches his mattress with one hand. "I was about to tell her the day she showed up...Anyway."

"Jess," Talia waits for me to look up. "She'll come around once she knows why you did it. I mean, she came to see you here, didn't she?"

It does seem crazy that we've managed to find each other twice since we first met. But none of that matters now. "There's something I need to tell you, Talia." She sips from the cup, I wait for her to sit down on the chair.

195

"Me too. You go first." She says, looking at me with those green eyes that have almost always brightened my worst days.

"Oh. Okay." I take a deep breath. "I, uh, want to be a pilot."

"Really?" My little brother's got himself a dream! "That's great."

"Thanks," I say, returning the smile. I clear my throat before saying the hard part. "One way is to join the Air Force, and the basic training is…in Texas."

My sister's gaze drops to her lap.

"After the training, which takes eight or so weeks, they could station me at a base closer to Chicago. But…they might not. And this is all banking on if I actually get accepted." After I figure out how to get a valid birth certificate and I.D.

"When are you planning to leave?" Talia asks.

Because she doesn't try and stop me, I sense she understands. I need to move on. "As soon as I get outta here, and figure out my paperwork, I guess." There's no point in putting it off. "I have no reason not to."

"Not even…" And Talia points to the door. I'm guessing she's referring to Summer.

"She's the reason I even started asking myself what I wanted to do with my life. If anything, I hope she comes back one more time so I can thank her." That's the truth.

"Can I convince you to stay just a bit longer?" Talia clasps her hands together on her lap.

"Why? Are you, what, getting married or something?" I smile wide, hoping a little teasing might lighten the news of my leaving.

She shakes her head, no, but she's not smiling. "It's Dad." The elephant in the room just woke up. We haven't talked about Dad at all since Talia showed up. "I'm having a restraining order written up. And I'm going to press charges."

My hand moves to the back of my neck. I just finished burying his gun. I had no plans to face him now. I'm speechless.

"And I think we should do it together. Because…Well, two

stories would be stronger than one."

"I… umm… I don't know." I start with the truth. "I mean, what good will it do? He'll win. We both know that."

"I have to do this." Talia rises from her seat and walks to the window and looks out. Still facing away, she says, "All this time, I've been hiding. I'm through with running."

"Face to face. Are you up for it?" I ask. Talia turns to face me again, rubbing her hands like she's trying to warm them. Sunrays streaming into the room make the dust look magical.

"I've imagined it for quite some time now. Dreamt about facing Dad almost every night since I went to the shelter."

When she pulls her hair over to her mouth, I'm guessing the dreams were more like nightmares.

She tucks her hair behind her ears before she says, "And each time the judge asks me to say what happened," she continues. "Each and every time, my voice disappears. And all I hear is the sound of laughter. Dad's."

Should I tell her I had a plan to end that sound. One pull of that trigger and we'd never hear Dad laugh or scream or say the words, "Or else," ever again. The gun's buried. I'll leave the plan in the grave too.

Instead, I open up my night table drawer. "Maybe this will help you find your voice on that day." Holding the simple silver chain with a heart-shaped charm dangling at the bottom. The heart is made of glass. And it's blue. As I hold it up, the sun hits it and light refracts a dancing shadow on the sheets.

Talia lets the heart land in her palm, keeping it open between us. "Blue," she says. "For Mom."

"I picked this up, because it reminded me of you. Do you like it?" She nods, sniffling. Then turns and lifts her hair, letting me clasp the necklace behind her neck.

Talia hugs me and says, "It's perfect."

"I'm surprised I didn't lose it when I almost drowned." The moment the words slip, I realize I've opened the grave I just said I'd leave buried.

"What were you doing out there in the water, Jesse? You and I both know you never learned to swim." She's now looking at me with a similar glare that Summer just walked away with.

"Look," I need to clear one thing up. "I wasn't trying to kill myself, if that's what you think. I was, I… I just needed to, uh… clear my head. Get rid of a dumb idea."

"So you went swimming late at night? By yourself?" Talia's shaking her head. She doesn't buy it. "Jesse, if you're gonna tell the truth in court, start by telling me the truth. Now."

Did I agree to go to court with her? Would it mean I have to talk about everything? "The gun." I blurt out, chewing on my lower lip, my hand at the back of my neck again. "I stole Dad's gun before I left that day with Lagan. And I needed to get rid of it."

"Why did you take the gun in the first place? I mean if you weren't trying to take your own life, does that mean—?" Talia asks, but when we look into each other's eyes, I think she knows. "Forget it. I'm glad you got rid of it, and you're still alive." Talia pauses and adds, "It's not like I've never thought of a hundred ways to kill Dad. But…maybe there's a better way. A way to at least let him know we're not scared of him."

"But, I am." I say. I hate admitting it, and like a switch was flipped, the burns on my back begin to itch.

"I am too," Talia says, no judgment in her eyes. "But he doesn't need to know that."

"How much are you gonna say in court?" And moreover, how much will you show? I'm looking at my sister's arm. I've only seen it uncovered when Dad forced her to hold it across the sink.

Talia tugs at her sleeve and exhales deeply. "None of this will be easy. But then again," she pauses, our eyes meeting. "What has ever been easy for us?" Talia steps in closer, her hands on my bed railing. "Will you go with me? To court? To face Dad?"

I rub my back against the back of my hospital bed, aware that until the dude at Fred's hostel and now the hospital staff here, no one had ever seen my burns. I'm so lost in thought, I don't notice until she sits on my bed. Talia leans on my sheet, her sleeve pulled back. "It's always as ugly as I think it will be. Sometimes more. But never less." Talia stares at her own arm, and fiddles with her sleeve at her elbow, like she wants to pull it down, but she's forcing herself to wait.

And I know I have to move. Because I can. "I won't let you face Dad alone. We both have them," I say, and with that, I turn on the bed and inch my shirt up, exposing my back to my sister for the first time, her gasp audible even though I can't see her face.

The touch of her cool hand makes me flinch, and right away, she says, "Sorry."

"He told me to move. I couldn't back then. So he burned me. Every time I failed him. He told me I was a mistake. And he had the power to cross me out." I take a deep breath. "But the worst part is that he warned me that if I ever showed you, he'd burn you with matches too." I suck in my breath, reminding myself that it's over. "He's not here, now. It'll be okay." I clench my teeth, knowing it might never be okay, because I'll never be okay with what happened to me. To us.

Then her touch starts at my shoulder blades, and I can feel her slowly run her fingers over each and every dotted scar. Burns. Dad's anger. Making an X on my back, and then she wraps her arms around me, covering my scars with herself, her hands clasped over my chest. Talia squeezes in, and my hands fold over my chest to cover her arms.

"Jesse," my sister says, "The X. It's a lie. He lied to you."

Letting my chin fall to my chest, I turn, my shirt falling back over the scars, tears streaking down past my tightened jawline. "I. Know. I'll believe...I'm beginning, to believe it."

35
~ *Talia* ~

May 15th

Jesse and I talk about the upcoming weeks. I'll call Diana, start the paperwork with Jody, and find out everything we need to do. "And you concentrate on getting better," I tell him.

"For the next couple of weeks," he glances at the phone on the nightstand, "call me here. I'm not going anywhere."

Gazing out the window, the people look like ants below, all rushing here and here, maybe on their lunch breaks. When I look up at the cloud-peppered, blue skies, a few planes dot the sky. "My brother. A pilot, huh?" I turn to smile in Jesse's direction, and he just shrugs his shoulders.

"First things first." And on cue, Nurse Sheela knocks to tell Jesse it's time for his vitals. Lagan follows in behind her.

"Everything okay?" Lagan walks up to me by the window and reaches up, his hand gliding over my hair down my back. "Want me to grab us some food from the cafeteria so you can talk more?"

The mention of cafeteria food makes me giggle. That's where it all started for us. Sitting sort of across from each other, even though it was the high school café. "Now if you tell me you know the staff that works there, and you can get me an extra vanilla ice cream, I might just have to …"

"Kiss me?" Lagan fills in the blank.

"I was going to say, take you up on the offer." I shake my head, heat flushing my cheeks, wondering if Jesse heard. "And not unless they're serving tulips with turnips."

"It's been an eventful morning," Sheela says, "Why don't you two go to lunch and give the patient a couple hours to rest."

Jesse protests, insisting he's fine, but I can tell he's tired. "I'll come back soon." I look over at Lagan, smiling. He's my ride, and he nods, holding up four fingers by his side so only I can see them. I get it. He'd do anything for me. Four me.

It's my turn to do something for him. For us. I hug my brother goodbye, promising to call daily to check on him and keep him posted on the court details, and as we walk to the elevator, hand in hand, silently ride the elevator down, and walk out to the parking lot, we speak at the same time, both saying, "There's something I want to—"

But I say the word, "Show" and he says the word, "Tell."

Show and tell. Ha. Like back in kindergarten.

"Ladies first," Lagan says, opening the passenger side door for me.

"I think…I want to show you. Where it all started. Can you take me to Benton Harbor?"

Lagan pops in a piece of peppermint-flavored Trident and says, "Road trip!" Lagan turns the key, the car engine wakes up, and he pulls out of the parking garage. As we turn down Lake Shore Drive and head toward Michigan shores, Lagan tells me his story.

"Rani and I came to the lake a few weeks ago." Lagan looks forward, off to the water as I picture the tall, tan-skinned beauty I met in his Uncle's law office. His cousin whom he'd kept a secret from all these years. "I told her. About how I saw her get hurt. Touched. By our uncle when we were kids."

I remember that day under the willow, Lagan's head on my lap as he confessed the story of his hide and seek game turned dark when he hid under the bed and witnessed his uncle stealing touches from his cousin, at the time, just a little girl. Rani.

He told her? "How'd she take it?" This time, I reach for Lagan's hand. The one not on the steering wheel.

"For the longest time, she didn't say anything. I thought she was deciding how to phrase the words, 'I hate you,' or 'I'll never forgive you.' Then when she finally spoke, she simply said, 'Thank you.'"

That's odd.

"Weird, right?" Lagan glances at me then looks back at the road. "But then she said that she pretended it hadn't happened for so long, she actually believed that she had made it up. And that seemed far worse than if it were real. Because who makes up that kind of stuff for themselves unless you hate yourself or are looking for some kind of strange sense of sympathy. It's not like she was about to tell anyone either. But we were all invited to a family wedding last month, and she knew she would see him again, and if she thought it was just a story, she'd feel safe around him. And then she realized she felt even less safe not knowing for sure. The weekend I told her, she was alone because she faked being sick so she wouldn't have to go to the wedding. I had midterms, so my parents let me skip the wedding too."

Lagan lets out a huge sigh. "Now she knows it really happened. And now she's working up the courage to tell her mom. One step at a time, right?"

36
~ Jesse ~

May 15th

"You have every right to be mad, but will you give me a chance to explain?" I say out loud to the bathroom mirror in my hospital room. Alone. Repeating the line several times, I practice my apology to Summer. If she never shows up, I'll never get my chance. Looking over at the nightstand, the paper she scrawled her number on still sits there.

Sitting on the side of the bed, I pick up the phone and dial.

"I forgot my sweater," Summer says. She's in the doorway of my room. "Sorry. I'll just grab it and be outta here."

I'm holding the receiver in my hand, and she's pulling her phone out of her purse.

"Hello?" she says, and I can't help but smile.

"Hi," I say, speaking into the phone, my eyes on Summer.

"Very funny." She clicks her phone shut. "You don't have to call me to talk to me if I'm right here?"

"I...wasn't. I mean. I didn't know..." I exhale and try again. "I'm sorry. I have some explaining to do."

"Like why this whole time I've been calling you John, but your name is really Jesse?" Summer crosses her arms and then pulls out her phone in response to a text message alert. I place the phone back on the stand.

"That was my lab partner. She said we'll do the write-up tomorrow." Summer takes her sweater and walks toward the door, but turns before opening it. "What else did you lie about? Are you really working? Do you really want to be a pilot? Why did you bring me flowers?" The questions fire at me and I'm not sure which one to answer first. "And why did you take off that day at the library and never say anything?"

"Yeah. There's a lot I haven't told you. I guess my name would be a good place to start. My real name is Justice. But I go by Jesse." I wait for a response, but Summer just stands there, hugging her sweater to herself.

I continue when she doesn't say anything. "My dad named me." How do I explain a lifetime of anger toward the man who fathered me? "And I want nothing to do with him, so I, yeah. The day I ditched you at the library, he was there. And I didn't want him to see me."

Summer steps toward me, and takes a seat on the window ledge, crosses her legs, and peers out like she's looking for someone. She lowers her arms to her sides. "You ran away?"

"Something like that. I just want him out of my life. I want to move on."

"And the lake incident? Almost drowning? Are you gonna explain that?" Summer stands and takes a step toward me. "I mean, you said you weren't suicidal, but who does that? Go swimming in the dark, all by yourself?"

I stand up, steadying myself by holding the railing. "I know I haven't given you many reasons to trust me, but I'm telling you the truth. I just wanted to get rid of everything in my life that reminds me of my Dad. So I went into the water to bury the last thing of his I had. It was stupid. I'm sorry." I'm holding my breath, because I don't know what I'm going to say if she asks what the item was.

"I'm sorry too." Summer closes the distance, her hand reaching for mine. "I guess it's not like I gave you much to go on either." She's holding my hand, and it feels different than a handshake. A good kind of different. She lets go, ruffles my hair like she did days ago, and says, "All you know about me is I have two sisters, I'm a churro-addicted, pre-med student, and what else?"

"You like leaves, and, umm…you're always prepared for the rain." I say, pointing to the umbrella poking out of her bag. "Just surprised it's not purple." Wondering if there are purple roses in Texas.

A smile spreads across her face as she pulls it out and runs her hands over the length of the multi-colored umbrella. "It's the girly-girl in me. This way, no matter what I wear, if it starts to rain, my umbrella won't clash with my outfit."

I want to tell her that it reminds me of her. I've never told any girl something so personal, and as I rehearse the words in my head, they sound even more corny.

What?" she asks.

Is my face that easy to read? "Colorful." I say, the first word falling out.

She smiles so I keep going. "Colorful. Open. Pretty… just like you."

Summer giggles, puts her thumb under the button to snap off the strap, but I cover her hand with mine. "Isn't it bad luck to open up an umbrella indoors?"

"Well, then, maybe we should take a little field trip." She leaves the umbrella, walks out to the nurse's station and returns shortly. "Nurse Sheela says it's okay to wheel you out for a little fresh air. But I have to bring you back under the hour for your next treatment."

I move to the wheelchair—the closed umbrella lies across my lap. "Ready when you are."

As we wheel past the nurse's booth, someone whistles, and I turn to Summer. "Ignore them."

"Why?" Her smile breathes confidence as she shrugs her shoulders. "Maybe they heard the Churro Guy all the way over here."

"Churro Guy?" Did he tell her what he told me he would after all?

We enter the elevator and when the doors close, she leans

down and says softly in my ear, "He told me you liked me."

"Oh that." I nod, turning and now our faces are centimeters apart.

"His exact words were, 'John wanted to tell you he's all into you.'" Summer moves back and stands straight again, her stare straight ahead. "But now that you told me your name's Jesse, the message is a bit confusing, ya know."

The elevator doors open to the atrium, and I turn to face the greenery as Summer takes in the scent of flowers while all I can think about is her lips. So close to mine moments ago.

"But it's not raining?" Summer fiddles with the snap.

"Want me to open it for you?" I slowly walk over and pick it up again, hand it back to her and we hold hands as we walk to the corner wall of the atrium. The waves on Lake Michigan sparkle as the sun bounces off the water.

Summer lets go of my hand to unravel the umbrella as we both stand under it, and with her arms raised, her leaf tattoo shows fully.

"So you want to change the world?" I ask.

"Don't you?"

Remembering Texas, I say, "Well, I guess I do. But I'll probably have to leave Chicago to do it."

Summer smiles, lowers the umbrella to her side, and looks up. "Well, yeah. Never heard of any pilot flying a plane on the ground." She looks back in my eyes. "Doesn't mean we can't keep in touch. Of course, it helps to leave a number. An addy, you know. If we work on the basics, we might just have something here."

Something? "You're something."

"Yeah," she says. I look from the colors on the umbrella as she lifts it up over us again, back to Summer, right into those ocean blue eyes of hers. "And so are you," Summer says, and leans in, planting a kiss on my cheek.

Woah. "What was that for?"

"Because now I know for sure." She twirls the umbrella above us, the colors swirling into a whirlpool of rainbows. "Jesse, aka John, is definitely into me."

37
~ Talia ~

May 15th

Funny how you never forget the streets and sights once you've lived in a place for so many years. The stoplight close to the high school still takes forever to change to green. The cherry trees still rain pink blossoms all over the school courtyard. The basketball hoops in the park still have no nets and the fence lining the beach borders still leans too far to one side.

The midafternoon sun peeks overhead. "If we hang out long enough, this will be an S2S—sunrise to sunset date." Lagan's dimple-defining smile assures he's in no rush as he parks a few houses down from my old house. "This is it?"

I take a deep breath and stare at the house I grew up in. The new owners changed the siding from the earthy green to a deep, rusty orange, and the fence is now plastic white where a chain link wall used to line our yard. And mango orange Spanish tiles cover the black roof shingles Jesse walked on top of. And jumped off from. My eyes linger on the driveway, empty, smooth, freshly black-topped. I double-check the adjacent houses, and they appear unchanged.

"That's definitely it." I haven't budged from my seat though. "Maybe this is close enough."

Lagan's hand squeezes mine as he tosses the last of the candy wrappers into the grocery bag near my feet. "Take your time. Wanna talk for a bit? Or drive somewhere nearby, grab a bite to eat, and then come back, and maybe by then someone will be home."

My eyes stay glued on the window. Mom's bedroom window. The last place she looked when I longed for her to look into my eyes. My fingernails dig into the car seat.

"My mom." I swallow as Lagan turns the ignition on, then off. "My mom died in this house. I miss her. So much."

"Hmm." Lagan's eyes follow my gaze back to the house, his grip on my hand tightening. "Is her gravestone nearby? Do you want to visit?"

"I guess I should...bring flowers or something." The cemetery's two blocks away. "We could go there."

"We can do that." Lagan turns the key, the car engine comes back to life. Then waits a beat before asking, "Now?"

I nod yes, my eyes glued to the house. And as we drive past slowly, my palm slides down my side window, a landslide of rocks falling over my eyes as the memories bury me. "Stop!" I scream.

Lagan slams on the brakes.

"I mean." I'm hyperventilating, gripping onto the dash for balance. "I was talking to..." I bite my lower lip and the taste of blood grounds me. "The past."

"Should I...keep driving?" We're parked right past the house now. "I could wait."

A silver Honda Pilot pulls into the driveway, and we watch a woman, and three young children make their way into the house, backpacks in tow. The youngest is tugging on the woman's pant leg and pointing to Lagan's car. The lady starts walking over to us, and I'm frantically pulling at my sleeves.

"Excuse me, but can I help you with something? Are you lost?" The woman's two older kids disappear inside while the littlest holds tightly to her hand.

Lagan looks at me before answering. "Sorry to bother you, Miss. It's just that my girlfriend here, she used to live in your house. And she just wanted to show me where she grew up."

I nod to my lap, unable to make eye contact. "I see." The woman turns and looks back to her house. "My kids have to start homework, and I'm about to start dinner. Once my husband's home, you're welcome to come in if you want to take a trip down memory lane. That is, if you don't mind floors decorated with toys and couches covered in clean laundry."

"Thank. You." My voice cracks, but I manage to turn and smile at the lady, pulling her hair back into a messy bun as her youngest tugs on her leg again. "Actually, if we could just leave the car parked here for a little bit. So we could walk to the beach, would that be okay?"

"Mommy, are they gonna build a sand castle like the ones we build?" the little girl asks.

"I don't know, Peanut—" The woman picks up her daughter and turns back to us. "Of course. Take your time," she says, and they walk back to their house.

"Ready when you are." Lagan breaks the silence as we sit awhile longer in the car.

I know now that I'll never be ready so it's now or now. "Okay," I say.

He jumps out to run around and open my door for me. "Want me to carry you?" His arms are open wide.

"You'd do anything to get close to me, wouldn't you?" I find a smile and push him playfully aside. "I think I can manage to walk."

As we pass the house, the woman and her daughter walk down their front steps toward us, and the little girl waves a stem of green and white. "She insisted on it." The mother's arms are folded over her chest. "Okay now, Maya, just hand her the flowers and run back and let them alone."

Maya slows her trot to a walk when she's almost up to us. Without a word she holds the flowers out to me. A stem of daisies, some bloomed, some buds still closed.

"How did you know I love daisies?" I ask her.

"They're from our bush in the backyard." She beams a big smile at me, then looks at Lagan, and giggles, before spinning on her heels and running back up the porch steps into her mom's arms.

The door closes, and Lagan brushes my hair behind my ears. "That girl could tell, huh?"

"I know right?" I'm shaking my head, my gaze shifting from the flowers to the house, back to the flowers. "How'd she know I needed flowers?"

"I was referring to boy likes girl thing, but yeah. That too." Lagan looks down the sidewalk ahead, but he doesn't step forward till I do. I take a deep breath when we reach the T in the road. To the left is the harbor, the beach where Mom taught me to swim. To the right, two blocks down, is the cemetery. I turn right, squeezing Lagan's hand tighter as I step forward. We walk silently, and when we reach the cemetery gates, the manicured greenery reminds me of the garden I worked at, flowers blooming along the border, bouquets, fresh and wilting, lie in front of gravestones everywhere.

The plot where we laid mom rises above the ground, with a generic gravestone bearing my mother's name and the years she lived. No quote or line of poetry to hint at her story. As I inch closer to the spot, I let go of Lagan's hand and kneel to the floor, running my hand over the grass, imagining I'm stroking my mother's long black hair. A single teardrop lands on the back of my hand. Then another. And another.

"My mother," I say as Lagan crouches down next to me, sitting back on his heels. "She used to have the most beautiful long hair."

Lagan runs his fingers down a lock of my hair. "I could see that."

"Until one day Dad stole that too." Holding onto the blue heart charm Jesse gave me, sobbing and heaving, the memories spill. "And her back bled. And there were burns. And the bruises. And the time I washed her broken body. And Jesse...almost died when...the roof. The list. The hot iron near my face. The closet stench. The boiling water. The days I fed my mother with a straw. The wool hat she wore. The day I taped her hair around her face and painted her lips. The day I said goodbye, but..." Story after story. Stone after stone. Like an avalanche, I held on to them for far too long. And as I let them go, I can barely see through my tears. But I also see for the first time. I'm seeing through stones. And now I understand that this is why I came today. "Somewhere along the way, I made up her story. So I could deal with the fact that she left us. This..." My hand runs to the back of my necklace to unclasp it, a gift from Jesse and me, and I place the blue heart on the spot under which I imagine my mother's heart lies. "This is her story."

I take out the folded page in my back pocket, accepting I might never know more, dig out a small patch of grass, tuck it under the earth and cover it back up, patting it back in place. Silently I talk to her, telling her all I need to say, accepting I'll never know for sure if she hears me. I sign my confession with words I wish I had said more often. "Mommy. I love you." Then I take the daisies and lay them on top of the spot. "I'm ready now."

Lagan plucks one bud from the daisy stem and tucks it behind my ear and picks up the blue heart and rubs it between his fingers. "I think you should keep this. To remember today."

I came to let go. Not hold on. I shake my head no, reaching for the necklace so I can put it back, but Lagan closes his hand over mine. The hand holding the heart. "Just because you can't hold onto everything, doesn't mean you have to let go—of everything. It's okay to hold on to the good stuff. If she could see you now, Talia. Oh, if she could see you now."

As I rise to my feet, Lagan fastens the chain behind my neck, the blue heart falling over my chest. I brush my fingertips over the flower in my hair, raise fingers to my healing lips, and blow my mother a kiss goodbye.

38
~ Talia ~

May 15ᵗʰ Evening

After picking up some pizza slices and soda for the drive back, we travel most of the distance to Chicago in silence. Running my fingers through my long hair, I'm tickled by how Lagan reminded me this is one of the few things Mom and I had in common. And all this time I thought if I didn't find the strand, all would be lost. Lagan reminded me of the place where I can store my favorite moments. In between the pages of my story.

Every so often, my stare lights up Lagan's dimple-stamped smile, sending fresh waves of wonderful from my head to my knees. I picture the car sprouting wings, driving off the highway into the sky, and swimming through clouds to a secluded island, and then I remember. This time, Dad will do the swimming. To jail, if all goes according to plan.

At the first sight of the skyline, Lagan asks, "How close to the shelter can I get?"

Twilight paints her red Chicago sky above at eight in the evening. "Umm. Pretty close. You just can't know where it's at. How 'bout you drop me off a few blocks away. And I'll call you from Jody's phone to tell you I made it back okay?"

"I have a better idea." Lagan drives until we reach the

beach parking lot. The place our morning started. "I'll walk you halfway, then we'll text each other until you walk through the door. Cool?"

I unbuckle my seatbelt and on cue, he comes around to open my door. "SUS, okay, Lagan." I giggle, but as I brush my hair behind my ear, I notice it's gone.

Lagan feels around the passenger seat for my daisy, but no luck. "I guess that means I'll just have to buy you some flowers."

"Roses work too. If you can find blue ones," I say to keep him from mentioning tulips and my two lips yet one more time.

"Blue roses. Now there's a challenge I'm up for." Lagan makes like he's shooting a basketball toward an imaginary hoop. "And if I find them, what will I score?"

"A really, big, long, huge, mega, super-amazing…hug!" I push off his arm and walk backward, facing him, loving his look of shock.

"Well in that case, I'll have to find some blue tulips too. If they're out there, I will find them!" Lagan speeds up, scoops me up into a hug, lifting me off the sidewalk, and turns till he's the one facing backwards now. "Okay, lightning eyes. So don't you worry."

We walk hand in hand for several blocks, as I memorize the feel of his fingers entwined in mine, the scent of the summer night, the faint sound of his breathing.

I hate to say it, but rules are rules. "Here is good." About three or four blocks from the safe house, I let go of Lagan's hand, take a deep breath, and swallow. Not going to say it. Not this time.

"And no goodbyes this time, okay?" Lagan reads my mind. "It's S.U.S. from here on out." See you soon. "But any time you want to change it to S.U.N., you know I'm there." N For now. I wish.

Lagan steps closer and wraps his fingers behind my back, and as I nod, his lips rest on my forehead, like he means to stamp this moment on my mind.

"What's Jody's number?" Lagan pulls out his phone, types in the digits and seconds later, Jody's phone buzzes.

The words: *I miss you already* pop up on my screen on a digital Post-it.

I type back, *Of course you have a Post-it message APP* ☺ and hit send. He glances down at his phone, dimple awake and cute as ever.

My phone buzzes again, reading, *When Will I see You? Tomorrow's sunrise too soon?*

I look up, the first stars just starting to peek out, then type, *I'll ask. I don't see why not?*

Bringing tulips, just so you know, the next message reads. Except that the Post-it background changes from yellow to orange, and the smiley face sticker holds a flower across his lips.

And with that, I take one step away and leave him and take several steps before hitting send to the words, *And I'll bring the lightning* after adding a lightning sticker.

Several hundred steps more and I turn to see if he's still standing there or walking back. He's watching me, and I'm pretty sure he hasn't moved from where I left him. This time, instead of a message, I can hear him yelling the words, "Thanks for today. Can't wait till the sunrise!"

I hold up four fingers, spin on my heels and type, *Forevah doesn't seem so far away all of a sudden.*

A response comes back almost instantly, the words reminding me that there's still work to be done.

Let me know what Jody says. I want to know everything. And if I can help...

You have. I type back. Then add, *You do. And you're the first person I'll ask.*

Lagan looks smaller and smaller now when I turn. He must be walking back to the beach now. To his car. His next message comes through:

If tomorrow doesn't work out, I'll check in on Jesse for you, okay?

Thanks, I reply. A small, blinking light moving across the sky above makes me think of Jesse. And water. And Summer.

Are you at the beach yet? I can see the street lamp that marks the last corner before I turn down the street the safe house lies on. I'm less than two blocks away.

"Come home, Talia." The words stab me from behind. I don't bother turning. I just run, shoving Jody's phone in my pocket.

But my pace is no match for Dad's, and his hand grabs my left arm, twisting my wrist and forcing me to slow down. The scream I practiced in my dreams fails me. Only whimpers escape my lips and as his free hand clenches my chin, rotating my face till I'm looking in his eyes, his glare pushes me down a well.

I'm floundering in dark waters that mean to drown me when the buzz from Jody's phone reminds me I'm not alone. Not completely. Lagan texted back, but Dad's grip on my face keeps me from looking at his message.

Exhaling quick breaths, lips quivering, I stumble for the response I've never said to my dad. "I c-c-can't."

"Did you get the flowers?" His grip on my wrist tightens as he lets go of my face to unbutton the top clasp of his suit jacket. "Because I didn't want you to think I forgot about you. I'll never forget that you walked away, Talia. I never forget. No more hiding."

I look down the empty streets, at the gaps in the sidewalk, and then upward. The grey clouds move across the night sky over the moon, making it disappear and then appear again. Exhaling a deep breath, I say, "I'm not hiding. Anymore." I pull the cell phone out of my pocket, my hand shaking even as I lift it in the air. "I'm not alone. It's over, Dad. Let me go."

Dad snaps the phone from my hand and starts reading the messages, but with his hands off mine, I take off running down the street, back toward the last place I saw Lagan. *If I can get to Lagan before Dad catches up to me.* Afraid looking back will slow me down, I pound forward, speeding up as I repeat words in my head: "I will not burn. I will not burn. I will not let him burn me again."

A car pulls up next to me, and Dad's voice yells out of the

window. "Talia. Get in the car. Now!"

I stumble forward at the sound of his voice and eat it, my knees skidding over the sidewalk, my pants tearing on the concrete, my palms hitting the pavement. I bolt up and continue running, refusing to look in his direction. But the car door opens and he's running behind me now, on my tail.

A yank of my hair and my run comes to a halt as Dad pulls me back toward him, panting and sweating. "If you think a little run can stop me from getting you back…"

A whimper escapes. He's gonna cut my hair off. Punish me with a bald head like he did mom. He yanks so hard, I feel like he's ripping my hair out of my scalp. "What will it take for you to stop running? Don't you know I'm trying to protect you? I never wanted you to turn out like those other girls."

"What other girls, Dad?" Biting my lip each time he yanks my hair, I struggle to keep from crying. "And how did? Burning me…help you? Protect me?"

"Just like your mother." Dad drags me toward his car, but I punch backward, failing to hit him hard enough to make him let go.

I am not my mother. I will fight back. "I'm not going back. I'm never going back."

Pulling me toward the passenger side of his car, Dad acts like I didn't say a word. "She never understood how hard I worked to keep men from stealing her from me. No man wants damaged goods. I made sure you and your mother looked damaged. Always."

Car lights flood the sidewalk as the sound of screeching brakes comes to a smoking halt. Dad turns to look, loosening his grip enough for me to recognize the car. "Let go, Dad." I sputter the words, as Lagan races up to me, yelling street names into his phone. "It's. Over."

I can hear the sound of police sirens in the near distance, and I crumple to the sidewalk when Dad lets go of my hair. Lagan's hands hit Dad on the chest, shoving him backward. Again and again. "If you ever. Lay a hand." Another shove. "On Talia again? I swear, I'll…I'll…"

More flooding lights. Car doors slamming. Racing steps. And the uniformed policemen separate Lagan from Dad.

Dad brushes off his suit and straightens his collar as he reaches over to shake the taller Caucasian cop's hand. "Thank you, Sir. You arrived right before this fellow tried to break my neck."

Lagan pulls away from the shorter, African-American officer and dives back toward Dad, yelling, "What the hell are you talking about?"

"Isn't it obvious who's in the wrong?" Dad steps back while the cop restrains Lagan's shoulders to keep him from lunging. "Your hands were around my throat, young man. And I'm sure you'll have plenty of time to figure out your future. After you spend a few nights in jail to think about how to make better choices."

Is Dad saying Lagan never should have chosen me? That there's a better girl out there for him? More beautiful without burns. Less complicated with normal parents. Maybe he's right.

The cops are looking back and forth from Dad to Lagan. The tall, blond nearest Dad turns to Lagan and asks, "Weren't you the one who called Dispatch?" And Lagan nods, but his eyes pierce like swords, aimed at Dad's forehead.

"Miss," the older, dark-skinned cop, holding Lagan back turns to me, "This guy called in to report a potential assault on a young lady. Would you like to press charges against someone?"

I look over and Dad's shaking his head, no—his hands pushing back his jacket cuffs as he clears his throat and answers for me. "I think there's been a misunderstanding, officers." Dad focuses on the older policeman and says, "You're probably a father. You'd understand."

"Proud dad of four daughters, sir, but what has that got to do with anything?" The cop stands between Dad and Lagan now.

"I've told Talia, my daughter, that men are dangerous, and this young man's inappropriate behavior perfectly exemplifies what I've warned her about." Dad steps toward Lagan till they're eye to eye, the space between them only made up of the cop's stance. His hand rests on his revolver to warn both guys to keep cool.

Dad takes two steps back, waves to the blond cop and says, "I'd like to have this fellow arrested, but I'll decide in the morning if I'm going to press charges. Maybe a night of sleep is all we need to clear things up."

"What?" Lagan moves away from the officer dangling the cuffs. "You have it all wrong."

Dad turns to face me, eyebrows raised like he's searching for my approval. He's gambling with the man I love, and if I place my bets correctly, Lagan will only spend one night in jail. At least that's what I gather from what he just said.

"No." The word leaves my lips as a whisper at first.

"Miss," the shorter officer offers me a hand, but I ignore it, staying crouched down. "Are you okay? Was someone hurting you tonight?"

"I said, 'No.'"

I can see the taller officer putting handcuffs on Lagan and it all seems so unreal. He turns to me, eyes pleading, "Talia. Tell the cops what happened. Tell him the truth. Why are you saying, no?"

And this time I look straight at Dad and repeat the word. "No. No. NO!"

Dad tries to put his hand on my shoulder and move me away from the group, whispering, "Talia, let's talk, just you and me."

"NO!" I scream, brushing his hand off my shoulder.

No means no! I will not sleep on it. I will never sleep under your roof again. I will not wait for the morning to change my mind. I will not act like everything's okay and everything's gonna be fine.

"Enough," I say, because that is the bottom line. I've had enough.

The officer stops cuffing Lagan, one hand still free, and Dad clasps his hands together and says, "I agree. Why don't we all go home. Forget the charges, officer. I'll drop the charges.

We can talk, just the three of us. I've handled far more complicated cases than this, I think I can manage my family affairs."

"Attorney Vanderbilt." The taller cop says to the shorter one who is busy unlocking Lagan's cuffs. "I thought I recognized the face."

"This guy's famous." The African-American cop responds with even more enthusiasm, Lagan walking toward me, rubbing his wrist. "He's a lawyer. I say we let him handle his business. Everyone okay with that?"

"No." I say one last time, ignoring the cops and their sudden awe of the man I despise. "I won't let you hurt me again. I…I…He…"

Dad chuckles like I just finished telling a joke. I can't stand up to him, not the way his laughter rips into me like a victory chant, taunting me with a lifetime of lost battles. I cover my ears and close my eyes, and I'm back in the garden, fire surrounding me, trapped and tortured by a future where Dad burns me.

The gardener, who once showed me the way out without words, isn't under the rocks anymore. A survivor himself, he's waiting on the other side, telling me I don't need to say much.

Just show them.

I squeeze my eyes tighter still when I pull up my left sleeve, exposing my badly scarred arm.

The blond officer says, "Woah. What happened to your arm?"

Dad lunges toward me like he means to yank my sleeve down, but Lagan steps between us, and Dad moves till he's blocking the cops from seeing my arm.

"Talia." Dad growls. "You pull that sleeve down, or else." Darting glances between the officers and me, he clears his throat and says, "Why don't we go and see someone, say a … plastic surgeon… see if we can't make it better. I can afford it, and if that's what it takes…"

"Are you gonna pay to erase the X on Jesse's back too?" I leave my arm uncovered. Seeing Lagan wince at the sight of the burns stings, but I want Dad to know I choose tonight. Even if I agreed, I know Dad and all the money in the world will never erase my memories.

The African-American cop grabs Dad by the arm. "Miss, did he do this to you today?" The same cop dangles the cuffs with his free hand not holding onto Dad. "Because we'll throw this famous jerk behind bars…yesterday."

Yesterday. There's a place I don't want to go back to. A time I can never change. But the truth is, and Lagan knows it too, these burns are from weeks ago. I don't bother answering and lower my gaze to my knees.

"Thank you, Talia," Dad says, I think for the first time in my life. "Let's go home, now."

"Not so quick." The shorter cop tightens his grip on Dad's arms, the cuffs still visible to all. "Did this man do that to you?"

Blond cop raises his arms to usher us toward the cars as he adds, "We can either move this discussion to the police station or everyone sleep on it and we can talk about it in the morning. Half the street's awake now. Let's let the citizens of Zion go back to bed before I have to arrest everyone here for disturbing the peace."

I stay crouched on the sidewalk. I speak loud enough for Lagan to hear. "I can't go home with him."

With his freed hands around my shoulders, Lagan glares at Dad and says, "You heard her, officers. She's not going anywhere with that monster. Can't you see he's lying?"

The CB from the squad car squawks and the taller cop attends to it and returns right away, his eyes on his phone. "With all due respect, Sir," he approaches his partner and says something to him so only he can hear. Then the two cops sandwich Dad when the taller officer says, "Dispatch just called and said a second citizen reported a disturbance on this street. The anonymous caller emailed in a short video clip exactly twelve minutes ago. It's a little blurry, but the streets are identifiable as are the plates on your car."

"That proves nothing." Dad blurts out. "It's a free country.

220

And there are no signs saying I can't park here."

"See for yourself."

The cop holds his phone out as I rise and we all inch in closer for a better look. When he presses start, my life replays in front of my eyes. A silent movie of pain and fear and loss.

The black cop looks right at Dad and asks, "Well, then, Mr. Vanderbilt. Can you please explain why the guy who got out of your car is seen chasing a young lady and then dragging her back by her hair? I mean, unless someone stole your car in the last hour…"

All eyes are on Dad, and for once, he is speechless.

I move behind Lagan, holding tightly to his hand, and say, "The girl in the video. That's…um…me." I take a deep breath. "And the man hurting me is my father," I point to Dad, and say, "Him."

Dad backs away toward his car, but one officer grabs him from behind and the other pushes him toward the squad car, pull his hands behind him, and throw cuffs on.

I hear the words, "You have the right to remain silent…" as Lagan turns to face me, and I collapse in his arms. Like landing on a trampoline, for the first time ever, I'm falling. Free. And bouncing back.

Over Lagan's shoulder, Dad glares at me as the white cop presses on his back to guide Dad into the backseat of the police car.

The black officer approaches and says, "Miss, you okay? Sorry for all the confusion." Lagan turns to face him as the policeman shows me Jody's phone. "I believe this is yours?" I nod, and look back, but Dad's not visible through the tinted windows of the squad car.

"Thanks," I say, my hand shaking as I retrieve the phone, a hundred missed calls lit up. All Lagan.

The cop returns to talk with his blond partner who's sitting in the squad car. House lights flood the sidewalk. Neighbors lurk in their doorways and on their driveways, awoken by the commotion. Some peek through curtains. I see them. And they see me. And…it's okay. I'm okay with it.

One bravely approaches from across the street, reads Dad's plates that boast his famous name, and says, "Looks like Attorney Vanderbilt has a wild card he never planned to lay down." The man wearing a robe and slippers shakes his head. "You okay?"

I nod my head, and inch closer to Lagan, noticing the man is staring at my burnt arm.

"She's been through enough, sir." Lagan glares at the stranger, and he takes two steps back. "If you don't mind..."

"Not at all. Just wanted to make sure the lady was okay." He turns to leave, takes one step off the curb and turns to say, "Makes sense now how a guy who treats a young woman in public like that would deny the existence of human trafficking on national TV. By the way, that video is about to go viral. And MOD Hotels and Gerard Vanderbilt are goin' down. In my opinion." Then he nods a good night to us and to the African-American cop who just returned, and then the stranger walks back across the street up his driveway.

The officer jots down something on his clipboard and then says, "We need both of you to come down to the station to make a statement. Will you be able to follow in your friend's car?" He's directing his gaze to Lagan.

"Statement?" *As in speak?* My throat gets dry and my hand slips to the back of my head, soothing the soreness where Dad pulled my hair.

"I'll drive her," Lagan assures the officer. Then he turns to me, holds both hands, and says, "We'll call Jody and let her know everything that's happened. Then I'll take you to the precinct and all you have to do is—"

"Tell them exactly what happened," I say, nodding slowly. "And Diana and Jesse. I want to tell them too. Because, I'm ready."

With eyes locked, my face cupped in his hands, Lagan leans in, our foreheads touching. "You sure 'bout this?"

"I'm ready to fight back. And..." Nodding again and again, arms slipped around Lagan's neck, I know I'm ready for so much more. "Now's a good time."

"Now?" Lagan raises an eyebrow, but his dimple-lit smile tells me he gets it. Because he gets me. The new me.

I'm in his arms. Swimming through clouds. Seeing through stones. Looking into those eyes that promised to wait for me.

"Yes," I say. "Now's a good time...to start forever."

39
~ Jesse ~

May 16th

I'm on the roof. Of the hospital. Alone. And as I walk to the wall overlooking Lake Michigan, I imagine my eyes become telescopes, and I can see past the rocks, through the water, and into the sand. The gun that once occupied so many of my minutes awake—sleeps now.

I close my eyes, push myself off the roof, but this time, I have no intention of falling. My arms spread like wings, and I take flight.

I stand alone on the roof, open my eyes, and fall back. Into my wheelchair. Roll toward the elevator and press down. Talia called me last night, telling me how Dad hurt her, and I wanted to fly over there with matches and dare him to try again. And then I stopped myself. And savored the image of Dad's hands being linked by cuffs. Finally a little justice. I guess after all this time, I've learned to appreciate my name. But I still prefer to go by Jesse. And I told a certain pretty girl that each time she slips up and calls me John, I owe her another churro.

The elevator doors slide open. Yesterday's fires are out. It might rain tomorrow. Today calls my name. And I'm answering.

ACKNOWLEDGEMENTS

In the distance I see the red carpet. It turns purple. Then blue. Blue for Talia. Now I can walk forward.

And thank everyone in my life who has patiently cheered me on as the sequel to *Swimming Through Clouds* spread her broken wings, returned four plus times for makeovers, and finally leaves the nest.

Some lists are good, Talia. Here's one that I'm sure will be incomplete, but I'll try my best to remember all of you!

First and most importantly, thank you, God. You wrote the best love story of all, and I'm so grateful to be a part of it.

For the love of my life, Santhosh. You are my anchor, my real-life Lagan. Thank you for fighting for me. For us.

For my children. I can't stop the clock, so promise me you'll always be my little girls. Hannah, Nitha, Lydia and Sarah—you are my gifts. Thank you for daily filling Mommy's life with hugs and kisses and grace.

For my family and friends. You remind me that we laugh and cry together. Cheer each other on in the good times and hold each other in the rough seasons. You are my treasures.

For my niece, Deepa, musician, dancer, and artist extraordinaire. Thank you for helping me with my book cover! You are our first to venture off to college. Go paint up some rainbows, beautiful young lady. The world is your canvas.

For my best friend, Roopa, and writing crit group: Renee, Liz, Emily, Selene and Lisa. Thank you for being my first readers. You help me see things in my story I would have never noticed and continue to make me a better writer.

For my primary editor, Beth Jusino. Where do I begin? Okay, maybe I should start by saying thank you to my agent, Chip MacGregor. Chip, thanks for your honesty when I handed you the first draft of *Seeing Through Stones* and saying, "Raj, now don't jump out of the window, but it's not the right story." Then you introduced me to Beth!

For the last year, Beth, you have patiently walked alongside me as we searched for the right journey for my characters. The best thing you ever said to me was, "Be brave and let go." And as I erased and chiseled and wrote and rewrote, and rewrote some more, you asked me questions, made me dig deeper, and encouraged me not to quit. And if this is anything like running a marathon, I feel like we finished four or five (I lost count!) together. You're a gem I won't share with anybody. Okay, I guess that's not really an option. ☺ But I am so thankful for you and your investment in my writing.

And for my line editor, Hwee Goh. Funny how life had us cross paths after meeting back at Northwestern. Working with you felt like hanging out with a good friend. You have no idea how much I appreciate you cleaning up the final manuscript and championing my writing. I heart you!

For the women I met at Manavi's national conference, Aarohan (translated, "rising up")—a weekend dedicated to allying organizations fighting for South Asian survivors of Domestic Abuse. You inspire me with your dedication to the silent hurters. The stories I heard make my fictional tales dim in comparison. Thank you for walking alongside these women and children on their roads to recovery.

For Diana Mao, Supei Lui, Alissa Moore and all the women who pour hours of time into Nomi Network. Your work in India and Cambodia and New York, empowering women at risk of human trafficking and survivors of red light districts reminds me daily why I write. To give these beautiful girls and ladies a voice.

For the medical staff at North Shore LIJ at Glen Cove Hospital. Thank you for your friendships and fielding my 101 questions about hospitals and injuries.

For the Playlist Fiction agents and authors: Amanda Luedeke, Sandra Bishop, Jennifer Murgia, Laura Anderson Kurk, Laura L. Smith, and Stephanie Morrill. Can't imagine starting out my writing career with a better team! Each and everyone of you has impacted my life through your motivation, wisdom, and writing.

For my Launch Team and Playlist Fiction Street Team, and countless Bloggers who graciously agreed to feature my books. Thank you for standing on the sidelines as I exit the gate to my second book release. Your feedback, reviews, and comments help calm my doubts, over and over again!

For you. Yes, you. The person holding this book. Thank you from the bottom of my heart for giving this newbie writer the time of day.

And finally, last but not least, thank you Peter and Liz over at the Gly Café, who guard my writing corner with their lives. Thanks for carving out a little spot for me to pen my stories, sharing my out loud "YES!" moments, praying for me in my moments of panic, and keeping me awake with the best coffee in town!

I continue to see through life's stones, because of all of you.

Sincerely aware that great stories change lives,

Rajdeep

ABOUT THE AUTHOR

Rajdeep decided to be a writer during her junior year in high school after her English teacher gave her an "F" but told her she had potential. She studied English Literature at Northwestern University, and she writes Masala-marinated, Young Adult Fiction, blogging at rajdeeppaulus.com.

When Paulus is not tapping on her Mac, you can find her dancing with her four princesses, kayaking with her hubs, coaching basketball or eating dark chocolate while sipping a frothy, sugar-free latte. Find her on Twitter, Instagram, Tumbler, Goodreads, and Pinterest @rajdeeppaulus.

ABOUT PLAYLIST FICTION

Playlist Young Adult Fiction provides your YA fiction fix. With new books and offers available every month from some of the best indie voices in contemporary teen fiction, there's never been a better reason to download the drama.

Discover great books at www.PlaylistFiction.com!

And follow us @PlaylistFiction and on Facebook to hear about deals and new releases.